CHARMING THE CAPTAIN

❖

Hearts of Cornwall

K. LYN SMITH

Davenwood Press, USA
Paperback ISBN: 979-8-9911573-2-2

GET A FREE BOOK

Subscribe to K. Lyn Smith's newsletter at klynsmithauthor.com and receive a copy of the Hearts of Cornwall prequel novella, *Discovering Wynne*.

CHAPTER 1

CORNWALL, LATE SUMMER, 1820

GABRIEL MARSH EYED his man with dismay. "A putrid throat? How does one treat such an ailment?" It wasn't his habit to rely on his groom for doctoring advice unless the patient was of the equine sort. But, having learned the day before that Newford's only surgeon was "away to Truro," he had little choice.

"A mustard plaster and beef tea, sir," Hadley said. "A purgative might work, or a camphor rinse, but best to start with the plaster and see if that don't do the trick." At Gabriel's doubtful frown, Hadley tugged his ear. "You never had a putrid throat, sir?"

"Never."

A soft whimper came from the bed, where Emilia slept in the manor's only clean linens. Owing to some confusion with the domestic agency, their small party had arrived ahead of the servants to find Penhale cold and dark, the covers not yet removed from the furnishings.

Under ordinary circumstances, the lack of servants wouldn't have concerned him. He'd spent years on the battlefields of the Peninsula and could do for himself. But nothing about his life was ordinary now—not since the arrival from Portugal mere weeks before of this dark-eyed girl of seven years, delivered to his London doorstep by a colleague in the Foreign Office. Along with this unexpected package, Hugo Brightwell had also brought news that Gabriel's estranged wife was gone—killed while racing her carriage.

Of the two revelations, the knowledge that he had a daughter had been the most startling, and Gabriel still couldn't bring himself to believe it. He saw much of Mariana's beauty in the girl's raven-wing hair and finely-arched brows, but little of himself.

Brightwell had been eager to relieve himself of his task and return to Lisbon. "We were set upon twice before we sailed," he'd confided in the privacy of Gabriel's library. "Someone did not want your daughter to leave Portugal."

Someone. Gabriel didn't know what manner of people his wife had surrounded herself with in the years since their estrangement, but it would hardly surprise him to learn the villain was Vasco Ribeiro.

Gabriel had a years-long animosity for his wife's lover, a man he was reminded of daily when his shaving mirror reflected the scar from Ribeiro's blade.

But Ribeiro had already taken Gabriel's wife. Did he mean to have his daughter as well? To what purpose? The obvious answer—that Emilia was Vasco's daughter and not his own—was one he would not contemplate.

After extracting a promise from Brightwell to keep him apprised of Ribeiro's movements on the Peninsula, Gabriel had turned his efforts to managing his young daughter. With a soldier's efficiency, he fed her and paid his landlady to keep her while he continued his duties at the Foreign Office.

A daily examination of the *Times'* advertisements produced a governess who agreed to join them once her current position ended. He'd made it plain to Miss Templeton that she mustn't delay. He knew nothing of children, and he could scarcely tend to Emilia's needs himself. Her crooked plaits were proof enough of that, and now he'd let her catch a putrid throat.

Thick lashes fluttered against her pale cheeks before lifting to reveal dark eyes bright with a touch of fever. Gabriel took her hand. It was warmer than he thought it should be. He'd seen fever among his injured brothers on the Peninsula—the sort that produced hot, raging delirium. Emilia was such a small thing, and he knew nothing of what her slight child's form might withstand.

He stood and crossed to the nursery window. "Keep the fire up," he said to Hadley, "and see if you can find more linens that haven't been eaten by moths."

"Where are you going?"

"I'll ride to the apothecary then procure something for our supper. Fear not, Hadley. We'll bear up."

"The village may have someone who can help with the girl, sir. A maid, perhaps."

Gabriel shook his head. "Maids talk. I'll not have anyone finding Emilia because of some local gossip." It was gossip, after all, that had prompted their hasty departure from London. That, and the unsettling sense that someone had been asking questions about his daughter. Whispers were one thing; pursuit was another.

Gabriel had long known the power of rumor, both to protect and to destroy. As a captain in His Majesty's Army and lately an aide in the Foreign Office, he had often traded in rumors and speculation. More than once, village gossip had saved him and his men. It was one of the ironies of his life that he now found himself on the other side of it. Even now, he could still hear the whispers in London.

The wife left him for another.

They say he killed her and took the girl.

The child isn't even his.

How he could have killed his wife in Portugal while living in London was beyond him. He was sorry for her death, but by the time he learned of it, any passion he'd once felt had long since faded. It certainly wasn't the sort to drive a man to murder.

Now, with his task before him, he saddled his horse and rode to the apothecary, where he procured the needed plaster. *And* a castor oil purgative and camphor rinse, hopeful if not confident that with all three to hand, *something* might alleviate Emilia's discomfort.

Before returning to Penhale, he stopped at the Fin and Feather Inn, a modest but tidy coaching house, where he requested meat pies, a round of cheese and a jar of beef tea. The innkeeper, a pretty female with red curls, eyed him curiously as she gave his order to one of the maids.

While he waited, he wandered into the coffee room. The tables there were clean, and in one corner, a pair of gentlemen played at draughts. The innkeeper followed him and drew a mug of cider behind the oak bar. Though he'd not ordered it, he didn't argue when she pushed it across to him.

"Are you needing a room as well, sir?"

"No."

"Just going through, then. D'you travel to Falmouth?"

Gabriel's presence at Penhale would be known soon enough. Best to get it done with. In a repressive tone meant to discourage questions, he said, "I've leased Penhale."

"Penhale! 'Tis very good, sir. I'm Mrs. Teague, and the fellow just there"—she indicated a tall man emerging from the cellar stairs—"is my husband."

Gabriel already knew her name, and that she ran an efficient inn, along with her husband. He'd learned the husband had once had ties to smuggling and had even been suspected of some foul business years before, though he was now viewed with a friendlier eye.

"If you require anything," the innkeeper continued, "you've but to ask. Roddie and I—we'll see to't you have what you need."

Gabriel set down his mug. He'd thought to send Hadley down on market day to see what could be done to fill the larder, but that wasn't for two days. His daughter would require more than meat pies and cheese.

"What can you do to address my larder?"

Mrs. Teague, proving herself an astute businesswoman, assured him she'd see his larder filled with every necessity. Then, taking up a cloth, she wiped the already-immaculate bar.

"Penhale is a fine manor," she continued. "My grandfather, Alan Kimbrell, is your nearest neighbor at Oak Hill. He can tell you the property's history if you care for that sort of thing. 'Tis a fine history, too—from smugglers to kings, many have hidden within its walls. How d'your wife and children find it?"

"I don't have a wife."

She ceased her motions with the cloth. "But what can a bachelor want with a place like Penhale?"

"Solitude, ma'am." His tone was curt, bordering on rude, and her eyes widened. Before she could recover from his brusque reply, he inquired about the direction of the local farrier. From there, he kept the conversation on ordinary topics until the kitchen maid brought out his pies wrapped in paper and tied with a string. He stood and slid a half-crown piece across the bar and tipped his hat to Mrs. Teague.

Back at Penhale, he applied the mustard plaster to Emilia's thin chest and throat then persuaded her to take a few sips of the tea. When she fell into an easier sleep, he set aside the castor oil and camphor for another day and warmed the pies over the fire.

Behind him, his daughter muttered in her sleep. "*Mamãe*."

The word settled like a weight in his stomach.

He'd spent the last years not thinking of Mariana, but the arrival of their daughter made it impossible to keep her from his mind.

For all the contempt he held for the gossip in London, he couldn't deny the rumors had their root in truth. Mariana *had* left him. He could still recall the moment he learned of it.

He'd returned to his lodgings in Oporto from a week's campaign, weary from the saddle, to find his brother-in-law waiting for him. Miguel Alves, who'd never approved his sister's marriage to a British lieutenant, sat at Gabriel's desk, a glass of port in his hand.

After a moment's confusion, Gabriel noted the unnatural stillness of his quarters, the missing traces of perfume. He'd known, even before he dropped his bag and strode to the chamber he shared with his wife. Her wardrobe hung open, its contents emptied, and Mariana's mirror was gone from the dressing table.

He returned to the parlor where Miguel lifted his glass in a casual salute. "She has gone, my friend."

She has gone. As if Gabriel had lost a glove rather than a wife.

CHAPTER 2

BRONWYN KIMBRELL, WHO was rarely at a loss for words, found herself bereft. She stood at the window of her cousin's shop with her friend Kate, watching a man ride past on a long-tailed dapple-grey with black points.

Such an animal among the pedestrians and wagons of Newford's high street was an uncommon sight. Across the way, even Mrs. Tretheway, who would never be caught standing in the lane, slowed her march, and the blacksmith reined in his wagon.

But if the horse had caught Bronwyn's eye, it was the man who'd caught her tongue. He sat the saddle with ease. Gloved hands held the reins loosely, and it was no hard task to imagine the strength of his arms beneath the fine blue wool of his coat. From the tall crown of his beaver to the nicely shaped leg above the top of his boot, his figure was a nice one.

"Who do you think he is?" asked Kate, who was visiting from London and should have been unmoved by such sights.

"I'm sure I don't know."

"He's the new tenant at Penhale," Morwenna said as she arranged a pair of bonnets in the shop's case.

Bronwyn flicked a doubtful glance in her cousin's direction. The manor above Newford had stood empty for more than a year, and Mrs. Pentreath—who led the charge on any gossip worth mentioning—had declared a new tenant twice before, only to be proven wrong.

"I would not set any stock by Mrs. P's reports," she said. "I imagine he's merely a traveler who's lost his way to Falmouth." The man had nearly reached the post office; soon, he'd be gone from view. She leaned closer to the window.

"No," Morwenna said, "I had it from the gentleman himself."

Bronwyn and Kate turned in unison. "You've met him?" Bronwyn said.

"Has Penhale truly been let?" inquired Kate.

Morwenna retrieved a box of ribbons and set

about sorting the spools into their drawers. "Aye to both," she said.

"But where—when—?" Bronwyn asked in disbelief. How had she missed such a momentous event? Little enough happened in Newford that the addition of a stranger to their numbers should not have escaped her notice.

"I daresay you've been busy with your preparations for the fair," Morwenna said. "But I encountered him at the apothecary two days agone. He requested camphor, castor oil and a mustard plaster, and I overheard him give his direction for the bill. He is most certainly installed at Penhale."

"Heavens," Bronwyn said. "He purchased all that? He doesn't look sickly."

"Does he hail from London?" Kate said.

"I wonder how he came by such a distinguished animal. He must be flush."

Kate waved a dismissive hand. "Never mind the horse. Is he a bachelor?"

"I don't think Ben would appreciate your interest in our stranger's marital situation," Bronwyn reminded her.

"I ask merely from curiosity."

Morwenna held up both hands. "I don't know his origins, his health or the state of his purse. I know only that he is Captain Gabriel Marsh and that, according to Wynne, he does not have a wife."

"Wynne has met him, too?" Bronwyn said with a gasp.

"And Merryn, I believe."

"My *brother*? Oh, but that's too much!" Bronwyn straightened her gloves. "What say you, Kate? Do you not have an errand at the post office?"

They left Morwenna's shop, and Bronwyn urged Kate to hurry. The high street had resumed its usual pace, and a cart rumbled away from Mr. Clifton's bakery. Captain Gabriel Marsh and his fine horse, though, were nowhere to be seen.

"Where d'you think he's gone?" Bronwyn said.

"I thought you were resolved to be done with meddling."

Bronwyn frowned as a farmer's cart blocked her view of the high street. "This is not meddling," she assured her friend. "This is a morally appropriate interest in our new neighbor. 'Tis our duty to offer hospitality… to stand as ambassador for our fine hamlet… to…" She abandoned her argument at the skeptical look on her friend's face. "Oh, I suppose now that you've a bit of Town polish, you think me a goose."

"I do not! But why are we in such a pelter? You know nothing of this stranger, and I always thought you too sensible to be taken in by a handsome figure on horseback."

"Oh, hardly that. Have you been gone so long

you've forgotten what little is required to enliven our days? 'Twill be diverting to have a new soul about. Only think, Kate! You'll return to London soon, but where does that leave me? Here with no one but my own cousins and brother for company. And now, here is someone new, who hasn't heard the stories of how I ate a beetle on a dare when I was ten, or the summer I fell out of a tree and broke my arm."

"You were spying on your brother, I believe—"

"Irrelevant to the point, which is that this gentleman"—she waved a hand toward the post office—"does not know any of my past follies."

"I daresay a day or two in Newford will resolve that."

"Aye, but until then, he is unspoilt!"

"But you know nothing of his situation or his family, his prospects or—"

"You are putting the cart well before the horse, Kate. I don't aim to *marry* him. I'm content as a cat with my situation. It suits me very well."

And it did. At four and twenty, she had the running of her mother's household. She came and went as she pleased, so long as she took a maid with her. She'd gained a certain freedom in her majority, and she wasn't eager to trade it for a husband.

That wasn't to say she was wholly uninterested in the origins of a handsome stranger.

"I merely wish to—to broaden my acquaintance," she said as they reached the low steps of the post office.

But on entering the small timber-framed building, her nose wrinkled with disappointment. The post office, which also served as the village shop, held only her cousin Cadan behind the counter and Mrs. Tretheway. There was no handsome stranger in sight.

Still, as post-master, Cadan knew more about the goings-on in the parish than most. He guarded the King's post very seriously, but perhaps she might still learn something. She pulled Kate toward the shelves and busied herself inspecting a tin of paints.

Cadan retrieved a letter from the bins behind him and passed it to Mrs. Tretheway. The lady, dressed in her usual brown wool and white cap, complained over the cost of the post and how every pinch-farthing Kimbrell aimed to lighten her purse.

Cadan patiently explained that if the lady's grand-niece had made use of the penny post, she might have spared her aunt the expense.

Finally, the lady finished her business. As she turned to go, her cane fell to the floor with a heavy clatter, and Bronwyn knelt to pick it up. "Allow me, ma'am."

Mrs. Tretheway accepted her stick with a curt nod. "Miss Kimbrell." The frost in her tone was unmistakable, though it had been more than a decade since Bronwyn had dressed the lady's pug in a periwig. Despite Bronwyn's very pretty and mostly sincere apology, Mrs. Tretheway's manner had not thawed a whit. To any who speculated the lady's memory had begun to fail her, Bronwyn could argue such was not the case.

"How d'you do, ma'am? I trust you're in good health?" she said, confident that a cheerful greeting never did anyone a bad turn. And, if Newford's matrons found such a manner vexing, then she would count that an additional triumph.

"I'm as well as can be expected," came Mrs. Tretheway's grumbled reply, the lines around her mouth flowing south like the rivers on a map.

Bronwyn held the door for her. "Allow me, ma'am."

"I'm not infirm, girl," the lady said with a swing of her cane, which Bronwyn barely avoided with a neat skip. As Mrs. Tretheway's backside crossed the threshold, Bronwyn was tempted to let the door swing a little too quickly, but she checked the impulse.

"Ladies," Cadan said once Mrs. Tretheway had gone. "How can I assist you?"

"Kate wishes to know if she's any post from London," Bronwyn said, for which she received a narrow-eyed frown from her friend.

"Let me check," Cadan replied before consulting the bins behind the counter.

"It's not enough to drag me with you," Kate whispered, "but now you must embroil me in your lies?"

"'Tis all to a good purpose."

When Cadan returned with the news that, regretfully, he had no letters for Kate, Bronwyn turned them to the question at hand. She set the paints atop the counter and laced her fingers over the tin. Casually, as if she merely commented on the weather, she said, "I hear Penhale has a new tenant."

"Aye," came his short reply.

"A Captain Marsh, I believe."

With a laugh, he said, "Cousin, you're as obvious as the matrons. Mrs. Clifton was here this morning, and 'tis certain Mrs. Tretheway came to pick news from me rather than letters."

His phrasing put her in mind of a buzzard picking flesh from a rabbit's bones, and though she couldn't like the comparison for herself, she thought it rather apt for the matrons. Straightening, she said, "I will thank you not to liken me to the matrons."

"'Tis a proper shame a man can't sneeze in Newford without half the parish flapping about it."

"I've no interest in whether he sneezes or not," she protested. Although, he *had* purchased a noteworthy number of purgatives and cures... She let that go for the moment to say, "But don't you feel any curiosity for our newest neighbor? Why, he could be a… a duke in disguise or an *American*."

"Perish the thought," he replied, "though I'd venture to say 'tis doubtful."

"Why? D'you know something?"

Her cousin merely laughed and turned to record Mrs. Tretheway's coin in his ledger.

"D'you not find it the least bit curious that a single gentleman should set himself up in a house like Penhale?"

"I don't find it curious at all," he said without looking up. "Or peculiar or interesting or any other adjective you might wish to use, because I don't give it a thought. Nor should you."

"I don't understand how you can have not a single thought on the matter."

"Will you be purchasing the paints?" he said, and she realized she still held the tin.

"If I buy them, will you make an introduction when Captain Marsh comes for his mail?"

"Bronwyn!" Kate whispered, her propriety offended by this bit of bribery.

"Well, to be sure, he's met the gentleman," Bronwyn said reasonably. "Why could he not perform the introduction?"

"The post office is a serious establishment," Cadan said. "'Tis not an assembly room, and I am not your master of ceremonies to be making introductions."

"Oh, don't put yourself in a pucker," Bronwyn said. Nevertheless, she slid a coin across the counter for her new paints.

CHAPTER 3

GABRIEL ROSE EARLY, lit a lamp and dressed quickly. The house was still, save for the faint creak of the floorboards beneath his boots. In the kitchen, he warmed more of Emilia's beef tea and cut a wedge of cheese before setting off for the nursery.

He listened at the door, but there was no sound from within, and he'd not heard Emilia crying in the night, though he'd climbed the stairs more than once to listen. He knocked softly, waited a moment, then entered.

She was sitting up, her slight frame propped against the bed pillows. Her hair sprouted at angles around her face, the plait having long since abandoned its duty. She rubbed sleepy eyes, and he was pleased to see they'd lost the sheen of fever.

"Good morning," Gabriel said in English.

She blinked but didn't respond. Gabriel nudged the door wider with his tray, and she watched him warily as he set it on the table beside the bed then stoked the fire.

"I've brought more of the tea. Hadley tells me it's not bad, as beef tea goes." When Emilia made no move to reach for it, he said gently, "Take a little; it will help you feel better."

Her gaze went to the window, where a sliver of pale morning light seeped round the curtain. For a moment, he thought she might refuse a direct order, but then she held a hand out. The imperious motion was so reminiscent of Emilia's mother that Gabriel hesitated before passing her the cup.

She took three sips, so dainty he doubted she'd got any in her, then thrust the cup back.

"That's a good girl," he murmured, relieved at her compliance.

She eyed the tray and the wedge of cheese, so he broke off a piece and gave it to her. She chewed slowly, swallowed, then finally spoke.

"I want to go home." Her voice had lost the raspiness from her illness. He was relieved to know she was not a languishing, sickly thing.

She spoke in Portuguese, and he replied in kind. "I know, but your home is with me now."

"Why can I not go to *Tio* Vasco?"

Gabriel swallowed. This was not the first time she'd asked the question, but he couldn't fob her off indefinitely.

Setting the cheese aside, he took one of Emilia's hands in his. When she would have pulled away, he held her more firmly. "Emilia, Vasco is not your uncle. And while I know you wish to go to him, he is not the sort of man who should care for a child."

Emilia's defense was sharp. "He is kind and good, when it suits him."

Gabriel drew a breath through his teeth. He didn't doubt her mother had told her that; Mariana had once accused him of the same thing. "That is hardly a recommendation."

"You don't know him."

"I know enough," he said evenly. "You must trust me in this."

The silence stretched, and when Emilia pulled her hand again, he let her go. She betrayed no emotion for his words beyond a tiny furrow that creased her brow. He refused to think her compliance could be so simple, but years in His Majesty's Army had taught him to take his victories where he could.

The sky beyond the curtains was lighter now. Rising, he collected the kettle from the fire and prepared a basin of warm water at the washstand. Emilia watched him wring out a cloth with an unreadable expression. He'd never had occasion to care for a little girl before, and the past weeks had done little to grow his confidence. Surely, Miss Templeton would arrive soon, and he could leave

Emilia's toilette in the governess's capable hands.

For now, he injected a brisk authority into his voice and said in English, "A bit of fresh air always makes one feel better. Why don't we go exploring?"

The furrow returned to her brow. Still, she didn't refuse him outright, so he pressed on. "I understand from the land agent there's a fine park beyond the terrace where a body can view the ocean. What do you say we investigate it together?"

Her gaze flicked to the window, betraying the merest interest before she pulled it back to him. Gabriel waited, letting the suggestion linger until she gave him a small, imperial nod.

"Excellent," he said with more enthusiasm than a walk in the garden warranted. "Come near the fire, and we'll see you dressed."

She shivered while he scrubbed her pink, and he hurried to dress her in petticoats, wool stockings, and a pale grey frock. He laced up tiny half-boots little bigger than his hand, then, with a fortifying breath, he considered her hair.

Her expression was resigned, as his must have been, when she sat on a low stool and passed him her brush. His fingers, which could load a flintlock in seconds, were awkward with the task. He winced as the brush pulled at the tangles. It was long minutes before he had her hair re-plaited and tied off with a ribbon.

When he would have wrapped her tightly in her cloak, she shook him off. Going to the wardrobe, she rummaged about before emerging with a length of ribbon. She held this out to him, her gaze more challenging than hopeful.

He negotiated the thing, wrapping the sash below her tiny bodice and fumbling the ends until he finished with a perfectly uneven bow. It would do.

"*Perfeito*," he assured her.

Emilia's eyes met his in the mirror as, with a precise flick of her fingers, she twitched the loops into perfection. The little imp! She'd taken delight in his torment.

"*Piqueno diabo*," he murmured as he held her coat.

Emilia collected her mother's handkerchief, a square he'd tried without success to pry from her so it might be laundered. Tucking the cloth up her sleeve, she finally consented to leave the nursery with him.

Stepping into the brisk morning, they crossed the terrace and followed a graveled path to a paneled gate. It resisted when he pushed, so he leaned his shoulder into it until the hinges yielded with a loud creak.

As the gate swung back, he drew an audible breath. The garden—the land agent's "fine park"—had fallen into ruin. Brambles choked the paths, and decay lingered in the air. Gabriel muttered an oath under his breath, forgetting for a moment the tender ears at his side.

Emilia stopped inside the gate, her small, wool-wrapped form frozen as she took in the wild expanse. Her dark eyes narrowed, and she tucked her chin.

Gabriel crouched until his eyes were level with hers. "It will be right as a trivet soon," he assured her. Resolving to request the agency add a gardener to his staff, he said, "We'll bring in a groundsman, and the gardens will be restored in no time. Until then, would you like to see the stables?"

Emilia glanced at him before returning her attention to the garden. For a brief moment, he thought he saw a flicker of something in her gaze—interest, perhaps, or a hint of excitement—but it was gone as quickly as it had come. Without waiting for him to follow, she passed through the gate, her small boots crunching on the gravel.

"The gardens, it is," he murmured.

To one side of the path, beyond the crumbling stone wall, a copse of trees divided Penhale lands from those of his neighbor.

Emilia marched on as surely as if she had a destination, and Gabriel obliged her. Soon, fleeting glimmers of the sea appeared through swaying branches. They passed a crumbling stone sundial before reaching a bench beneath a twisted apple tree.

Emilia's steps didn't falter, and though he tried

to stop her—"Are you certain you wish to sit? You'll stain your cloak."—she moved aside the vines covering the marble seat and settled herself on the cold stone. With her profile outlined by the sun's first rays, she was the image of her mother.

Clearing his throat, Gabriel asked in English, "Do you enjoy the view?" She tilted her head but didn't look at him. He'd caught glimpses of understanding in her gaze before, so he didn't think she was unfamiliar with the English language, merely stubborn like her mother.

He said gently, "You'll need to practice your English. I imagine few here speak Portuguese."

She didn't respond. When the wind tugged at the hood of her cloak, Gabriel adjusted it more securely. She stilled under his touch, and he dropped his hands.

"I know all of this must be upsetting," he began.

She was silent for a long moment before lifting her chin and saying in Portuguese, "My mother enjoyed her garden." Her expression was one of defiance, as if she dared him to argue.

He replied carefully, "She did."

Emilia didn't offer any further comment, but he thought the tautness in her shoulders might have eased a fraction.

Gabriel eyed the cold bench beside her and, flicking his coat tails aside, he sat.

CHAPTER 4

BRONWYN'S BROTHER PROVED no more helpful than Cadan when she pressed him about Penhale's new tenant. He confirmed his men had been summoned to repair a leak around the library windows, but he knew little about the man or his purpose in Newford.

Then, gaze narrowing, he advised her not to call on the captain. Proper ladies with an ounce of sense—here, she lifted a finger in protest, which he preempted with a scowl—did not pay calls on gentlemen. If she insisted on making the man's acquaintance, he would take her himself when he could.

She replied that surely, for his favorite relation, he could find time to do this one little thing.

"Of course," he said, "and when my mother desires my escort, she shall have it."

He left her then, dodging neatly when she would have boxed his shoulder while their mother smiled over her needlework.

That had been two days ago, and Bronwyn disliked waiting.

She'd been restless since Kate's marriage in the spring, her thoughts eager for any distraction.

Though she'd promoted the match between her dearest friend and cousin Ben, she hadn't expected the discontent that followed when Kate set up her house in London. Why, she'd been at such loose ends of late, she'd thrown herself into the fair's Preparations Committee with more vigor than usual. (Anyone with eyes could see the thing needed managing, and with Mrs. Pentreath called to her sister's bedside in Helston, Bronwyn had leapt into the breach.)

Now, the mystery of their new neighbor offered the possibility of diversion, but she could do little but wait for one of the men in her life to make an introduction.

Unless… Granfer. With her cousins Jory and Anna away to Bath, she'd promised to call on him to see how he fared. And as Penhale's nearest neighbor, surely he'd met the man.

She checked the clock. It was early yet, but if she left now, there would be time to visit her grandfather and persuade him to pay an afternoon call on his neighbor. Decision made, she collected her hat and ordered her pony hitched to the cart.

Merryn, who was off in full career to attend some business matter in Truro, stopped long enough to give her a look of deep suspicion when she told him she was driving out.

Drawing on her gloves, she let him stew a moment before saying, "Worry not, brother. A proper lady *with an ounce of sense* does not take a pony cart to a place as grand as Penhale. I mean to call at Oak Hill."

She was mildly insulted by the disbelief in his gaze. Then she noticed the lines around his eyes—lines she was certain had not been there before. He must be working too much, worrying over his business and the necessary bills and contracts and whatnot that accompanied such an endeavor.

There was a bit of remorse in his tone when he said, "I will try to take you to call at Penhale soon."

She was almost back in charity with him—until, striding toward the hall, he added, "Be sure to take a maid with you."

Really! As if she were so ramshackle to abandon all propriety. With brisk motions, she tied the strings of her hat.

"Jenny is airing the carpets with Mrs. Tilbury," her mother called from the parlor. "You'll have to take Beth."

Bronwyn's grandfather welcomed her with his usual good humor, but to her dismay, she found him tucked up in his morning room, a quilt wrapped about him and a warm compress atop one knee. His cane leaned against the sofa, and despite the day's warmth, a robust fire burned in the hearth.

He was in no condition for social calls, and her fabulous plan crumbled beneath the weight of her concern.

"Granfer," she said, hurrying across to him, "'tis your rheumatism that pains you?"

"Demmed knee," he grumbled. "But don't worry yourself. 'Twill pass soon enough."

"Can I bring you anything? Shall I send for Dr. Rowe?"

"No, no. Parsons has me well in hand. That man," he confided, "hovers worse than your grandmother ever did. Have you had your luncheon? 'Tis devilish close in here if you'll pardon the language. I could do with a bit o' sunshine."

With Parsons' help, Bronwyn soon had her grandfather settled on Oak Hill's broad terrace, where they lingered over lemonade and sandwiches. Late summer bees hummed in the garden, and the sea *shushed* faintly below the cliffs.

They spoke of the uncommonly warm weather and the insects that had threatened her grandmother's roses before Oak Hill's gardener finally bested them. She offered congratulations for the victory, then, as naturally as she could, brought the conversation round to Penhale. Though her grandfather might not be fit for making calls, surely, he could tell her something of his neighbor.

But Alan Kimbrell, who knew more about Newford's inhabitants than any of them would like, had still not met the gentleman. He'd called twice, but both times, his neighbor had been out.

"Dashed odd the fellow don't have more servants to do for him in a place the size of Penhale."

"He doesn't have servants?" Bronwyn asked in surprise.

"Aye, I met a groom, o' course—the man keeps a fine stable. But there was neither housekeeper nor footman to open the door. A body'd need some dozen or so to keep up the place. A bit rackety if you ask me."

Bronwyn nibbled a sandwich of butter and ham and considered this. What sort of man leased a place like Penhale without a proper household? Was he under the hatches, as her cousins liked to say, and fleeing the moneylenders? Or did he fancy himself an artist or a poet with the soul of a recluse?

Hmm. Newford's newest resident presented a fine puzzle. Her curiosity, which had been stirring before, was now whipped into a proper froth. Before she could voice her musings aloud, though, she was interrupted by a wet stick, placed carefully in her lap by her grandfather's wolfhound.

"Oh! What have you got there?"

Brioc laid his chin atop his offering and turned hopeful brown eyes on her as his tail threatened a potted palm.

"Brioc's been bedoled since Jory's taken Trout," her grandfather said, adjusting the quilt across his lap. "The servants exercise him, but I daresay he misses his lady."

"Poor doggie," Bronwyn said, cupping the wolfhound's large head with her hands and giving his ears a gentle scratch. She murmured more condolences and as her reward, Brioc nudged the stick closer, ears perked forward with self-abasing eagerness. Bronwyn gave her grandfather a questioning glance.

"Go on then," he said. "I'll enjoy a rest, and you'll gain an admirer for your trouble."

Bronwyn lifted the stick from her lap with two fingers, and Brioc wriggled with excitement. Stepping onto the lawn, she threw the thing, and he bounded after it.

They repeated this exercise for a quarter of an hour until Brioc returned with a larger specimen than the one she'd thrown and laid it at her feet. Tail sweeping the grass, he invited her to give this new, better stick a good toss.

"Really, now," she said with a laugh. "Did you think I wouldn't notice such a trick?"

Brioc only responded with an eager bark.

Her grandfather roused from his nap. "I've told him a reserved manner will win him more favor, but he insists on playing the fool."

Parsons materialized with a wet cloth for her hands. Some minutes later, Bronwyn pulled on her gloves, promising to return for Sunday luncheon. With a kiss for her grandfather's whiskered cheek, she sent for her cart and collected her maid, no more advanced in her campaign to make the acquaintance of Captain Gabriel Marsh than when she'd arrived.

———

GABRIEL REACHED FOR the dish on his dresser and frowned—he'd misplaced another handkerchief, the third in as many weeks. He muttered a curse for his carelessness and pulled another from the drawer, his fingers briefly grazing the linen-wrapped oval tucked at the back. He had no time to worry over such things as lost linens; there was still much to be done to see them settled at Penhale.

As the innkeeper had suggested, the manor was more house than a bachelor—a *widower*, he reminded himself—could require, but it was all the land agent had available on such short notice. And the lease was more than fair, owing to Penhale's remote location.

At the time, it had seemed the solution to his needs. Now, he wondered if he'd misjudged, but he was determined to make the best of their circumstances. Summoning Hadley from the stables, they set to work.

Some hours later, Gabriel surveyed the drawing room with satisfaction. Hadley had got the covers off the furnishings, and Gabriel had spent the better part of the morning putting the fireplace to rights and wiping away the dust that had collected on every surface.

The rugs still needed washing, or whatever it was maids did with rugs, and the curtains would have to await an expert's touch. But on the whole, he was satisfied with his efforts.

It wasn't that he meant to do any entertaining, but the light coming through the French windows was bright and warm, and the room would make a nice place for an afternoon of reading. He had no desire to take up housekeeping as a permanent occupation, though, so he'd sent Hadley into Newford to inquire after the day's post. Again. If the domestic gods favored him, he'd have word from the agency soon, or Miss Templeton. Both, even, though he wouldn't expect such good fortune.

He turned at a sound to find Emilia at the threshold, her slate in one hand and chalk dusting her fingers. Owing to her illness, he'd allowed her some leisure these last days, but like all soldiers, she must have something to occupy her time. Idle hands and the devil's mischief and all that.

To that end, Gabriel had taken on the role of tutor. Although he was better suited to providing instruction in marksmanship, riding and map reading, he'd begun with lessons in English. Miss Templeton, when she arrived, could address deportment, needlework, music and anything else a girl of seven required.

"Have you finished your translations?" he asked.

Emilia offered her slate and he took it. Her dark eyes watched him as he assessed her work.

He couldn't tell if she cared for his opinion, but he gave it to her anyway. "You've done a fine job," he said with a smile. "You've correctly translated the words for *dog* and *dress*, but do you recall what we said about the word *Papá*? It is the same in English."

Emilia shook her head. "*Capitão*."

Gabriel sighed. Emilia's reluctance in addressing him—and her formality in calling him Captain when she did—was unsettling. But they were still finding their way around one another, and he'd no wish to do battle over the matter. So, with a gentle hand to her shoulder, he said, "You will master the language yet. English can be stubborn, but I perceive you are as well. Why don't we try our hand at numbers next?"

———

PIPPIN'S TAIL SWISHED lazily as Bronwyn drove down the lane, and Beth's chatter filled the air with an amusing story from Oak Hill's scullery maid about the cook's mischievous cat. "Caught the little pilcher, she did, nickin' scraps from the pantry while the mice roam free in the stable."

Bronwyn paid only partial mind to this tale as Penhale's broad drive appeared ahead, marked with sturdy stone pillars and clumps of heather and gorse. *I am a proper lady with an ounce of sense.*

The cart rolled past the entrance without slowing, and she was pleased with her restraint, though she'd hardly admit as much to Merryn.

Her warm feelings of self-approbation were forgotten some yards later though, when an alarming crack split the air, and the cart gave a shuddering lurch.

Startled, Bronwyn reined in the pony, and the cart wobbled to a stop. She looked over the side but quickly righted herself when the vehicle tilted precariously toward the ditch.

"Oh, miss! I was that afeared we'd fly straight int' the ditch!" Beth's eyes were wide, one hand pressed to her cap as if it might fly away.

"There's nothing to fret over," Bronwyn soothed.

She motioned for Beth to climb down before following the maid, careful not to tip the cart any farther toward the ditch. Once on the lane, she spied the problem readily enough. They'd hit a stone, and two spokes in the rear wheel had snapped.

She eyed the lane ahead. She could abandon the cart and lead the pony to Newford some three miles below.

Frowning, she turned and looked behind them toward Oak Hill. Her grandfather's stables would have the parts needed to make the repairs. That was a far more attractive option.

But then... Penhale was closer still, its drive mere *steps* from them while Oak Hill lay half a mile back, at least. Whether Penhale's stables would have the necessary tools was another matter, but surely Captain Marsh's groom could manage such a repair.

"You'll have to hold the pony," Bronwyn said, passing the reins to Beth, who squeaked at being given such a task.

"Why? Where are you away to?"

Bronwyn nodded at Penhale's entrance. "I am going for help."

Beth's head swiveled toward the pillared drive

and back. "What? Up to Penhale, miss? But the cook at Oak Hill, 'er be sayin' the new man be an odd sort. Keeps to 'isself, 'e do, like 'e's too grand to be consortin' with the likes o' Newford. D'ye think 'is lordship'll hold with strangers 'pearin' on 'is doorstep?"

Bronwyn gave her skirts a twitch and smoothed her hands over the front of her dress. Righting her bonnet, she said, "We shall know soon enough."

She left Beth with firm, determined strides, ignoring the maid's protests. The wind whispered through the ancient trees lining Penhale's drive, but there were no other sounds as she walked. No birds called to one another. No squirrels or rabbits stirred the undergrowth. The shadows swayed and lengthened until Bronwyn, who was not prone to nervous fits, felt her first prickling of uncertainty.

No one knew anything of this Captain Marsh. What if he were an angry sort of fellow? A criminal, even? He'd not appeared to have a rough disposition, but was a fine figure not the perfect disguise for a man bent on mischief? Why *had* he come to Newford, of all places?

Then she bent her thoughts to the supplies he'd procured from the apothecary. Camphor, castor oil, mustard plasters. To be sure, someone at Penhale was ailing.

What if he had a wife after all, despite Wynne's

intelligence? A sickly female he kept in his attic.

In his *attic*? Bronwyn rolled her shoulders. She was not such a goose. Her cart had broken spokes. That was all. She merely needed the assistance of Captain Marsh's groom, and then she would be on her way.

With martial resolve, she took the final steps into the manor's broad forecourt and stared up at Pen-hale's stately facade. The afternoon sun struck at an angle, carving stark shadows where the east and west wings met the main house. Before the steps, a circular fountain stood dry.

The stables, some distance from the house, lay quiet, and the wide field beyond them stretched empty. No one appeared on the portico to greet her. Was there truly no footman?

That was when she noticed the door's bare face—the knocker had not been put up.

She considered turning back. She could still do it—slip through the trees, cross the field beyond and be back on her grandfather's terrace in a wink.

But she was not a craven sort of female.

Lifting her skirts, she climbed the steps and rapped firmly on the door. Silence. She knocked again, harder this time.

At last, footsteps sounded from within, followed by the scrape of bolts being drawn back.

CHAPTER 5

"ONE, TWO, THREE..." Emilia recited her English numbers in her soft, child's voice. Gabriel had no sooner settled her in the nursery with a fresh slate of translations when a faint knock sounded at the entrance below.

Gabriel went to the window. He couldn't see the door from this vantage point, but he had a full view of the forecourt. It was empty. There was no carriage or horse on the packed gravel. He scrutinized the trees lining the drive, but they were still.

He was wondering if he'd mistaken the sound when the knock came again, soft but insistent. A *female* knock. Had the governess—bless the heavens—finally arrived? Why had she not written?

He hurried from the nursery, stopping long enough to collect his coat from his room before descending the stairs. He shoved his arms into the sleeves as he reached the marble entry and paused to adjust his neckcloth in the mirror. He didn't wish Miss Templeton to think she'd arrived in bedlam, but there was nothing to be done for the dust on his trousers or the lack of a proper retainer at the door.

Drawing the bolts, he opened the door himself to find a dab of a female on the threshold.

Garbed in a simple dress of pale muslin, her person was well-formed, her countenance distinguished by a pair of large brown eyes, a little nose and a firm chin.

She didn't immediately speak. Instead, her dark brows fell together in a fleeting frown at his appearance.

The reaction wasn't wholly unexpected, given his dust and the long white scar that bisected his left eyebrow and half of his cheek. Gabriel imagined her impression of him must have been divided between revulsion and curiosity. The sooner she resolved herself, the sooner she could begin her duties. He cleared his throat.

"You're the governess, I presume," he said in cool tones. "Miss Templeton?"

Her eyes widened, and she found her speech. "I beg your pardon, sir—the governess?"

Her voice was clear with an easy lilt to it—her rolling consonants more aligned with the accent of the local populace than with a London governess. It was then he noticed she had no bag or trunk, nor traveling cloak.

"My apologies," he said. "I have mistaken you for someone else."

She glanced swiftly at her skirts. "Oh! Heavens, no. I'm not a governess, a fact for which we must all be grateful. I think I must offer *my* apologies for my ill manners, though. I'm not usually at a loss for speech. 'Tis only"—she paused, squinting at him—"you are not what I expected."

"Not what you expected?" he repeated, his wry condescension apparent even to his own ears.

"To be sure, you seem perfectly respectable, of course—very fine, really! But you're... older than I anticipated. Oh, dear, that was wretchedly done, wasn't it? What I meant was, when I saw you in Newford, I had the impression of someone a bit younger. Oh, and now I've made it so much worse, and you must think me rude beyond measure, which I promise you I am not. You are not so very old at all, of course. Only... not so young as I thought."

She thought him *old*? He'd only passed his thirtieth birthday last month. Regardless, this female couldn't be a day less than twenty-four. In a generous mood, he might allow twenty-three, but certainly no less than that. There were not so many years between them.

"I'm afraid you have the advantage of me, Miss—?"

"Miss Bronwyn Kimbrell," she said with a broad smile, extending a hand for him to shake.

Her steady gaze as he did so was direct enough to put most junior officers to the blush. *He* was not a junior officer, though he was still at a loss regarding the reason for her visit. If she was not the governess, then where was her companion? Surely, she hadn't called on a gentleman by herself.

"What, Miss Kimbrell, brings you to Penhale?"

She gave a heartfelt sigh. "The road," she said dramatically. "To be sure, 'tis riddled with stones and misfortune, both of which have brought me to your door to beg your assistance—or your groom's rather, if you can spare him. I'm fully aware that, as you are newly arrived, it ought to be *you* receiving kindnesses from your neighbors, rather than the other way round. But, you see, my cart has cracked a spoke. Two, rather. I've left my maid to hold the pony, but I don't know how much longer Pippin will suffer standing in the lane—Pippin being the pony, not my maid. He's been ancient for *ages*, and while he's not precisely indolent, he is not often inclined to do that which he doesn't wish to do. At any rate, the long and short of it is this: I find myself stranded just beyond your drive and, well... yours was the nearest dwelling."

The fascinated horror with which he heard this tale convinced him the woman had escaped her keepers. She folded her hands demurely at her waist, which he took as a signal that her speech had reached its end. He followed the thread of it back to the start to decipher what she wanted of him.

"My groom has gone into Newford," he said. Her brows fell at this, and he held his sigh. It wasn't his habit to leave ladies standing at his door, much less stranded on country lanes, so he added, "I, however, have fixed a broken wheel or two in my vast years on this earth."

She didn't miss his dry tone, and her eyes sparked with humor. "Only one or two? I would have thought an ancient man such as yourself would have encountered far more than that."

He didn't respond to her attempt at levity but said only, "If you care to wait in the drawing room, Miss Kimbrell, I will collect my gloves, and we'll see what's to be done." He stepped back, and she entered his home, her gaze swiveling left and right. There were no coy attempts to hide her curiosity.

"Oh!" she said, glancing up. "Now, who is this?"

Gabriel followed her gaze to where Emilia watched them from the first-floor landing, slate in one hand and her mother's handkerchief in the other. A frown creased her forehead.

So much for keeping to themselves.

With a sigh for the inevitability of it, Gabriel made the introduction. "This is my daughter, Miss Emilia Marsh. Newly escaped from the schoolroom, it would seem. Emilia, this is Miss Kimbrell."

"How d'you do, Miss Marsh? 'Tis a pleasure to make your acquaintance."

Miss Kimbrell made a small curtsy, which earned her little more than a blink from Emilia. Gabriel was certain his daughter knew her manners better than that, but he sensed her unease with their unexpected visitor, so he allowed the lapse.

He spoke in Portuguese, assuring her the lady was no one of any consequence. After a brief hesitation, she turned and retreated to the nursery.

Miss Kimbrell's smile remained firm throughout, though her fizz had fallen somewhat. Her thoughts were far too easy to read—she was regretting the necessity of their meeting. That was just as well, for the last thing he wanted was a string of curious villagers turning up at his door.

CHAPTER 6

BRONWYN WAITED IN Captain Marsh's drawing room while the gentleman collected his hat and gloves. He'd offered neither conversation nor refreshment— not that she would have taken any with Beth and Pippin standing in the lane, but the offer would have been nice.

Turning in a circle, she examined the room. Furnished in blues and cream, it was much as she remembered from her visits with her mother, when they'd paid calls on the previous owner. A damask settee with matching cushions sat opposite a pair of overstuffed chairs, and a chaise near the hearth was done up in pale stripes.

But if there'd been any question about the presence of a housekeeper, she could put that to rest. The dust motes that rose from the curtain when she nudged it aside spoke eloquently of the lack of servants. And the carpets… to be sure, they required a proper beating. But curiously, the table, when she pulled a finger across it, showed no dust. Someone—surely, not Captain Marsh himself?—had cleaned it.

This turned her thoughts to her host and the scar marking his smooth brow and cheek. She hadn't noticed it from Morwenna's window, but seeing his face fully for the first time had sent a dozen speculations through her mind about how he might have come by the wound.

A fresh wave of distress washed through her, and she pressed a hand to her middle—only to recall with mortification how she'd stood at his entry gaping at him like a perfect goose. Even worse, she'd suggested it was his *age* that had rendered her speechless! As if she were fresh from the schoolroom and he a member of her grandfather's set.

She shook her head. Sometimes, her tongue escaped before reason had a chance to catch it.

He did seem a trifle older than she'd expected, though not in an unappealing way. The impression came, perhaps, from the immovable line of his jaw or his masterful nose. Or perhaps in the steady way he held his hazel eyes on her. She suspected it was experience rather than years that had put the look on him.

Her musings were cut short when the captain returned. "Shall we?" he said with a curt motion toward the door.

She dismissed her thoughts, summoned a smile, and stepped lightly through to precede him from the house. He led her to the stables where he collected some tools. She looked round in some surprise as the stables were as fine—or finer than—the man's drawing room, with clean-swept floors, bright light coming through the upper windows and a fresh patch in the roof.

She made the acquaintance of Captain Marsh's horse, a spirited stallion with the odd name of Fogo, as well as a mare and two equally magnificent carriage horses. Fogo was even more stunning up close, and after an initial, high-handed attempt to chew the straw of her bonnet, he allowed her to stroke his nose, his ears twitching as she whispered compliments in them.

Captain Marsh frowned, unaccountably displeased by his stallion's capitulation. "Do you enjoy horses?" he said.

"Oh, how could a body not? Especially one as fine as your Fogo. There's something so noble about them, don't you think? May I give him an apple?"

Reluctantly, it seemed, the gentleman passed her an apple from a nearby bin. She fed it to his horse, adding with a laugh, "I think you must never let Fogo stand near my pony, though. Pippin has always imagined himself to be grander than he is, and I fear the comparison will cause his consequence to suffer."

The captain almost—very nearly—smiled at that, but it seemed she'd found the extent of his humor. He should know, though, that she was not so easily put off.

She had many questions—why was he in Cornwall, and what had become of his wife? What was the language he'd spoken to his daughter? It was not Italian, she thought, or Spanish.

As they walked down the drive to the lane, their steps crunching the gravel, she began with something easier. "From where d'you and your daughter hail, sir?"

There was a brief pause before he replied somewhat tersely, "London."

She waited, but no further details were forthcoming. "And d'you stay through the rest of the year? I hope you will be here in the autumn at least—the cove below the cliffs is a sight to see when the bracken turns to copper. And the scent of the gorse when it blooms—"

"The duration of my stay is undecided."

"Oh, of course." Bronwyn frowned. Aside from Newford's matrons, she'd rarely encountered anyone quite so... thorny. Or so unaffected by a friendly manner. But, she acknowledged, how strange it must be to remove to an unfamiliar place with no acquaintances or family. Surely, he could use a friend. Someone to guide him at the very least.

She tried again. "Captain Marsh, I apologize if I overstep, but I could not help but notice the lack of servants in your home. If you would like some recommendations—"

"They come soon, Miss Kimbrell."

"I beg your pardon?"

"My servants will be here soon." Then, with a sigh, he added, "There was a muddle-up at the agency, but I am assured of their earliest possible arrival."

"Their arrival… you have hired servants from… from *London*?"

"Well, yes," he said, his cheeks hollowing.

"Oh, but incomers will never do! Not if you wish to get on properly. You must have good Cornishmen and women to see to Penhale. I can give you the names of some excellent housekeepers, and Mrs. Jones—she's our cook, you know—she will tell you that her sister makes the best fish stew. My cousin will argue there's none better than the Feather's, but truly, you cannot go wrong with Mrs. Davies in your kitchen. Oh! And our housemaid's sister used to work at Penhale! 'Tis certain that, between my cousins and me, we can give you a list of the best—"

"I thank you, but I am confident the agency has assembled a suitable staff. We will endure until they arrive."

"But—"

"If I should change my mind, I will be sure to let you know."

Bronwyn closed her mouth with a frown. It was his house, after all—his peace that would surely be cut up if he didn't hire the proper staff. But on the matter of his daughter, she could not remain silent.

"But what of Miss Marsh's governess?" she said. "Miss… Templeton, was it? Is she also embroiled in your agency's 'muddle-up'?"

"No, Miss Kimbrell. Miss Templeton assures me she will join us as soon as she's concluded her current post in Suffolk."

A London staff and a governess from Suffolk. This had all the makings of a proper disaster. Biting her tongue, she said only, "Well, I should hope she arrives soon. Young girls should not be long without a governess. There is no telling what sort of mischief they might find if their studies are permitted to lapse."

"Do you speak from experience, Miss Kimbrell?" he said dryly.

"Ha! You are making a joke. But yes, to answer your question, I do speak from experience. Let me be your cautionary tale, sir. My governess took off with the squire's gardener when I was ten, and my family had the devil of a time finding a suitable replacement. I beg your pardon for my language, but I am well acquainted with the mischief that can be found with even the merest bit of effort. Your daughter most certainly requires a governess, and they do not grow on every bush in Cornwall. If your Miss Templeton does not make good on her promise, then you will have wasted all this time."

"You make a sound argument, Miss Kimbrell. I shall be sure to consult you, should I find myself in need of your governess recommendations."

Bronwyn counted to five and waged a silent but thorough debate regarding the differences between meddling and advising. (They were numerous.) In the end, she held her tongue against any further *advisement*.

The adage was true, it seemed: one woman could lead a horse to water, but twenty could not make him drink.

They reached the end of the drive, and Bronwyn left the horse—the captain, rather—to go to Beth.

The maid released an audible breath on spying her. "Oh, miss," she said, "there you be. I was that worrit you'd been 'napped by 'is lordship—" Her words ended with a squeak when Captain Marsh emerged from the drive behind Bronwyn. "Er, I was that worried you'd got yourself lost."

"Beth," Bronwyn said, "this is Captain Marsh. He has come to help us with the wheel. Here, let me take the reins and relieve you of Pippin. There's a good pony. The wheel, sir—the one with the broken spokes—is just there."

CHAPTER 7

BRONWYN ACCEPTED HER cup from Kate in the Feather's private parlor. They sat with Wynne and Morwenna, a bracing pot of tea and a plate of Wynne's raspberry tarts between them.

Beside the table, sleeping in a basket, lay Wynne's infant daughter, exhausted from being passed round her female relations. Young Elowen snored softly as Bronwyn recounted her broken wheel of the day before, and how she'd been obliged to seek aid from Penhale.

She described her encounter with the new gentleman there, including the unexpected appearance of Captain Marsh's daughter—a revelation as surprising to her companions as it had been to her. She also told them how the gentleman had spoken to the girl in a language she didn't recognize, which they all agreed had been rude, and how his words had sent the silent Miss Marsh back to her turret.

"And you say the girl doesn't speak?" Morwenna asked with a frown.

"I don't know that she *doesn't* speak," Bronwyn admitted, "only that she did not on this occasion."

Wynne added that, with a mysterious daughter in his attic and a manner that was surly at best, Captain Marsh put her in mind of "the villain from that tale in Morwenna's periodical… *The Vampyre*… what was his name?"

"Lord Ruthven," Morwenna and Bronwyn supplied.

"Aye, our stranger certainly has a brooding air about him."

"Menacing," Morwenna agreed.

And Bronwyn felt compelled to add that while Lord Ruthven left one with the impression of a pale sort of fellow, "Captain Marsh looks as though he spends a deal of time out of doors. I do not think him as cold as Ruthven, nor prone to vice, nor did I ever say he keeps his daughter in his *attic*." Chewing her lip, she reviewed her accounting and amended, "Although I can see how my words might have given that impression."

"But you did say the girl hasn't a governess or a nurse, nor does she seem acquainted with the basic civilities. What sort of cruel monster is this Captain Marsh, to neglect his daughter so? Why, when the matrons learn of this, they'll land on Penhale with pitchforks."

Bronwyn straightened and set her tea aside. "I said her governess has not yet *arrived* and that Miss Marsh's manner toward new acquaintances is one of… of caution and reservation. I most certainly did not give any indication that her father is a monster—oh!" she said, finally detecting the gleam in her cousins' eyes. "You are having me on! You're perfectly horrid, the pair of you!"

And when Kate lifted her cup to hide her own smile, Bronwyn added, "And you—my dearest friend! I think you must be as wicked as my cousins, to let me go on when you knew they were quizzing me."

"You cannot deny us our fun," Wynne argued.

"I would have a care, though, in telling your tale round the matrons," Morwenna added sensibly. "Their scrutiny is already piqued, and we know how swiftly they can turn such things into matters of propriety. If they scent anything irregular—vampire or not—Captain Marsh may find Newford less tranquil than he anticipated."

Bronwyn shifted uneasily on her chair. "You must credit me with more sense than to set the matrons on him."

"Must we?" Kate asked demurely over the rim of her cup.

Her friend's softly spoken question reminded them it hadn't been so long since Mrs. Pentreath and her circle had found Kate in compromising circumstances with Bronwyn's cousin Ben, an incident which *might* have begun with Bronwyn's poorly-planned (but well-intentioned) actions.

"Are you not enjoying the happy glow of newly-wedded bliss?" Bronwyn said a touch defensively.

"I am," replied Kate, making a study of the contents of her cup.

Bronwyn cast her eyes toward the ceiling as a ridiculous blush stained her friend's cheeks. Then, unable to ignore the temptation Morwenna had set before them, she said, "What *do* the matrons say?"

The conversation then shifted to the rumors that had been trotted round Newford regarding Captain Marsh's possible origins—if a charge of vampirism couldn't be laid at his door. Some whispered he'd fled London after crossing a vengeful husband, while others claimed the man had fallen in with a notorious ring of thieves—both of which Bronwyn added to her list of his scar origins.

Morwenna, who was privy to all manner of conversation in her shop, had overheard heated whispers that morning between some of Newford's matrons. Mrs. Tretheway suggested Captain Marsh was a lost heir to some noble house, come to claim his birthright—though Morwenna's well-placed ears had yet to uncover why he thought to do so at Penhale, of all places.

Mrs. Clifton had firmly rejected this theory, claiming she had it from *Mr.* Clifton that the newcomer was a disgraced royal—a royal!—fleeing a scandalous past. Mrs. Tretheway's lips had pursed over such ill use of their village.

From which point, it was only a small hop for Bronwyn and her cousins to decide he was an aristocratic highwayman, seeking redemption in their quiet hamlet. They weren't so lost as the matrons that they didn't know their speculations were ridiculous, but it was amusing nonetheless to imagine the most ludicrous scenarios.

When their laughter faded, Wynne brushed a stray crumb of pastry from the table. "D'you think we ought to offer aid to this duke-turned-highwayman? I know Keren has been pleased with her brother's governess—per'aps Miss Litton could recommend one of her friends from Truro, at least until Miss Marsh's own lady arrives. To be sure, Captain Marsh must welcome any assistance with his daughter, and I imagine *she* would appreciate another female in the nursery. I've never known a man who could tie a proper sash."

Bronwyn explained how, in the least meddlesome way possible, she'd offered whatever aid the gentleman might require in securing both his household and his nursery staff—and how her generosity had been flatly rebuffed. "And though I doubt his sense in doing so, he is the master of his house, and I accept his choice."

The silence round the room was absolute as she lifted her cup to her lips and took a sip of tepid tea. Finally, Morwenna found her voice. "And that's to be an end to't?" The disbelieving hitch in her tone was hardly flattering.

"What?" Bronwyn said. "D'you find it so hard to imagine? I assure you, I've far more important things to do with my time than press sound advice on a man who doesn't wish't."

Elowen woke and expressed doubt at this pronouncement. Wynne lifted her from her basket and added her opinion. "I confess to some surprise," she said slowly, "and, truth be told, a bit of disappointment. I would not have expected you to abandon the field so easily. Truly—you've no plans to contrive another meeting?"

Bronwyn tucked her chin. She'd resolved not to meddle in Captain Marsh's household when he'd made it so abundantly clear that her opinion was not needed. But as for contriving another meeting… well. Was that not the purpose of dropping her handkerchief in his drawing room?

——

Gabriel watched as Hadley, whom he'd promoted from groom and coachman to groom, coachman, cook and footman, strode triumphantly up the drive. The lightness in his step could only mean one thing: the post had come.

Did he bring a letter from the domestic agency? Miss Templeton? Or had Brightwell sent word of Ribeiro's untimely demise?

Gabriel left Emilia to her sums and hurried from the nursery, reaching the first-floor landing as Hadley entered the front door.

"Well?" he said without preamble.

Hadley, long accustomed to his employer's directness, merely grinned and withdrew a letter from his coat. When Gabriel reached the entry, he extended it with both hands as one might a gift.

"Your post, sir."

Gabriel took the letter, turning it over to find his direction written in an unfamiliar hand. An unfamiliar, *masculine* hand, so it was not from his governess. Nor had it come from Brightwell, whose pen he would have recognized. It must be from the agency.

His gaze flicked to Hadley, who showed none of the reserve expected of a footman and remained eagerly at his side instead. Gabriel couldn't fault him.

They were both well acquainted with the hardships of the battlefield, but the past days had taxed the limits of their patience in new and unexpected ways. Housekeeping and laundry—domains any good soldier should have conquered with a few creative curses—had proven far more challenging with a young lady in residence. A young lady who came with bows and lace and all manner of furbelows that did not bear up well to their masculine efforts.

"Well, Hadley," Gabriel said, his voice wryer than he intended, "let us see whether the agency has sent us more than apologies this time."

He broke the seal with a decisive motion, unfolded the paper, and read.

Captain Marsh,

Let me begin by assuring you that your custom is our agency's utmost priority. You have our deepest regrets for the unfortunate delay you've suffered…

However, it is now my unhappy duty to inform you of a far graver situation…

In a tragic and unforeseen mistake, the staff assembled for your home were erroneously dispatched to a country manor in the north…

Be assured, the clerk responsible for this deplorable error has been relieved of his position without a reference… I am assembling a new complement of household servants, which task I anticipate being completed inside of a month...

In compensation for your inconvenience, the agency is pleased to offer the services of an additional kitchen maid, at no expense to your household...

Gabriel's stomach sank. He lowered the letter and marshaled his expression before relaying the contents to Hadley. Hadley, who'd been with him from the siege of Almeida to their victory at Toulouse, who'd remained loyal and stalwart as bullets whistled around them... But this was asking too much. His groom would surely tender his notice now.

"A month?" Hadley said in a horrified whisper that mirrored Gabriel's own sentiment.

Gabriel thought again of Miss Kimbrell and her offer of aid, given without a moment's hesitation. She seemed the worst sort of managing female, but he didn't doubt she'd take his household in hand with a mere word from him.

But there was Emilia to consider.

He meant to keep their presence in Cornwall from making the rounds of local gossip, a feat that would be nearly impossible with local servants. He'd already overheard a few speculations at the apothecary, enough to confirm the townspeople were beginning to weave their tales about him. So far, though, none had mentioned his daughter.

He certainly didn't wish to call attention to the

fact that there was a young girl of dark Iberian looks in residence. The last thing he wanted was any sort of gossip that might find its way to Ribeiro. He didn't know if the man still searched for her, but until Brightwell confirmed otherwise, Gabriel would remain on his guard.

No, he would not accept Miss Kimbrell's aid—however tempting the notion of a well-ordered house might be.

Clearing his throat, he summoned his most rallying captain's voice. "We will manage, Hadley. No—we will *triumph*. We are capable of great things, and we will not be defeated by a bit of lye and dust."

Hadley's slow nod betrayed his disbelief. "Might be best to lower your expectations, sir." Then, with the grim resolve of a man pinned behind the enemy's line, he added, "Shall we try our hand at the laundry again?"

Gabriel couldn't help but smile at his groom's generous use of the plural "we." While Hadley had spent the last days tending to the stables, Gabriel had taken on the laundry. For his efforts, they now slept on board-stiff linens, and he'd turned more than one of Emilia's shifts an unfortunate shade of yellowish-brown.

His brisk attempt to convince his daughter it was "in the English style" had only earned him more of her frowning silence.

"I would rather empty the chamber pots than attempt the linens again," he said wryly. "I've my dignity to consider, after all, but let's see what's to be done in the kitchen."

CHAPTER 8

AS IT TURNED out, Bronwyn's fallen handkerchief, left so artfully behind in Captain Marsh's drawing room, failed miserably in its mission. Nearly a week passed, but the gentleman made no move to return it. Not that she expected he would, she reminded herself for the fifth time. He did not seem the sort to seek a lady out, but then, he'd not seemed the sort to abandon all civilities, either.

Curiosity, however, was a difficult beast to tame, especially when tantalizing bits of overheard conversation were dangled before it.

While placing an order with the chandler, she'd heard Mrs. Tretheway recounting a chance meeting with Captain Marsh outside the bakery. The lady's smile was smug as she shared the details, doling them out like a bishop giving coins to beggars. Bronwyn had felt no shame in listening; *listening* was not the same as meddling.

And in any case, there was little of interest in Mrs. Tretheway's report. The most noteworthy detail was that the captain had tipped his hat—a nice beaver—then held the door for her. As if any gentleman might have done less!

Bronwyn had bitten her tongue against her questions. She could—she *would*—ignore them. It was nothing to her, whether Captain Marsh's London staff had arrived, or his daughter's governess. Her curiosity was an ant beneath her boot, insignificant and easily squashed.

Today was Sunday. After church, she and her mother would drive to Oak Hill for her grandfather's weekly family luncheon. The fine weather promised to hold, so they would dine on the back lawn where the children and dogs could play. She would not be surprised if her grandfather had invited his new neighbor.

Which, of course, was no concern of hers.

As she put the final pin in her hair and collected her shawl, she paused to give her reflection a frowning glance. Could she truly be mistaken for a governess?

Not that there was anything *wrong* with being a governess—she'd had several, all respectable and intelligent females, but they were also sensible. And if there was a single word that had never been applied to Bronwyn Kimbrell, it was *sensible*.

She tilted her head, scrutinizing her reflection. In her experience, governesses went about in sober-hued wool dresses made high to the neck, without any frills or flounces to soften the edges. Her own dress was a pretty shade of pale blue, but the line of it was simple and undeniably practical. There was the tiniest flounce at the hem, but only the most discerning eye would ever notice it.

Blast it all. She *did* look like a governess.

The case clock in the parlor chimed the half hour. They would soon be late. She reached for her gloves but paused again.

It wasn't that she minded being taken for a governess. It was simply that she had more dash.

Pleased with this entirely reasonable justification, she called down the hall for Beth before throwing open the doors of her wardrobe. She ruffled the contents with an impatient hand until, at last, she found a soft muslin gown in a jonquil hue. It had a narrow bit of Honiton lace edging the bodice and puff sleeves, and the neckline was modest enough for church—though she suspected their vicar's brows might lift at the color. But with an ivory shawl, she might escape his notice.

Beth came in and frowned at the dress in Bronwyn's hand. "What is't, miss?"

"I must change," she said, hopping as she removed her blue slippers.

"But miss, what be wrong with the blue? Per'aps a different sash —"

"Too sensible," Bronwyn said, to which Beth merely replied with an open-mouthed nod.

The jonquil dress, which she usually reserved for social outings, earned a questioning look from her mother as she descended the stairs, and a frown from Merryn when her brother joined them.

As expected, their vicar's forehead did furrow upon finding such a cheery lamb among his flock. Like two caterpillars, his eyebrows crawled upward before settling back together. When his sermon took a turn from the divine gift of forgiveness to the follies of vanity in youthful hearts, Bronwyn turned her attention to a loose thread.

Once the service was finished, when it looked as if the vicar might be aiming his steps in her direction, she hurried her mother along.

"Mama," she said, rushing them through the churchyard, "we'll be late if we don't hurry."

"But I see your aunt waving —"

"You'll see her at Oak Hill, where you can have a proper gossip. Come along, now."

———

BRONWYN FOUND A place on one of the thick blankets on her grandfather's lawn. She'd just set down a plate piled with slices of cold chicken and cheese, and a bowl with enough syllabub to earn a teasing remark from Kate, when Morwenna's voice reached them.

"Grandpapa, did you extend an invitation to your new neighbor?"

Bronwyn paused, a bite of chicken halfway to her lips. Lowering her fork, she tilted her head and feigned an interest in a loose thread at the blanket's edge.

"'Course I did. Parsons sent one of the footmen off with a note to Penhale. Marsh declined, though—politely, I'll grant him. Seems the man prefers his own company," he added with a chuckle.

Bronwyn's hand tightened on her fork. He'd declined? What sort of man declined a direct invitation from a neighbor? It simply wasn't done, especially when the neighbor was Alan Kimbrell. Did he not realize that her grandfather—and the larger Kimbrell clan—owned much of Newford?

"What sort of gentleman keeps to himself like that?" she blurted, forgetting for a moment that she did not care what Captain Marsh did.

Just then, a piece of chicken fell from her cousin Alfie's fork and was promptly seized by Brioc with a loud, wet snort.

"A man of uncommonly good sense," replied her grandfather mildly, "if he's any notion of the company to be found here."

There was laughter at that, and Bronwyn returned her attention to Kate, who'd been recounting a humorous encounter with a London jarvey.

Though her friend's tale was amusing, Bronwyn found her thoughts straying back to Penhale's reclusive tenant. Even if the man had no wish to socialize with his neighbors, what of his daughter? Surely the girl would benefit from an afternoon of sun and games. Several of Bronwyn's young cousins were present. They would have made suitable companions for Miss Marsh.

"Bronwyn?" Kate's voice recalled her attention. "You haven't heard a word, have you?"

"I beg your pardon. I was wool-gathering."

Kate smiled. "About a certain gentleman, perhaps?"

"Not at all," Bronwyn replied primly. "I was merely thinking that"—she cast about—"that Brioc has grown rather round of late. I daresay someone has been feeding him pastries again."

Upon hearing his name, the wolfhound abandoned his watch over Alfie's plate and lumbered to her side, collapsing with a dramatic sigh. She scratched his ear, but when his eyes rolled hopefully toward her syllabub, she wagged a finger in warning.

"You would do me such a rude turn, after I scratched your ear and tossed your disgusting stick?

Or have you forgotten that kindness so soon?"

His ears perked at the word "stick," but detecting reproof in her tone, he dropped his head between his massive paws, looking up at her with doleful brown eyes.

"Oh, no. If you think I'm to be so easily gammoned by your poet's eyes again…" His sigh was so forlorn that it stopped her mid-admonishment.

"Blast."

Sensing victory, Brioc bounded up and away, only to return with a choice stick which he dropped without ceremony onto the blanket.

"Oh, very well," she muttered, "but I won't have you spoiling my dress." Sighing in resignation as she rose, she handed her bowl with its uneaten syllabub to a waiting footman.

Alfie grinned around a mouthful of squab pie. "'Twould appear you've landed a beau at last."

With an arch glance for her cousin, she said, "Brioc has a fine address, and any lady would be pleased to keep company with him."

Alfie waved his fork toward the departing footman. "Does this mean you won't be eating your syllabub?"

She didn't honor this with a reply as she followed the dog onto the open lawn. Brioc's tail wagged furiously as Bronwyn drew her arm back and threw the stick. It sailed across the lawn and the wolfhound charged after it, sending children scattering with cries of laughter and protest. When he nearly upset the table of cider and lemonade, she took their game farther afield, beyond the lawn and away from the children's cricket ground.

After several tosses, she muttered, "You are relentless. What d'you say to a nice, calming stroll through the gardens instead?"

The dog, unmoved by the prospect of such tame diversion, thumped his tail against the ground. His gaze moved from her to the stick and back again, and when she didn't comply, he lifted an encouraging paw toward her skirts.

Taking a little hop backwards, Bronwyn held up both hands. "Now, that is a bit too forward," she admonished him. Then, with a sigh, she threw his stick again, and again, until her arm tired and her face flushed from the effort.

The game carried them farther from her grandfather's luncheon, away from her cousins' laughter and the *thwack* of the cricket bat, toward the quiet wood that separated Oak Hill from Penhale.

Heavens, had they come so far?

She glanced back and could barely see her grandfather's lawn, hidden as it was beyond a small rise. Here, the noise of her family's gathering was replaced by the shushing of wind through the trees and the occasional trill of a distant bird.

Brioc's stick landed at the edge of the copse, and he raced happily toward it, tongue flopping. Through the trees, Bronwyn could make out the line of Penhale's garden wall.

That was when she heard it: a faint and melodic tune, coming to them on the breeze. She stopped, listening. The singing was soft, the voice that of a child. Though she couldn't make out the words, the language carried the same lilt as the one Captain Marsh had used when speaking to his daughter.

Brioc heard it, too. His ears pricked up, and his tail stilled before he let out a sudden, booming bark, so out of place in the quiet wood that Bronwyn's heart skipped.

On the other side of the wall, a girlish yip of surprise followed, and the singing stopped.

"Brioc!" Bronwyn hissed in a harsh whisper, but the dog was gone, crashing through the copse toward his new quarry.

Bronwyn hurried after him, brushing aside a tangle of ivy and ignoring how it pulled at her dress. She soon found herself at Penhale's old stone wall, while ahead, heavy paws crunched the leaves.

She followed the sound until she came to an iron gate, hanging drunkenly on loose hinges. It revealed a gap wide enough for a dog—*and* a smallish female—to slip through.

CHAPTER 9

"Where have you gone, ungrateful beast?" Bronwyn muttered, hoisting her skirts as she stepped carefully through the gate's opening. The stones of the wall were slick with moss, and her gown caught on the brambles more than once. By the time she squeezed through, the soft muslin of her gown was streaked with dirt, and the hem was surely ruined.

Penhale's garden sloped up toward the house on her left, and down toward the cliffs to her right. She recognized the small figure of Miss Emilia Marsh, standing rigid atop a marble bench near the path's edge. She clasped her small hands at her chest, out of reach of Brioc, who danced and panted eagerly below.

"Brioc," Bronwyn commanded. The dog responded with a deep-throated bark to come meet his new acquaintance.

To the girl, Bronwyn said, "'Tis all right, Miss Marsh. Brioc won't hurt you. He's large, to be sure, but harmless. He thinks himself a puppy still, though we've all tried to convince him of the truth of't."

The girl flicked wary eyes at Bronwyn, before returning her attention to the beast circling below.

"Brioc," Bronwyn said more sternly.

Chastised—and in front of his new friend, no less—the dog lowered his ears and trotted back to her side.

More gently, Bronwyn said, "You can't let high spirits get the better of your manners if you wish to make a fitty impression. Now, make your bow to Miss Marsh like a proper gentleman."

Relieved not to have lost Bronwyn's favor altogether, Brioc fell into a pose of such fawning submission, his hindquarters high and great front paws splayed wide in the dirt, that a grin escaped Miss Marsh. She clapped her hands over her mouth to catch it, her wide eyes darting to Bronwyn before she lowered her hands back to her chest.

That was when Bronwyn spied the embroidered corner of a linen square peeking from the girl's little fingers. "Why, you found my handkerchief!"

The amusement vanished from Miss Marsh's face so swiftly Bronwyn thought she must have imagined it. The girl angled a defiant chin at her before pocketing the handkerchief in her pinafore.

Bronwyn blinked at this blatant larceny. But though Miss Marsh's chin remained high as she pressed the pilfered square in her pocket, Bronwyn spied the merest flicker of uncertainty beneath her stubborn gaze.

"Oh! Well, per'aps 'tis only one that *looks* like mine, but I'm certain you've the right of't."

Brioc gave a happy bark, recalling their attention to where he still bowed, awaiting someone to accept his invitation to play. Bronwyn smiled at Miss Marsh.

"D'you see? Brioc is quite harmless. A handsome fellow, truly, though I won't deny his manner, 'tis a little forward. You sing very prettily, by the by."

Miss Marsh didn't acknowledge the compliment. Her gaze remained fixed on Brioc, though now there was more curiosity than fear in it. Bronwyn moved closer to the bench and Brioc padded behind her.

"Would you like to pet him?"

The girl hesitated, and Bronwyn wondered if she understood English. Miss Marsh had yet to speak, but she seemed to understand Bronwyn's assurances. Certainly, she'd comprehended Bronwyn's claim to her handkerchief.

Finally, the girl extended a hand toward the dog. At a soft word from Bronwyn, Brioc approached the bench and nudged the small, proffered palm with his nose.

"Oh, well done," Bronwyn said to the pair of them as Miss Marsh gently ruffled the dog's ear.

Brioc, in raptures over this treatment, placed one paw on the bench and rose on his hind legs so Miss Marsh might reach his favorite spot. The girl didn't hesitate to oblige him, a smile lifting the corners of her mouth as Brioc tilted his head to give her the best angle.

A deep, masculine shout interrupted them. Miss Marsh stilled and the dog dropped onto his haunches with embarrassing haste. Bronwyn looked around Miss Marsh to see the girl's father coming at them, the capes of his coat flying behind him. His dark gaze was fixed on the wolfhound, and Bronwyn's stomach dropped at his thunderous scowl. A lesser female might have fled at this stage, but she was made of sterner stuff. But really, was it any wonder the French had been vanquished?

When Captain Marsh reached them, he gave Bronwyn a swift measuring-up from head to toe, his gaze too dismissive to be flattering as he took in her stained gown and torn hem. Then, in a voice that was more of a growl, he said, "Is this your mongrel, Miss Kimbrell?"

Brioc, sensing conflict if not the insult, rose to stand between them, his hackles lifted ominously.

Bronwyn laid a reassuring hand atop his head and lifted her chin to meet Captain Marsh's gaze.

"No, sir," she replied firmly. "That is, he is not a mongrel. I daresay Brioc's lineage can be traced further back than"—she caught herself before she said *yours*—"than that of most gentlemen. At any rate, he belongs to my grandfather, and I'll have you know he was a gift from—"

"I don't care if he was a gift from King George himself. I want to know why the beast was attacking my daughter."

"Attacking! Well! Brioc may be a trifle over-eager, but I assure you—"

"*Pare*," Emilia said softly, drawing all eyes to her. Even without a knowledge of the language, Bronwyn sensed by her fierce frown she was urging them to silence.

Gingerly, Emilia climbed down from the bench and approached Brioc, despite her father's stern warnings. She reached for the dog's ear and gave it a gentle stroke. The wolfhound's hackles relaxed at this treatment, and his tail thumped in ecstasy.

Bronwyn fought a superior smile, though it escaped anyway. "There," she said to Captain Marsh. "'Twould seem your daughter has found a friend, and Brioc, a champion."

The gentleman glanced from his daughter to Bronwyn. His expression was unreadable, though his tone remained clipped as he said, "I'll thank you to keep your grandfather's dog off Penhale property, Miss Kimbrell."

"I shall be pleased to do so," she replied with a smile that felt a trifle brittle.

For a moment, Captain Marsh looked as though he might argue the point further, but then he sighed—a deep, resigned sound—and turned to his daughter who was now receiving Brioc's wet and unashamed kisses. "Take your leave of Miss Kimbrell and join Hadley in the stables. It's time for your riding lesson."

He spoke in English, and the girl's brows dipped in displeasure. Then he said something more in the tongue Bronwyn didn't recognize, and Miss Marsh proved she could make a proper curtsy before leaving them.

Brioc whined to see his new friend go, and when Captain Marsh turned back to Bronwyn, she called up a conciliatory smile. "My apologies, sir, for the inconvenience. I will endeavor to see that Brioc remains on his side of your wall, though per'aps you might consider repairing the gate."

"I will see to it," he replied shortly.

"Excellent."

"Excellent."

With nothing more to be said, Bronwyn summoned Brioc and walked back the way they'd come. Captain Marsh's sigh stopped her before she stepped through the gap.

"Miss Kimbrell."

She turned, wondering if he might offer to drive her back to Oak Hill by way of the lane. It was not very gentlemanly of him to send her climbing back through the brambles in one of her best dresses, though she didn't know how she would explain returning to Oak Hill by the front door.

His expression, though, was not that of a gentleman offering his escort. It was stern, his scar thin and white across his cheek as he said, "Does your offer still stand? That is, are you able to recommend servants for Penhale?"

Bronwyn's heart skipped. This was even better than his escort. He wanted her *help*. It wouldn't do to prostrate herself like an over-eager wolfhound, though.

Drawing a breath, she gave him a perfectly normal smile without any hint of excessive feeling. "I should be happy to offer what aid I may, if 'tis your wish."

———

GABRIEL THOUGHT MISS Kimbrell's smile was far too pleasant for the task he'd set her.

"'Tis Sunday," she said, "so not the best day for hiring staff, I'll admit. But have no fear, Captain Marsh. I am certain a few words in the right ears will have a cook on your doorstep before the supper hour."

Her words were calm, without the animation he'd witnessed during their first encounter, and he felt like a cad for his earlier rudeness. It was clear she was holding the reins on her natural energy.

But the reins soon slipped, and her enthusiasm for the task (which was a mystery in itself) overtook whatever resolve she had to present a decorous front. She began to pace, marking items off her fingers as she went. Her strides lengthened—too resolute to be maidenly—while the dog watched her movements with avid interest.

"You'll require a kitchen maid," she continued. "I imagine the squire's cook must have a suggestion or two. And a housekeeper, to be sure—Mrs. Forsyth raised six daughters; she'll know how to go on with Miss Marsh until your governess arrives. And then a man for the door... someone to tend the grounds... This garden is dreadful." She spared a frown for the tangled vines surrounding them.

"The grounds can wait," Gabriel said. "The laundry, however, cannot."

"Oh, without a doubt! Beth's sister Lizzie works the laundry at the Feather with Mrs. Thatcher. I'm confident my cousin can be persuaded to lend her for an afternoon or two, until we can achieve a more permanent solution."

She paused, turning to face him. "Oh, you're frowning. 'Tis an unacceptable plan? I assure you, my cousin's inn is first-rate, and her staff are the most efficient you'll find this side of Truro."

Gabriel forced his expression to ease. He'd been told more than once that his frown could stop an enemy's bullet, but this petite female merely gazed up at him with a question in her dark eyes.

He couldn't fault her plan—he was the one who'd added a laundry maid to her list, after all—but he was keenly aware of the impropriety of the situation. An unmarried lady did not manage a gentleman's household—and certainly not without a formal introduction.

But that was the least of his concerns, for it seemed a lot of people would be consulted to secure his Cornish staff. Worse still, she spoke of bringing in people from the inn. The *inn*—a crossroads where strangers of all sorts passed through. His household would be a topic on far too many tongues for his peace of mind.

"Miss Kimbrell," he began, "for reasons I cannot disclose, I prefer—I *require*—a discreet presence in Cornwall."

She made a scoffing sound. "Well, 'tis rather late for that."

His frown deepened.

"Oh, you're serious! But truly, I think 'tis a fair

bet that particular goose is already dressed and cooked."

"What do you mean?" he said around the hot unease rolling in his gut.

Her brows came together, and she folded her hands at her waist. "Why, because 'tis Newford. Gentlemen of unknown origins—especially handsome gentlemen such as yourself—will always cause talk. Talk which, if you'll permit me to say it, has only been encouraged by *your* efforts to maintain a 'discreet presence.' You've presented us with something of a riddle, Captain Marsh, and I—*we*, that is—love nothing more than an engaging puzzle to sort."

Her cheeks dimpled a little at this confession, a fact he might have found intriguing if her words hadn't caused him some alarm.

"What are people saying?" he demanded.

Miss Kimbrell frowned at his tone, and the wolfhound growled low in its throat. The lady laid a hand atop the dog's head. With a glance toward the gap in the gate, she said, "Captain Marsh… are you engaged in something… nefarious?"

He'd unsettled her, though it was not his intention to do so. With a steadying breath, he forced a measure of calm into his voice. "No, Miss Kimbrell. I assure you, I am not engaged in anything nefarious, but I would know what is being said about me. If you please."

She studied him for a long moment, weighing his words. He waited impatiently for her to complete her assessment. At last, her frown fell away, and she dipped her head in a short, decisive nod.

"Very well," she said, waving the air between them. "No one is saying very much that's useful, to be sure, but there is speculation. It ranges an impressive length—with you as the lost heir to a dukedom at one end and a notorious thief at the other." Her dark eyes brightened with mischief. "And, of course, there's the usual speculation of vampirism."

"Vampirism!" He blinked. "That's... usual?"

She shrugged. "We are a creative lot."

Clearing his throat, he said as evenly as he could, "And what do people say of my daughter?"

Understanding crossed Miss Kimbrell's features. "'Tis *her* presence you wish to conceal... not your own." She waited for him to confirm this, but when he remained stalwart, she continued. "I would ask again if you're involved in something criminal—if you've taken her from her family, per'aps—but anyone can see she is your relation. To address your question... I do not think many are yet aware of your daughter's presence." Her nose wrinkled. "Though I feel I should confess... I have mentioned the pair of you to my cousins. And Kate—but Kate is my cousin by marriage now, and my dearest friend. She would not for the world betray a confidence if she knew it to be such."

His alarm must have shown, for she quickly added, "Should I ask them to hold their silence?"

Gabriel released a heavy sigh and spread a hand over his forehead, pressing his temples. It was clear now that maintaining a discreet presence would prove impossible—especially once he had a local cook in his kitchen and a maid from the inn washing his linens. He ought to have stayed in London, where at least he might have hidden Emilia among thousands of anonymous faces.

Miss Kimbrell's thoughts seemed to travel a similar course.

"Silence," she said, "is not the surest way to achieve your aim." Tilting her head, she considered him a moment longer. "May I suggest, Captain Marsh, if you truly wish to avoid notice, you would do better to make yourself—and your daughter— known. Take your place within the community, if you will."

"You suggest I become a Newforder?" he said doubtfully.

She laughed, a light sound that fell over itself like a pocketful of coins. "Well, no. Mrs. Dauntry and her husband came down from"—she waved vaguely at the rest of England—"from Devon or thereabouts some thirty years ago, and Mrs. P still calls them incomers. So, no, unless you are born into Newford, or you marry into Newford, you are never really *of* Newford. But 'tis still possible to have a place here.

"The truth is, Captain Marsh, 'tis the excitement of a stranger that will keep tongues wagging. That's not to say we don't enjoy some gossip about our neighbors, but most of us are loyal when it matters. If 'tis the notice of those *outside* of Newford which concerns you…"

"Then I ought to make friends within," he finished grimly.

"Precisely!"

The dog bounded at Miss Kimbrell's enthusiasm, eager for whatever new game was afoot. Then, from beyond the wall, over the rise between Penhale and Oak Hill, came the sound of male voices.

Gabriel tensed, his hand reaching for the hilt of his missing sword until he realized a party must have come in search of Miss Kimbrell.

She leaned close to whisper, "I must go. I will send a cook to you before tea, and a housekeeper by week's end. And when my grandfather next invites you to Oak Hill, do not cry off."

Gabriel did not readily agree to this, but he held a branch aside for Miss Kimbrell to pass through the crooked gate.

Contrary feelings of relief and doubt clouded his thoughts. Relief that he'd soon have a cook, and doubt that mixing with the local inhabitants was the best way forward. As a wartime strategy, the tactic had merit. It was one he'd used before to great effect, though it hadn't been without its complications.

The last time he'd made friends with the local citizenry, he'd gained a wife, and he knew how well that had turned out.

CHAPTER 10

BRONWYN WOKE TWO days later, having enjoyed the sleep of the virtuous, her mood buoyed by the success of her domestic efforts on Captain Marsh's behalf. Despite her easy assurances to the gentleman, securing a cook *and* a laundry maid on such short notice—to say nothing of a housekeeper—had been no small task.

Given the captain's insistence on discretion, she'd taken particular care to find individuals who were not inclined—or rather, were *less* inclined—to gossip, which had been no easy feat. In the end, she was pleased to have assembled a capable, if rudimentary, staff to see to the running of Penhale:

Mrs. Forsyth, housekeeper.

Mrs. Davies, cook.

Lizzie, housemaid *and* laundry maid, the poor dear. (Persuading Wynne to part with the Feather's laundry maid, even temporarily, had cost her an afternoon of sorting linens at the inn when she ought to have been sorting details for the fair.)

John Trewin, first footman and de facto butler. (John, a grandson to Penhale's former butler, had been seeking a position in Truro. He'd assured her he would be some pleased to stand as first footman in the manor where he'd spent so much of his youth.)

If she'd yet to secure a gardener, she thought her grandfather's worthy groundsman might provide a suggestion or two to tame the plantings.

To put a finish to all these efforts, she'd just asked her grandfather to extend another invitation to Captain Marsh for Sunday luncheon, certain the gentleman would find time in his calendar to accept. Her grandfather's doubting squint was followed by a noncommittal grunt.

"Don't think your industry on behalf of my neighbor has escaped my notice."

Bronwyn considered her reply before giving his hand a squeeze. "Of course it hasn't. Little in New-ford would dare to do so. But Granfer, when I first encountered Captain Marsh—quite by accident, mind—his household... Well, he has suffered the most shocking incompetence you can imagine. I suppose 'tis to be expected from a London agency, but I thought it only neighborly to offer what assistance I could. I know you would wish for Penhale to prosper."

Her grandfather shifted in his chair, and the blanket over his knees slipped. Bronwyn reached to adjust it, but he batted her hand away.

"You are the most managing female," he muttered, though not unkindly. "I suppose your grandmother would have been proud of your capable manner, though she'd have agreed with me that a proper introduction should have come first. As the head of this family, it is my obligation—my privilege—to do this."

Bronwyn thought it best not to remind him of his rheumatism, which had prevented her from requesting the introduction he so earnestly wished to make. Instead, she offered, "Yes, well, 'tis an unfortunate fact that circumstances—and broken wheels—don't always allow for proper introductions. But if you should extend another invitation to Captain Marsh, and if he should accept, then I would be pleased if you do the honors. I shall pretend never to have met the gentleman, if 'tis your wish."

"Don't be impertinent, and there's no need to resort to dramatics."

"Pity," Bronwyn said with a smile.

He merely harrumphed. "Anyway, 'tis already done."

"What is done?"

"I have directed Parsons to issue another invitation."

"Oh, splendid!"

"Do not be disappointed if he declines."

"Oh, but he won't. I particularly told him—well, that's neither here nor there. But Granfer, we must do what we can to help Captain Marsh and his daughter feel welcome."

She soon left him to doze on the terrace, and her afternoon ramble with Brioc wound them, rather predictably, toward the wall at Penhale.

Today, no sounds came from the other side. No singing or gruff shouts.

Brioc bounded toward the crooked gate, tail wagging, and Bronwyn followed at what she hoped was a more decorous pace.

But at the gate, Brioc whined and Bronwyn frowned. Captain Marsh's gate stood firmly shut against them. New hinges reinforced it, and a heavy iron padlock secured the whole.

A padlock!

The nearby shrubbery had been clipped back, and even the trees overhanging the wall had been trimmed—as if a body might have climbed an oak to gain the other side. (A body *might* have considered such a course, were it not for the encumbrance of a dress.)

Well. Perhaps Sunday luncheon would not come

to pass after all. She was disappointed but not wholly surprised at this development, given Captain Marsh's irrational aversion to socializing.

Brioc, undeterred by such things as padlocks and pruned branches, pawed at the dirt beneath the gate. Bronwyn nudged his shoulder, but when that failed, she called his attention to a lovely butterfly.

Duly redirected, Brioc bounded ahead in pursuit.

As she turned to follow, Bronwyn spied something pale caught between two stones in the wall. Moving closer, she perceived a folded slip of paper. Glancing to either side, she slid the note from its resting place and was surprised to find her name written across the front.

Unfolding the paper, she smiled to read the sparse words inked in a bold, masculine hand.

Thank you for sending troops. Your cousin's maid has proven capable with the linens. — M.

——

DESPITE HIS MISGIVINGS about Miss Kimbrell's plan, Gabriel couldn't deny his household was running smoothly. Two days ago, he'd given her leave to proceed, and this morning his hall had smelled of lemon and beeswax. He'd scarcely had time to enjoy it before John brought Alan Kimbrell's invitation to him.

Tea at Oak Hill.

Take your place within the community, Miss Kimbrell had urged. And while she was right—the surest way to forestall gossip was to make himself and Emilia as commonplace as possible—he didn't have to like it.

But it was only tea. He'd penned his acceptance before he could think too long on the matter.

Now, as they approached Oak Hill, he was pleased to see Emilia's blue sash was (more or less) straight, and the braids he'd tucked beneath her bonnet remained (relatively) intact. How a child could appear rumpled simply from *sitting* was a mystery beyond his understanding.

He'd given his daughter the forward-facing seat, and her gaze followed the shadows along the lane during the short drive. She held her handkerchief in one hand, her fingers curling and flexing around the linen. He shared her uncertainty.

The carriage rocked to a stop at the end of an oak-lined drive, where Oak Hill, a manor in the Tudor style, sprawled. There was no other word for it, for the house threw its heavy limbs every which way. The army captain in him bristled at such disorder, but the man in him was intrigued. There was a carelessness to the structure that reeked of privilege—not the privilege of wealth or class, but the privilege of belonging so completely to a place and time that it mattered not what others said.

A footman let down the steps, and Gabriel helped Emilia alight. Kimbrell's butler greeted them at the wide entry and led them past a winged staircase framed by a gallery. Emilia's eyes were bright as she took in the house and its furnishings.

Oak Hill lacked Penhale's faded elegance. Where Penhale was chintz and gilded plaster, his neighbor's home was made of rough stone and dark wood and rich velvet. Without apology, the walls were uneven, with not a right angle to be found.

The butler guided them along a whitewashed corridor held up by dark oak timbers and lit by panes of colored glass. Finally, they emerged onto a rear terrace, where a man with sharp eyes and thick side-whiskers, rose stiffly from his chair.

"Forgive my slowness," Alan Kimbrell said, "but the rheumatism has ahold of m'knee."

Gabriel thanked him for the invitation and introduced Emilia when a bark came from the lawn. Turning, he spied the dog—Brioc—racing for the terrace, tongue lolling and ears bouncing.

And, beyond the dog, strolled Miss Kimbrell.

She lacked a hat and lifted one hand to shade her eyes. When she spied them on the terrace, she stopped. It was possibly the most still he'd ever seen her, but the stillness didn't last. She was soon moving again, her steps brisk and purposeful as she strode across the lawn.

He was pleased to see she'd found his note.

"Bronwyn, m'dear," Kimbrell said as she came onto the terrace. "Come meet my new neighbor properly."

Miss Kimbrell's smile was warm, and her curtsy just proper enough to satisfy convention.

"Captain Marsh, Miss Marsh. How lovely to see you again." She straightened and added, "I trust Mrs. Davies' cooking has met with your approval?"

"It has indeed," Gabriel said. "As has Mrs. Forsyth's management." He hesitated, then added to Kimbrell, "I confess I owe your granddaughter a debt of gratitude. Had it not been for her aid, I fear my household would still be in chaos. It was generous of her to act on my behalf—particularly given the… unconventional nature of our acquaintance."

Miss Kimbrell's expression flickered with a hint of surprise—whether for his admission or his manners, he couldn't say.

Her grandfather gave a dry chuckle. "Aye, well," he said, gesturing for them to be seated. "My granddaughter's never been one to stand on ceremony if something needs doing. But Mrs. Forsyth, m'dear? An excellent choice, though I confess to some surprise you lured her from her daughter's home."

"Really, Granfer." She passed him a cup of tea. "Mrs. Forsyth has been yearning for a change these past months, and you know't well."

Her grandfather's mouth twitched. "Indeed. Now then, Captain Marsh, tell me what you make of Cornwall."

———

BRONWYN APPROVED OF her grandfather's scheme. Tea at Oak Hill was, after all, a far less daunting introduction for Captain Marsh and his daughter than the ordeal of a Kimbrell Sunday luncheon would have been. She couldn't even fault him for not informing her that his invitation was for *that* afternoon, for had the Captain declined once more, she would have been sorely disappointed.

They sat down to tea and cake, and Brioc made an enthusiastic invitation to Miss Marsh to join him in a gambol. After a hesitant look toward her father, who gave his nod of approval, Miss Marsh accepted, and the pair were soon exploring the lawn.

As the conversation turned to the ramshackle state of Penhale's gardens, her grandfather suggested Bronwyn show their guest Oak Hill's neat rose beds. So, Bronwyn led Captain Marsh down the graveled paths, his hands clasped behind him as she pointed out how her late grandmother had arranged the roses to shield them from the sea winds.

"You received my note," he said.

"'Twas cleverly done, sir. I'm glad the arrangements meet with your approval, though I'm even more pleased you've ventured out."

They reached the center of the garden, where her grandmother's first rose bush grew in a place of honor. She gestured to the aged plant with its gnarled stems and fragrant pink blooms. "This, Captain Marsh, was my grandmother's favorite—*Rosa gallica... officinalis* or something like that. The Apothecary's Rose, I think, though she always called it 'Alan's Blush.' As if my grandfather ever did anything so ordinary as blush. He had it planted when they first came to Oak Hill, and though it has weathered more than fifty Cornish winters, it still blooms every summer. She always said it reminded her that even in the harshest of gales, there's a spot of beauty to be found."

"It seems a... hardy specimen," he replied dutifully.

And Bronwyn, who had many more things she wished to discuss besides the hardiness of her grandmother's roses, blurted, "Your daughter speaks another language, does she not? 'Tis not French or Italian, I think. Nor German—"

"Portuguese."

"Portuguese! I might have known. The sound—

'tis very like Spanish, but not the same at all. I gather her mother is from the Peninsula?"

Captain Marsh did not immediately reply, and Bronwyn moved on to a collection of vibrant China roses, tossing a smile over her shoulder as she went. His jaw shifted to one side as he stood in silent imitation of one of the garden statues until, finally, he followed.

"Yes, my wife was Portuguese."

Was. His use of the past tense was not unexpected—he had a child but no wife, so it stood to reason he was a widower. But hearing his words spoken aloud, with very little feeling to them, caused her breath to catch.

"I—I'm sorry," she said, contrite. "My cursed curiosity leads me to open doors I shouldn't. You've my condolences for your loss."

"Thank you," he said, his tone clipped.

When it seemed as if he wouldn't say more, she ventured, "I lost my father to an accident when I was young. Though 'tis not the same, I think, as losing a spouse, I remember the… the emptiness of it all."

He gave a curt nod, his expression hardening. "My family's situation is unusual. I'd prefer not to discuss it, if it's all the same to you." The scar was taut across the shadow of his lean cheek, and there was such a pinched look about his eyes that she knew not what to say.

Uncertainty, she decided, was an uncomfortable feeling.

Turning, she pointed out the cabbage roses, which her grandmother had always described as flightier and a vast deal more fun than their damask sisters.

They walked on in silence, and soon returned to the terrace, where her grandfather was teaching Miss Marsh the proper way to throw a stick for Brioc. As they settled into their chairs again, Miss Marsh demonstrated her newly acquired skill, sending the stick sailing in a graceful arc that had Brioc bounding after it with enthusiasm.

"Well done!" Bronwyn said. "Though I should tell you about the time my cousin Alfie and I discovered the perfect throwing stick for his hound in Widow Chenoweth's field. We thought ourselves quite clever until we learned 'twas her favorite weeding stick!"

Her young friend's eyes widened. "What—what happened?" she asked in English, a feat of such proportions that her father went unnaturally still beside Bronwyn.

Bronwyn fluttered a hand carelessly. "Oh, Alfie's hound chewed it to bits, you can be sure, and the widow bade us work in her garden for a *month* to compensate for a new one. Though," she added in a whisper, "I think she merely enjoyed having two pairs of young hands to pull her weeds for her."

Captain Marsh observed his daughter as she heard this tale, and Bronwyn noticed how the hard line of his shoulders eased slightly when Miss Marsh ventured a tiny smile. Encouraged, Bronwyn spun another story—this one only slightly embellished—about the time she and her cousins had collected crabs on the beach with her aunt's best bonnet as a net.

"Did you catch any?" Miss Marsh asked.

"Oh, yes! We had a fine supper that night! Though I'm afraid the bonnet was never the same after its swim in the tide pools."

Her grandfather chuckled. "Your aunt was beside herself."

"Indeed, she was," Bronwyn agreed with a sigh. "No matter what I said in my own defense, she could never believe it was Alfie's idea. But she forgave us, as she always did. Now, Miss Marsh—I can talk an awful lot, but you must tell us something of Portugal. Surely you've left behind many friends there."

The girl nodded faintly but said little of her life before coming to England. Bronwyn made a few more attempts to draw her out, but these proved equally unproductive. Sensing Miss Marsh was more comfortable hearing stories rather than telling them, she asked what she knew of Cornish smugglers.

Miss Marsh's eyes widened. "Smugglers? Like the Silva in Lisbon? They are wicked men who hurt people and steal things."

"*Not* like the Silva," Captain Marsh added meaningfully. "I'm certain Miss Kimbrell's smugglers are all honorable gentlemen."

"Oh, to be sure!" Bronwyn agreed. "There aren't many left on these shores, but in their day, 'tis said their honor was far stronger than their greed. There's even a tale of one—Black Jack, they called him—who was a terror to the revenue men but a saint to the people. His men never took a shilling from the poor, and he had a rule that any smuggler under his command must leave a portion of his earnings for the widows and daughters of lost sailors. 'Tis how they say he met his bride, though few know the full truth of't."

Captain Marsh merely lifted an amused brow, and her grandfather shifted restlessly until his knee found a more comfortable position. Miss Marsh, though, was a rapt audience. "But why doesn't anyone know the truth?" she said.

"Well, to be sure, smugglers like their secrets," Bronwyn continued. "They hold them close, and the coast of Cornwall is particularly well-suited to keeping them. 'Tis full of hidden crevices and caves. Why, many of the houses on the cliffs even have tunnels beneath them—passages leading from the sea straight up to the cellars, where a man could spirit away his tubs before the Preventives laid ahold of him."

Miss Marsh brightened, and Bronwyn realized her mistake when the girl turned to her father. "Are there tunnels beneath Penhale, *Capitão*?"

"No," her father answered hastily.

"Oh no," Bronwyn agreed, "not at Penhale. I think any passages there must be bricked up by now. And even if they weren't, they would be terribly dark and damp—certainly not the sort of place for a young lady to go wandering."

"Not even for a little look?"

"Certainly not," her father said.

Bronwyn wrinkled her nose. "Your father is right. Besides, you wouldn't wish to encounter the bucha-boos, would you?"

"What are the… bucha-boos?"

"Ghosties," she said impressively.

Gasping, Miss Marsh replied, "But there's no such thing!"

Bronwyn gave the girl a teasing wink, which earned her matching harrumphs from the gentlemen.

The conversation turned to lighter matters then, and when tea drew to a close, Miss Marsh gave them a shy farewell. And her father's half-bow, Bronwyn was certain, was slightly less stiff than it had been.

CHAPTER 11

THE MORNING AFTER their visit to Oak Hill found Gabriel pacing his library, a restless habit he'd acquired during his years of command. Each turn brought him past the window overlooking Penhale's unkempt gardens, where Emilia sat with one of her dolls beneath the gnarled apple tree.

She'd not spoken of yesterday's tea, but she *had* surprised him at breakfast by asking—in English, no less—for more butter for her bread.

He paused at the window, his thoughts returning again to Miss Kimbrell. Her forthright manner with Emilia had accomplished more in a single afternoon than his clumsy attempts these past weeks. The way she had drawn out his reserved child with tales of misadventures and crabs caught in bonnets...

The woman was probably—*undoubtedly*—a poor

influence on an impressionable mind. She was too forward by half and too busy, but his household was running smoothly and his daughter was speaking.

"Devil it," he muttered, resuming his circuit of the room. He'd not lied when he told her grandfather he owed her a debt. Courtesy demanded some acknowledgment of her kindness.

Settling at his desk, he penned a note:

Miss Kimbrell,

As I told your grandfather, I am in your debt for your efforts on behalf of my household. If I may be of service to you in return, I would be honored to do so.

The missive was too brusque, but it would serve. He folded it in careful quarters, then made his way through the garden. After leaving his note at the wall, he forced himself to return to his library rather than loiter about like a schoolboy awaiting a reply.

And yet, he found himself back at the wall before luncheon, gratified to find another twist of paper in place of his note.

He unfolded the smudged page, taking several seconds to make out the words—Miss Kimbrell, it seemed, did not pride herself on a careful, elegant hand. The letters were bold slashes and tangled crossbars, each stroke an obstacle barely tolerated in the writer's impatience to commit her thoughts to the page:

I assure you, Captain, the pleasure of a problem solved is its own reward. There is no debt to be satisfied.

How fares your daughter? I do hope she enjoyed herself at tea. Your Emilia has quite won Brioc's heart, I think. He pines. Yes, good sir, pines.

P.S. You really ought to permit me to bring someone to see to your (I hesitate to say it) garden. The weeds are dreadful, and I fear the brambles will swallow Miss Marsh when your head is turned. Perhaps you might borrow my grandfather's groundsman. Mr. Patterson is a fair wizard with dirt. Or my cousin-in-law Kate—she has a way of persuading compliance from even the most reluctant patches of earth.

Gabriel's lips twitched. The lady prattled as much on the page as she did in person. But she'd given him no hints as to how he might repay her efforts. If she wouldn't accept his gratitude, then what could he do?

He stared at her note, one hand bracketing his jaw, her words fading as he considered his options. Then, inspiration struck.

During their first meeting, he'd perceived how her eyes had lit at the sight of his prized Portuguese mounts. She'd watched them with an appreciation that reminded him of his own reaction on first seeing the breed.

Fogo would never do for a lady, but Amante was a gentle, well-mannered mare. Before he could think better of it, he withdrew a pencil from his coat and wrote out his reply:

Perhaps I can tempt you with a ride on one of my mares? That is, if you keep a riding habit.

P.S. Thank you for your offer to tend my garden. It is unnecessary, but perhaps I will hear your Mr. Patterson's recommendations at some future time.

Her response was swift:

Of course I've a riding habit. This is not a backwater, sir. Your invitation is most generous and I accept with pleasure. I confess I've been longing to see your magnificent horses again. I will, of course, be obliged to come properly chaperoned. I daresay my grandfather's groom can be persuaded to join us.

Concerning your garden, if the notion of Newford's generosity causes your hesitation, you needn't worry. I can suggest to Mr. Patterson that he charge you a ridiculous fee. Between us, it will be worth it. Worry not—I will arrange all!

Gabriel stood at the wall far longer than necessary, turning his pencil between his fingers. What the devil was he doing? His correspondence with Miss Kimbrell had the tenor of a flirtation, of notes exchanged in secret. And inviting her to ride with him felt dangerously like… courting.

He most certainly was *not* courting Miss Bronwyn Kimbrell.

He had no wish to burden himself again with the trials and torments of the married state. But it was only one ride, and one ride did not a courtship make.

———

BRONWYN SWEPT INTO Morwenna's shop with such vigor that the bell above the door clanged in protest. Finding the front empty, she hurried toward the back, where Wynne rocked a sleeping Elowen while Morwenna attached a sleeve to a bodice.

"Morwenna," she said breathlessly, "I need a riding habit."

Wynne laid the infant in her basket and settled back in the pose of one attending a theatrical performance. Bronwyn ignored her.

Morwenna, without glancing up from the cheery blue poplin on her worktable, continued plying her needle. "And a good afternoon to you, cousin. Why, dare I ask, d'you need a habit when you've not been atop a horse these last years?"

"One doesn't forget how to maintain a proper seat," Bronwyn said with a touch of impatience. "'Tis only been some years since I've had occasion to do so."

The corner of Wynne's mouth lifted. "And you've occasion now?"

"Captain Marsh has invited me to ride with him on one of his fine horses. That is, he will ride his own horse, and I shall have a separate mount."

Morwenna's needle paused mid-stitch. "I should hope so."

Wynne tipped her head to one side. "You're to ride out with our mysterious Captain Marsh? To what purpose?"

"He wishes to thank me for assisting with his household, I suppose, though I assured him no such gesture was required. 'Tis simply what neighbors do."

"But what if he makes off with your person and spirits you away to his evil lair?" Wynne asked. "Are you not the least concerned for your safety?"

With an exasperated sigh for their teasing, Bronwyn informed them she would have a proper chaperone in the form of their grandfather's groom.

"But Edwen is half deaf!" Wynne said.

"He doesn't need to hear to observe the proprieties," Bronwyn replied. Then, in case they needed further persuading, she reminded them of the captain's eye for horseflesh. "Or did you not see the fine mount the captain rides? I've never seen such carriage. And he has more of the breed in his stable! To ride such a creature… Why, my father"—she paused to swallow an unexpected lump—"I daresay he'd have been impressed with such specimens. You know how he enjoyed talking horses with the squire."

A moment of respectful silence passed before Morwenna recalled them to her workroom. "And this urgent request of yours, 'tis on account of the gentleman's *horses*? It has nothing to do with the gentleman himself?"

Wynne chuckled and Bronwyn counted silently to herself. "Morwenna. Can you or can you not contrive something suitable?"

"Aye," Morwenna said at last, setting the bodice aside and motioning to the dressmaker's platform. "Up with you then. Let's see what's to be done."

Bronwyn obediently stepped up and loosened her sash as Morwenna fetched her measuring ribbon.

"I've a ready-made piece of worsted green wool," Morwenna mused. "I'm confident it can be altered to your shape, though the jacket may be troublesome. I expect 'twill take some three days—"

"Three days!" The cry flew from Bronwyn before she could stop it. Her cousins stilled, and heat filled her cheeks. "That is to say… surely something can be readied sooner?"

Morwenna's eyes narrowed. "When is this ride to take place?"

"Erm… tomorrow?"

Wynne snorted and Morwenna gasped. "You agreed to ride *tomorrow* when you haven't a habit?"

"Well, aye. Hence my presence in your shop."

Morwenna pressed her lips together, considering. "I don't know…"

"What if I help?" Bronwyn suggested. "You know I can sew a proper seam."

"'Twould require most of the afternoon, but I suppose with your help, and Wynne's if Roddie can spare her"—Morwenna cast a questioning glance at Wynne, who nodded—"I daresay, it can be managed."

Bronwyn pressed her hands together, more relieved than she cared to admit. While she could contrive some tragic tale for Captain Marsh about her best riding habit being devoured by moths or shredded by squirrels, she'd rather not.

She was looking forward to riding Captain Marsh's mare.

She was looking forward to riding *with* Captain Marsh. Gabriel. Gabriel Marsh—his name had a rather nice sound to it.

Without pausing to inspect that thought too

closely, she beamed at her cousins. "You are angels amongst mortals, both of you. A lady couldn't hope for better relations. I knew I could count on your resourcefulness and your good nature—"

"Too brown, m'dear," Morwenna said.

"I thought it might be. I should warn you, though, if we're to work into the evening, I shall talk endlessly about gaits and paces."

"Better that," Wynne said, "than languishing sighs over Captain Marsh's mysterious scar."

Bronwyn, now down to her chemise and stays, directed a quelling frown at her cousin.

"You should know I don't languish or sigh," she said primly. "Such sentimental behavior is neither productive nor becoming."

"One day," Wynne predicted ominously, "you, too, shall sigh."

"Arms out," Morwenna instructed.

CHAPTER 12

GABRIEL GUIDED FOGO alongside Miss Kimbrell's mount as they crested the rise beyond Penhale. The wide path trimmed the top of the cliffs like a ribbon, with weathered heathland on one side and the distant thunder of waves crashing against the rocks on the other.

Behind them, Miss Kimbrell's elderly groom rode a sturdy cob. Gabriel's intelligence, by way of Hadley's questions in Newford, had uncovered the fact that the man was harmless but nearly deaf. This was confirmed with a few words exchanged at high volume between them before the fellow dropped back to follow at a respectful distance.

Gabriel observed Miss Kimbrell's form with the objective eye of a cavalry officer. After an initial tension in her frame, she'd settled into the saddle with a natural ease. She wore a green riding dress and hat that set off her dark hair and Amante's silver coat, and a salted breeze pinkened her cheeks. Indeed, she made a pretty picture against Cornwall's brilliant sky and rocky cliff.

Surprising himself, Gabriel said, "Your habit becomes you." Compliments, which he'd once given easily, were now awkward things with rough corners and edges that made him clear his throat. He avoided them when he could, but this one escaped without his permission.

"This old thing?" she said with an unassuming laugh. Then, with a sigh, she added, "Oh, bother. I cannot dissemble properly, Captain Marsh. The notion of riding one of your fine horses was too tempting to refuse, though I confess I did not, in fact, have a proper habit." At his raised brow, she explained, "My cousins, you see—they're the best a lady could wish for—they made sure I was properly turned out today. 'Tis they who deserve your compliments."

Her artless confession brought an unexpected smile to his lips. "Then you must tell them their efforts were successful."

She tipped her head in agreement, and they rode in silence for a few paces. He allowed himself to feel the sun on his cheek and the motion of the horse beneath him. "I trust Amante meets with your approval?" he said.

"Oh, but how could she not? She's magnificent!" Miss Kimbrell's face lit with delight, and her voice held a note of reverence.

"She was bred in the hills of Portugal," Gabriel said, adjusting his grip on Fogo's reins as the stallion shifted beneath him. "The bloodline is known for producing mounts with steady tempers and smooth gaits—ideal traits for both the battlefield and long days in the saddle."

"Amante is a beautiful name. What does it mean?"

Gabriel cleared his throat. "Lover."

Miss Kimbrell's expression faltered for a moment before she said, "Oh! Well, that's rather... 'Tis an intriguing choice. It has a musical sound, don't you think?"

"I did not name her," he said.

"But it suits her perfectly—she's a bit dramatic in appearance and no doubt prone to romantic fancies."

"No doubt."

"And what of your Fogo? Dare I ask what his name signifies?"

"In Portuguese, it means fire."

"An excellent, strong name! I daresay he strives to live up to it with his energy and spirit. Did you acquire them during your time abroad? I gather you served in the unfortunate war in the Peninsula?"

Gabriel hesitated, unwilling to open the box on

his time abroad. He wondered again what he was doing, riding out with Miss Kimbrell, offering compliments, when a note of thanks would have sufficed. Perhaps a simple token would have served to express his gratitude—a book perhaps, or a pretty fan.

But Miss Kimbrell waited, her expression open and earnest. To refuse to answer would be churlish. "Yes," he said simply, "to both questions. I began building my stable when I left Portugal. I was a captain in the 14th Light Dragoons."

He'd begun his stable with a pair of young colts of *Alter Real* stock, gifted to him by Lisbon's Regency after the war. Since then, he'd slowly acquired mares, and now his studs were nearing their prime. He would have to begin his breeding operation soon if he meant to do it. He'd just never thought to do it in Cornwall. Surrey, perhaps, or Norfolk. But Cornwall, so far from Newmarket and the society of London, had never even entered his list.

"Alas, I have never left Cornwall," Miss Kimbrell said with a heartfelt sigh, "though I shouldn't have liked to do so because of a war. How dreadful that must have been. Were you very much affected by it? Oh, but listen to me. Of *course* you must have been affected. I don't imagine a body can suffer the things you must have endured and *not* be altered in some way. I am only sorry for't." Then, frowning to herself, she added, "You've probably noticed I've a tendency to pry into things that do not concern me. I cannot help but speak the thoughts that pass through my mind, though I resolved again this morning to guard my tongue."

"Thank you, Miss Kimbrell. Your... delicacy is to be commended."

"Delicacy, ha!" She laughed, and the sea below caught the sound and carried it away. "You, Captain Marsh, would be the first to apply that particular word to me. Now, what if we apply ourselves to a more cheerful subject? I've filled my head with questions about your horses since first making their acquaintance in your stable. You must tell me more about the breed. Their temperament, their coats—oh! And that gait. What a striking way your Fogo carries himself!"

The lady's open expression drew a reluctant smile from him. "The expressive gait comes naturally to them, though proper training can enhance it. Do you notice how Amante carries herself, even at the walk?"

"Aye," she said slowly. "She feels more... springy... than I expected, but her pace is deliberate and graceful. 'Tis as if she moves through the steps of a minuet." She leaned forward slightly on her saddle. "Have you ever considered breeding your horses? Their progeny would be exceptional, and the bloodlines highly sought after, I think. Why, I can't imagine any gentleman of taste who wouldn't want such blood in his stable. I suppose the initial cost would be dear, but surely the returns would justify the expense!"

Gabriel guided Fogo carefully around a rough section of the path, skirting a place where the cliff had crumbled. "You've an uncanny perception, Miss Kimbrell. That is my aim when—" He stopped short of saying, *When the gossip around my family is ended*. The scar on his cheek tightened as he finished, "That is my aim."

"An ingenious scheme! I wonder I didn't think of it," she teased. "Penhale's stables would need expanding—nice as they are, they're hardly enough—but that could be managed. The lower meadows would be perfect for grazing. Have you spoken to my brother? He's clever with building plans and just finished a pair of loose boxes for our squire—though yours would need to be grander, of course. But think how splendid it would be! A proper breeding operation right here in Newford—"

"You'll recall my stay in Cornwall is temporary," he reminded her shortly, then regretted his tone. He added more evenly, "I have not decided where I'll settle."

"Of course, you said as much when we met, but—" She stopped and tucked her lower lip behind her teeth, clearly wanting to say more but restraining herself. "That is, of course."

The silence stretched between them, broken only by the horses' soft tread and the distant cry of gulls. Miss Kimbrell shifted, her movements suggesting discomfort—whether from their ride or his curt response, he couldn't be sure. Her unease pricked at his conscience. After all, she'd shown him and Emilia nothing but kindness, her prying nature notwithstanding.

Adjusting the reins, he offered a harmless observation on her riding skill. She accepted this with a smile, though it seemed a bit tight at the corners.

"My father always said I had an adequate seat," she mused, shortening the reins with natural ease. "I haven't had much occasion to ride these last years, but I don't suppose one forgets the basics of proper horsemanship."

"It was your father who taught you to ride?"

Her eyes softened beneath the brim of her hat as she shook her head. "'Twas Edwen who taught me," she said with a nod for the groom behind them, "though my lessons were at Papa's request. He earned his living as a builder like my brother, but his passion was for the horses." A fond smile touched her lips. "He spent every free moment at the races or the market near Bodmin." Her voice lowered to a near-whisper. "He would have marveled at your stable, I think."

"You said you were young when he passed?"

"I was twelve. Young, but not so young as your daughter when she lost her mother." The mare shifted beneath her, flicking an ear, and Miss Kimbrell steadied the horse. "There was an accident... My father was atop the Feather's stables, repairing the roof with my cousin Ben. He was there one minute, and simply... gone... the next." A moment passed before she added with forced lightness, "Well. The less said of that, the better, I think."

Gabriel studied her profile, noting the determined set of her chin. "I am sorry for your loss. I think we must both be a little altered for the things we've endured."

She was quiet for several moments, the silence between them an easy one, until she said, "We should make the most of our time, don't you think?"

She looked over at him. It wasn't the direct gaze to which he was growing accustomed, but a sideways glance that hinted at more beneath the surface of her words. He rolled a shoulder as she continued.

"If we can't know from one moment to the next if our existence will continue, aren't we obligated to embrace every endeavor and satisfy every curiosity? To ask all the questions and... and do all the things?"

Her query caused him a mild bit of alarm, and he braced himself for another interrogation. Truly, she could have been a force for the allied armies. "Within reason, I suppose."

They approached a place where the path widened, and Miss Kimbrell urged the mare into a longer stride. She called over her shoulder, "What do you say to a bit more speed?"

Before he could answer, she'd given Amante her head, and the mare surged forward. Pebbles skittered and tumbled over the cliff as they rode dangerously close to the edge. Gabriel's heart jumped against his ribs as he envisioned the lady's broken body on the rocks below.

"Miss Kimbrell!"

She couldn't hear him—or she ignored him—and rode on. Eventually, she reined in and turned, laughing, the wind tugging her hat. Her cheeks were flushed as she cantered back to him. The groom drew his sturdy cob next to Gabriel, an admiring smile on his weathered face.

"Did you see that madness?" Gabriel demanded.

Edwen cupped a hand to his ear. "What's that?"

Gabriel raised his voice. "I said—your mistress is reckless!"

Edwen squinted at Miss Kimbrell, then back at Gabriel. "Aye, even as a girl, her rode like the devil 'isself were on 'er heels." His eyes twinkled beneath craggy brows as he added, "Ain't a drop o' fear in 'er!"

Gabriel gave the older man a stern look. "That is hardly reassuring."

Edwen only shrugged. "The maid's got sense enough when it matters."

Gabriel must have still worn his frown when Miss Kimbrell reached them, for she said, "Oh, come now, Captain. Surely you don't think Amante would let any harm come to us?"

"You could not have known that," he said stiffly, though privately, he admitted she was right—Amante was far too sensible, even if the lady wasn't.

Still, the sight had sparked an unwelcome memory. Mariana had been similarly heedless one summer's day, galloping her mount along the harbor's edge until the horse had shied, nearly sending them both into the water.

Like Miss Kimbrell, she'd merely laughed, but where his wife's boldness had been calculated to shock, to draw attention and elicit gasps from their companions, Miss Kimbrell's seemed born of a genuine enthusiasm. She'd ridden like she had because she *liked* it, not for any other purpose.

She slowed Amante to a walk. The tip of her nose was pink from the wind, and a few dark curls had escaped their pins. The overall effect was rather… charming. He hardened himself against it.

"Your scar," she said suddenly, breaking into his thoughts. "Did you receive it during the war?"

"You are prying again, Miss Kimbrell."

"So I am." She didn't sound particularly repentant. "Though you must admit, such a dashing attribute does invite speculation."

Dashing? He ignored that to say, "I must admit no such thing."

"Well, of course, you must do as you wish. But as we're becoming friends—we are becoming friends, aren't we?—and as we've agreed we must ask all the questions, I thought per'aps…"

He couldn't help his bark of laughter. "I never agreed to such a ridiculous notion," he said, surprised at the lightness in his chest. Then, giving her a penny though she'd asked for a pound, he conceded, "As to my scar, I did earn it during a war of sorts, though not the one to which you refer." The old injury pulled as he spoke, a reminder of Vasco Ribeiro's blade and everything that had followed.

She opened her mouth in surprise before closing it again. "The captain wishes to maintain a bit of mystery," she said. Then, seeming to give this some thought and reaching a conclusion, she dipped her head in a gesture of compromise and turned them back toward Penhale. "Very well. You may keep your secrets, for now."

"You're too kind," he said dryly, holding his smile.

She glanced at him sidelong as they rode. "D'you

know, for all your desire to keep to yourself, I believe you can hold a conversation when you've a mind to."

He lifted a brow. "Thank you. I think."

Then, as though inspired by some fresh notion, she brightened. "I've just the thing! You ought to attend Newford's assembly—'twill be a fortnight hence, on the last Wednesday. It will give you an opportunity to meet more of your neighbors, and I'm confident I can persuade the committee to waive your first subscription."

Gabriel exhaled shortly, shaking his head. "I do not attend dances."

A flicker of disappointment crossed her face, but she smiled through it as she adjusted her reins. "Ah, well. 'Tis probably for the best. I imagine our country assemblies would pale against London entertainments anyway."

She urged Amante forward, and soon, they reached Penhale's stable yard once more. Gabriel dismounted and turned to assist Miss Kimbrell. His hands fit easily about her waist. Her gloved fingers rested on his shoulders, and her skirts brushed him as he lifted her down.

She smelled brightly of sunshine and lemons and the sea, a fact which reminded him how long it had been since he'd held a feminine form so near to his own. He stepped hastily away to see to his horse.

CHAPTER 13

"Are you certain Captain Marsh won't object to our invasion of his garden?" Kate asked as Bronwyn brought her cart to a stop at Penhale's entry and handed Pippin's reins to the waiting groom.

"Oh, pish. Once he sees how quickly we can set his garden to rights, he'll be glad the troops are come." She hopped from the cart and smoothed her skirts, giving Brioc a warning look when he made to follow. "You stay with Mr. Patterson."

Her grandfather's groundsman climbed down with a grunt. "Come along, then, beast. Let's see what manner of wilderness we've ahead of us." The dog bounded after him, tail wagging as they disappeared around the far wing of the house.

"I still think we ought to have waited for a proper invitation," Kate said, but Bronwyn was already mounting the steps.

"We'll be old and grey if we wait for an invitation from Captain Marsh. Besides, he's a neighbor—"

"To your grandfather."

"—and we shouldn't stand on ceremony with neighbors. Besides, our vicar would counsel us to, 'Turn not away from the stranger at our gate.'"

"But we are at *his* gate."

"Then the captain ought to 'Forgive his neighbor's trespasses.'"

Kate snorted softly, and Bronwyn rapped upon the oak panel, frowning to see the captain still hadn't found his knocker.

After a moment, John Trewin opened the door with a dignity more suited to a duke than a guest arriving in a pony cart. But he seemed pleased with his importance, so Bronwyn passed him their cards and said in her gravest tone, "Miss Bronwyn Kimbrell and Mrs. Benedick Kimbrell to see Captain Marsh."

"I will see if he is at home."

Once the door closed, Kate murmured, "Ten to one he is not 'at home.'"

"Ten to one—have you become a betting lady since removing to London?"

Kate's eyes widened. "Heavens, no! It's only since I acquired your cousins for my brothers-in-law that my language has turned so improper."

The door opened again, and John flashed a grin.

"This way, if you please."

He led them through the entry, which Bronwyn was happy to see gleamed beneath Mrs. Forsyth's lemon polish. "John," she whispered, "your livery is rather handsome."

His lips twitched. "D'you think so, miss?"

"Oh, indeed. You've pristine gloves, and the buttons have a lovely shine."

"As you say, though 'tis naught but borrowed togs from the linen closet. I only hope the captain might remain long enough to give Penhale a fresh look with new jackets. I imagine red or green would suit the place."

"Why, I daresay you're right."

He deposited them in the drawing room and pulled the doors to, pausing to give her a rogue's wink.

As Kate arranged herself on the settee, Bronwyn observed the drawing room curtains and rug had been cleaned. She bit her lip against a smile—self-congratulation was unbecoming—and folded her hands while they waited. And waited.

When Captain Marsh finally appeared, his expression was unreadable as he bowed to them both. "Miss Kimbrell," he said. "And Mrs. Kimbrell. It's a pleasure to make your acquaintance."

"As I indicated to you previously," Bronwyn began, "Kate has a sound knowledge of gardens—

Cornish gardens, in particular. I thought you might welcome her suggestions while Mr. Patterson examines your soil."

His brow lifted. "Mr. Patterson is here as well?"

"You did say you would hear his recommendations."

"I said I *might* hear his recommendations at some future date."

"Today is a future date, is it not?"

Kate rose. "I hope we do not intrude, sir."

"I am growing accustomed to Miss Kimbrell's whims."

Kate ducked her head. Bronwyn ignored her friend's poorly concealed smile when a sound from the doorway drew their attention. Emilia watched them, hands clasped before her, dark eyes bright with interest.

"Miss Marsh," Bronwyn said with a curtsy then introduced her friend to the girl.

"Have you escaped your studies? I cannot blame you—the outdoors are far more interesting than a boring old schoolroom."

"Miss Kimbrell," Captain Marsh said meaningfully, his glance flicking toward his daughter.

Belatedly, Bronwyn realized her error. "Of course, studies are very important for a young lady such as yourself—*extremely* important—but there's no reason you can't enjoy a respite on occasion. And a garden, I think, is an excellent place to learn."

She lifted an inquiring brow at the captain—
Better?

After a long pause, he relented. "Very well," he said, gesturing toward the door.

Together, they exited onto the rear terrace and entered the garden. Bronwyn was surprised to see much of the overgrowth had already been trimmed back, though the beds remained bare.

"You've already begun," she said.

"Do you think me incapable of wielding the garden shears?"

"Not at all. Though I confess myself amazed you found the time with your busy social calendar."

He laughed, the sound short and deep. The sternness fell away from his expression to reveal he had a pleasant smile. This was surprising, and an unexpected warmth filled Bronwyn's center for having caused it.

Before she could think more on that, Brioc's happy bark came from the back of the garden where Mr. Patterson examined the tangled limbs of a tree. The dog made straight for Emilia, who grinned as the wolfhound prostrated himself at her feet.

Bronwyn spread her arms toward the garden. "Well, Kate. What d'you think?"

"It's an ideal size—neither too large nor too small." Kate tapped her chin with one finger before taking the path to her left. She strolled for some moments before stopping near an empty bed by the crumbling stone wall. "Repair the wall, and this could be an excellent place for climbing roses. The salt air is a challenge, but the hardier specimens will thrive…"

She went on to explain the merits of particular roses, and her quiet enthusiasm had the captain nodding politely. Bronwyn couldn't help but smile to see how deftly her friend spoke of grafting and blight. Kate had always been quietly confident and happy in her life, but since her marriage, there was something… more… in her countenance. Joy, perhaps.

Bronwyn might dislike that her friend would soon return to London, but she couldn't dislike her happiness.

Kate looked up, and Bronwyn blinked away unexpected moisture. At Kate's questioning glance, she said brightly, "What d'you make of the sunny place there?"

"Peonies, perhaps. Do you agree, Mr. Patterson? They're rather hardy and prefer the sun."

Mr. Patterson joined them on the path. "Aye. Peonies'll do well enough here. Soil's not bad, considerin'. Needs work, but it ain't beyond hope."

"I've seen them arranged in the most intriguing parterres at Kew, though I think a less formal scheme will serve here."

"You refer to the Royal Botanic Gardens at Kew Park?" the captain asked.

"Yes, have you been, sir? My husband and I have gone there several times since our arrival in London."

Something in his face shifted at the mention of London, the scar on his cheek pulling taut. "I've not had the pleasure," he said curtly.

"The gardens are not to be missed, if you've occasion to see them, though I confess I do sometimes miss the simplicity of Cornish wildflowers."

As Mr. Patterson led Kate and the captain farther down the path to discuss the remaining beds, Bronwyn fell into step beside Emilia. "*Como se diz 'peony' em português?*" she asked slowly, the words tripping gracelessly from her tongue.

Emilia's eyes widened. "You speak *português?*"

"Ha! Hardly at all, to be sure. But can you believe I found a dictionary in my brother's library? I should like to learn a few words, if you'll teach me. How was my pronunciation?"

"You said it wrong," Emilia said, then widened her eyes at her own temerity.

"Oh, I have no doubt of that," Bronwyn said wryly. "You must teach me the proper way."

They paused beneath the apple tree, and Emilia carefully pronounced the words for her. Bronwyn repeated them dutifully until her tutor gave a smile of approval.

"So if a peony is *uma peónia,* then what is a rose?"

"*Uma rosa.*"

"And a… violet?"

"*Uma violeta.*"

"Well, it does not seem like Portuguese will be very difficult to learn at all!"

Emilia smiled—rather impishly, Bronwyn thought. "*Você tem uma folha no chapéu.*"

"Oh, heavens. What does that mean?"

Shyly, Emilia translated. "You have a leaf on your hat."

Bronwyn laughed, delighted with the girl's humor, and reached a hand up to remove the offending leaf from her bonnet. Emilia's smile faded as she watched her father, who stood with Kate and Mr. Patterson near an old sundial.

"*O capitão,*" Emilia said hesitantly, "he wants the garden to be beautiful, but he will make it English, like him. It won't be like my home." Emilia looked down at the toes of her little half-boots, acting for all the world as if her heart weren't ragged about the edges.

Capitão… That was what Emilia called her father, Bronwyn realized sadly. Not Papa, or even Father, but Captain.

She took in the garden—an expanse of dirt that

must have taken hours, if not days, to clear—before returning her gaze to Emilia. The girl's slim dark brows were drawn together in a frown, and Bronwyn's heart twisted unexpectedly—for the man who'd cleared a garden for his daughter and the little girl who couldn't see his efforts. She didn't know what had brought them to this corner of Cornwall, but it was clear they were cautiously feeling their way around one another and stumbling a bit in the process.

Swallowing, Bronwyn spoke carefully. "I think your papa is trying to make this garden special. 'Tis only that he doesn't know how to make it special for *you*. If you tell him about the flowers you miss, I imagine he'll be pleased to add them, if he can. D'you think you can do that?"

Emilia examined the dirt at her feet for a long moment more before giving a tiny nod. "I will try."

Bronwyn smiled, relieved, but then she felt the weight of the captain's gaze. She looked up to find a considering expression on his face as he watched them. She didn't doubt he wondered what mischief she was encouraging in his daughter.

———

GABRIEL LISTENED AS Patterson grumbled about the poor drainage in the northwest corner. The soil would require improving, he said, and the sundial would have to be moved, to which Mrs. Kimbrell agreed.

Gabriel looked up from their joint contemplation of the dirt, his gaze moving of its own accord to where Miss Kimbrell walked with his daughter. Her laughter carried as she untangled a leaf from her bonnet ribbons while Emilia moved more quietly, the dog at her side.

Though Miss Kimbrell's laughter had caught his attention, it was their conversation that held it. He couldn't hear the entirety of it, but the odd phrase reached him on the breeze, and he realized Miss Kimbrell was speaking Portuguese—or attempting to, rather. Her hands accented her speech with gestures that were unnecessary but wholly natural to her while Emilia's soft attempts to correct her pronunciation carried the barest hint of a smile.

He'd spent the past weeks persuading his daughter to improve her English. Her home was here now, in England, and she'd have a dreadful time with no one to speak to but him. But Miss Kimbrell had neatly outflanked his position without even trying, drawing his daughter out in the process. It left him feeling both gratitude for the effort and envy for the ease with which she did it—an uncomfortable situation on both counts.

Patterson, perceiving where his attention lay,

shook his head. "The lass could always coax wool from a sheep. Her charms 'ave had me an' the missus twisted round her finger since she were no bigger'n a sprig, no matter what mischief she found."

"Her charms, as you call them, seem to have a particular effect on my daughter," Gabriel said, his tone dry.

"Aye. You'd best keep a watch, Cap'n, else she'll have your girl clamberin' up trees and racin' frogs afore you know't."

Gabriel couldn't help a scornful snort, though he wouldn't mind seeing his daughter engaged in a bit of frivolous entertainment. Patterson and Mrs. Kimbrell returned to their discussion of the garden, but Gabriel only gave them half an ear. His attention remained on the pair near the apple tree until, excusing himself, he crossed the garden toward them.

"Captain Marsh! D'you come to test your Portuguese?" Miss Kimbrell said as Brioc tried to lick his hand. Gabriel held firm with the beast, who resigned himself to a polite pat on the head.

"On the contrary, I've come to prevent further injury to the language." His tone was dry, and though Miss Kimbrell laughed, Emilia looked at him with a faintly horrified expression. His daughter, he decided, was too serious by half.

Clearing his throat, he added, "I jest, Miss Kimbrell, of course, and I commend you on engaging such a superior tutor for your lessons."

"Oh, she is the best," Miss Kimbrell agreed. "Though I'll have you know I am an excellent student. Am I not, Miss Marsh? I expect I shall be fluent in no time."

Emilia's eyes widened at being implicated in Miss Kimbrell's self-delusion, but she nodded hesitantly, too polite to gainsay her friend.

They permitted him to walk with them, the dog padding softly behind, until they reached Emilia's bench. The view to the sea below was broader now, with so much of the brush cleared, and he was reminded of the gardens at Mariana's family home in Lisbon.

Ventos Antigos had overlooked the sea as well, and its terraces brimmed with fragrant orange blossoms, cascading jasmine and bougainvillea, and orderly rows of lavender. There were lemon trees to perfume the air, and shade beneath a tiled pavilion; beyond the garden's edge, the sea glittered.

The lushness of it was so far removed from the bare dirt beds and crumbling stone wall of Penhale that he nearly put a halt to Patterson's plans. This mean little village in Cornwall would never be a suitable consolation for what his daughter had left behind in Portugal, nor could a retired army captain ever think to stand in for her mother.

He scrubbed a hand over his face. When he opened his eyes, Emilia had taken her favorite place on the bench with the dog at her feet, and Miss Kimbrell stood beside him.

"Your daughter," Miss Kimbrell whispered, "might have some ideas about the garden... per'aps even some favorite flowers from her home in Portugal."

"I'm certain she must." His tone was sharper than he'd intended. But then, realizing his irritation was with himself rather than Miss Kimbrell, he added, "My apologies. You are right, of course."

From the corner of his eye, he caught the hint of a smile on her lips—the lady *would* like to be right—but when she turned to face him, her expression was carefully lacking in humor.

"Well, then?" she asked, nodding toward the bench.

Gabriel joined his daughter on the cold stone, nudging Brioc aside when the dog would have laid his damp chin on his trousers. Clearing his throat, he said, "Mr. Patterson was telling me his plans for this section. I thought I might suggest something different. Did you have any favorite flowers in Lisbon?"

His daughter glanced at him, then at Miss Kimbrell, and for a moment, he thought she'd remain silent. But then she spoke, her voice soft. "Jasmine."

He drew a heavy breath. "Jasmine. It was your mother's favorite."

Emilia's eyes widened at the mention of her mother, but she gave a wary nod.

"Then it's decided," Gabriel said. "We shall plant jasmine, there by the wall where it will be sheltered."

Emilia's expression was unreadable until, finally, she said, "By the wall… like at home."

—

BRONWYN PULLED UP before the door of Kate's father's house and set the brake. The groom stepped forward, but before he could assist Kate down, Bronwyn waved him off.

She sat quietly for a moment, gathering her thoughts. Kate turned, her brow furrowed in question.

"Bronwyn," she said, "is everything all right?"

"Aye," Bronwyn said softly.

Ben—Kate's husband and Bronwyn's cousin— came around then from the garden at the side of the house. His face was drawn in thought until he spied his wife in the drive. A welcoming grin replaced his contemplation, so barmy it must have been embarrassing for him.

"Go away," Bronwyn called. "You may have

your wife d'rectly, but for now, she is mine."

He halted, his gaze shifting between them. Then, without a word, he turned and left.

Kate's hand found Bronwyn's on the bench. "What is it?" she asked gently. "Is it your mother—does her health fail her? Or Merryn? I know he has been working rather diligently—"

"There is nothing wrong," Bronwyn said, returning the press of her friend's hand. "Quite the opposite, rather. Oh, Kate, 'tis only that I'm so happy for you."

"Th—thank you."

"Of course, I was happy for you and Ben when you first married. I knew you were meant for one another, but now I *see* it. I see how your marriage has brought out more of your... your light, I suppose. I couldn't be more overjoyed. Only, please don't forget me."

"Oh, Bronwyn!" Kate released Bronwyn's hand to throw her arms around her instead. "As if I ever could. You are my dearest friend and always shall be."

Bronwyn returned her friend's embrace and sniffed. When they parted, she said, "Well, that was a shocking display."

"It was, wasn't it?"

They sat quietly for a long moment, shoulders touching on the cart's narrow bench.

Kate's voice was thick as she said, "When Papa first brought us to Cornwall, you didn't care that we were incomers. You took my hand that first day and pulled me along with you. We skipped on the beach after you persuaded me to remove my shoes. Do you remember?"

Bronwyn's laugh wobbled. "Aye. You'd never seen sand before. 'Twas like watching a new puppy find her legs."

Kate laughed too, and Bronwyn felt something shift inside—like a glass too close to the table's edge had been slid back to safety.

"I know you're content in your life," Kate said softly, "but I do hope you find the sort of love Ben and I share."

Bronwyn dabbed her nose with a handkerchief. "What is it like—to be married, that is?"

Kate considered this in silence for a moment. "It's... strange at first," she admitted. "To wake every morning and know you belong to another, and he to you. But life feels... larger, somehow, when the joys and burdens are halved and shared. Don't mistake me—Ben can be maddening at times—but the day is brighter knowing he's there. It's truly the most glorious feeling." She reached for Bronwyn's hand again. "It's my greatest wish that you find such joy as well. Do you think Captain Marsh—"

"I don't know," Bronwyn said, cutting short her friend's question before Kate could voice it.

She spoke the truth—she didn't know if there would ever be any affection between herself and the captain. He kept a sturdy wall between himself and the rest of the world, but she sensed he was troubled by a sharp and jagged pain.

Her chest ached as she wondered if he'd found with his wife what Kate described—if his days were darker now that she was gone. She wasn't certain he'd ever allow her close enough to know.

She knew only that she was helpless to stay away.

CHAPTER 14

GABRIEL STOPPED IN the doorway of the nursery, arrested by the domestic scene before him. His housekeeper sat beside Emilia on the edge of the bed, weaving a tale of Cornish fairies while she worked a brush through his daughter's dark hair. The sight was so normal that his heart jumped.

His temporary household had come a long way in the past weeks, owing to Mrs. Forsyth's efficient management. Dust was gone from the corners, light streamed through clean windows, and the most delightful smells wafted from the kitchen at all hours, for the cook was forever baking bread or biscuits. He'd not heard the faintest whiff of gossip in the corridors, and he could hardly recall why he'd refused Miss Kimbrell's offer of aid in the first place.

Mrs. Forsyth's voice carried the rhythmic lilt of

Cornwall, rising and falling as she spun her tale to a rapt audience.

"… And the piskies, they do love a bit of mischief, see? But leave 'em a bowl of cream, and they'll 'elp with the churnin' come morning."

Emilia's shoulders, usually as rigid as chapel pews, had softened beneath the woman's gentle words. "Did you ever see one?" she asked.

"Oh, many's the time us've caught their little lights dancin' o'er the moor." Mrs. Forsyth set the brush aside to plait Emilia's hair with deft fingers. "Me own gran used to say they be partial to dancin' and music, especially on clear nights like this one, when the moon rises high. Why, once she swears she saw 'em holdin' their own assembly, with tiny fiddles made from cricket wings."

Assembly. Tonight was the last Wednesday of the month. Soon, Miss Kimbrell and her friends would gather at the inn. He recalled with a prick of unease her enthusiasm when she'd extended her invitation, and her disappointment when he declined, though she'd covered it cheerfully. He wondered if she knew how clearly her face betrayed her thoughts.

"Did the piskies wear fine clothes?" Emilia asked Mrs. Forsyth.

"The finest, to be sure! All spun from moonbeams and cobwebs, or so me gran said." Mrs. Forsyth secured Emilia's plait with a ribbon. "There now, Miss Emilia. Neat as a pin, and twice as pretty." She rose and turned down the bed covers. "In ye hop."

As Emilia slid between the sheets, her dark eyes found him in the doorway. Gabriel cleared his throat before stepping into the room.

Penhale's nursery was a modest space with whitewashed walls and a window dressed in green curtains, the panes now reflecting the small fire in the grate. Though warm and free of drafts, the room suddenly struck him as woefully uninspiring.

Emilia watched him with wary eyes, and he called up a smile. Since it pulled at his scar, he imagined the effect was less comforting than he intended.

"You've very few books," he observed. "Do you enjoy stories?"

She nodded, though her eyes remained on him.

Aside from the requirements of their daily lessons, his daughter's interactions with him were scant. He recalled with some frustration how easily Miss Kimbrell had drawn her out on the terrace at Oak Hill and again in his own garden. With a few artless questions, she'd encouraged Emilia's confidences. Could it truly be so simple?

"Did your mother read to you?" he blurted, which only caused Emilia's eyes to widen. Artless, hah! He certainly lacked Miss Kimbrell's easy speech, but his daughter's wariness whenever he mentioned her mother was odd, as if she expected him to steal her memories from her.

"She did," came Emilia's reply with a stubborn lift of her chin.

He advanced a little farther into the room and tried again. "Your mother had a lovely voice," he offered. "Which stories were your particular favorites?"

His daughter's gaze went to Mrs. Forsyth, where she received an encouraging nod. "Amadis," she confided.

"*Amadis de Gaula*? You've a liking for knights and adventure, then?"

"*You* read Amadis?" A measure of unflattering doubt laced her tone.

"Soldiers have many hours to fill, and one of my lieutenants read the tales aloud to the company. We all found them thoroughly diverting, especially the ones featuring lady Oriana."

She blinked at this revelation.

"Shall I see if I can procure a copy for your shelf?" he asked.

Emilia's small fingers pleated the counterpane until she finally admitted, "I would like to hear the stories again, and see the pictures."

"It is done then." He cleared his throat. "Well, I shall let you return to… piskies, was it?"

"Aye, sir. Fairies, some calls 'em," the housekeeper informed him.

"Good night, Emilia."

Her reply was dutiful. "Good night, *Capitão*."

As far as social exchanges went, it was not his finest, but his daughter had spoken to him with more than one-word sentences. He would count it as a victory.

He left them, and penned a letter to Hugo Brightwell in Portugal, beseeching him to send the finest copy of *Amadis de Gaula* that he could find—one with pictures.

With that task complete, he considered the evening ahead. He would eat his supper and then… what? He'd brought books on equine breeding that he meant to read again, but the drawing room took on a chill in the evenings, and the thought of another solitary night in Penhale's vast library depressed him. Perhaps he could persuade Hadley to a game of dice, but his groom had left him with a light purse the last time.

He ascended the stairs to change for supper, though he didn't know why he bothered when there was no one to please but himself. But he had no sooner reached his door when John appeared bearing a tray with the evening's post.

"These are just come, sir."

Gabriel took the letters and recognized Miss Templeton's perfect script on top. Throwing open the door to his chamber, he broke the seal and read her letter. His stomach fell. Emilia's new governess would not be accepting the post after all.

On further consideration of the challenges attendant on providing instruction to a foreign and motherless child, and after consultation with her governess colleagues, Miss Templeton did not believe herself suited to the task.

A foreign and motherless child. Gabriel crumpled the page and tossed it onto the fire. His anger for Miss Templeton's narrow thoughts was swift, even as his better sense told him he ought to feel relief. Clearly, the lady would not have made a fitting addition to his household, and it was better to know that now. He would not have any of his servants thinking themselves above his daughter or *consulting* about her with other households.

Gabriel sighed through his teeth.

John, a great hulking fellow, lingered uncertainly in the doorway.

"'Tis unfortunate news, sir?"

Gabriel cast him a frowning glance. "Yes, John, it's very unfortunate news."

"Right then. Beggin' your pardon, sir. My uncle says as how a proper servant ought to keep his tongue between his teeth, but 'twas plain as the sun—"

Gabriel pressed his temples. The man had a regrettable lack of address. "John."

"I'm doing it again." John drew himself up and said without inflection, "Mrs. Davies wishes to know, sir, if ye'll be taking your supper in the library t'night."

"The small parlor, I think."

"Very good, sir."

Gabriel crossed to his dressing room and saw that John had already laid out his supper clothes. His footman-butler, for his faults, was ambitious of becoming a footman-butler-valet. Gabriel undid his cuffs, but when he noticed John remained in the doorway, he said, "Was there something else?"

"Oh no, sir. 'Tis only that I wished to say… that is…"

"I prefer plain speaking, John."

Straightening, the man said in a rush, "Some of us asked Miss Kimbrell what she thought of our odds for a place at Penhale—a regular one, like— and I want to say how pleased we are ye be considerin' it."

Gabriel's brows came together. "Considering it? And how, pray, does Miss Kimbrell come to know my thoughts before I do?"

"I… that is…" John's face fell. "I didn't mean to speak out o' turn, sir, or cause trouble for Miss Kimbrell. Only, she said as how you're not the sort of employer to disregard a proper job."

Gabriel leveled his gaze at John. His patience, tried first by Miss Templeton's letter, frayed further at the notion of his servants consulting with anyone outside his household. What else had they been saying?

"John, if you're to remain in my employ — temporary or otherwise—you'll remember that your loyalty lies within this household, not with outside influences. I'll not have my staff discussing the affairs of this house with others. Is that clear?"

John straightened his shoulders and met Gabriel's eye squarely, his face tight with embarrassment but his voice steady. "Aye, sir. Ye'll not have cause to question my loyalty."

"I expect not," he said briskly. "Now, send in Hadley, if you please."

John bowed himself out of the room and moments later, Hadley replaced him. The groom wore an expression of mild alarm. "Sir? Has something occurred?"

Gabriel turned away from the window. "What are you hearing in Newford regarding my temporary staff?"

Hadley's jaw shifted to one side. "Not much— why? Do you suspect someone, sir, of bad intentions?"

"But there *is* talk?"

"A few comments here and there, mostly 'bout

your generosity in making places for them all."

His generosity?

Gabriel closed his eyes on a sigh. He hadn't even decided to *remain* in Cornwall, let alone make any permanent decisions about his staff. Perhaps the fault was his for leaving the household in an indefinite state. Still, it was his house to command.

Miss Kimbrell was too confident by half, but that didn't give her leave to speak for him—or worse, to discuss him with his servants. No matter her past kindnesses, the lady had overstepped.

After Hadley left, he paced his chamber for an entire minute before making his decision. Problems didn't improve with age. The sooner he took this matter up with Miss Kimbrell, the better.

He rang for John and when the man returned, subdued, Gabriel said tersely, "Have the carriage readied, and lay out my evening clothes. I'll be going out after supper."

John's eyes widened briefly before he mastered his expression. "Very good, sir. I've been keepin' your evening coat pressed, hopin' you might have a need fer't. Shall I help you dress? I can have you stripped up proper in no time."

"I've been dressing myself since before you were born, John."

"As you wish, sir."

John backed out of the room, and Gabriel went

to find his supper. Afterwards, he donned an ivory waistcoat and evening coat of dark blue superfine. Finding his handkerchief gone from atop his dresser, he retrieved another before descending the stairs to find John waiting with his greatcoat.

Outside, the moon was up, and Hadley waited on the drive with the carriage lamps lit, stamping his feet against the evening damp. His groom lifted one greying eyebrow at Gabriel's attire.

"If I might say, sir, it's good to see you stepping out again."

"This is not a social occasion."

Hadley made a noise in his throat that sounded like disbelief.

CHAPTER 15

Bronwyn laughed as her young cousin executed a turn with more enthusiasm than grace. "Mind your footwork, Matthew. Though I'll grant you're vastly improved since you nearly toppled poor Miss Carew into the punch bowl last month."

Matthew's cheeks reddened around his grin, making him look even younger than his sixteen years. The candlelight caught the copper highlights in his dark hair—the same shade many of the Kimbrells shared.

"You're mistaken, cousin. Surely, 'twas Daniel who forgot the steps of that reel."

"Oh! My apologies. How thoughtless of me to confuse you with your less accomplished twin."

"You're teasing me again."

"Per'aps, but only a little."

Beeswax candles burned in the Feather's upstairs

chandeliers, their light reflecting in the long windows that lined one wall. From the small gallery, fiddles played a rousing reel that had many of Newford's younger set bouncing and twirling across the polished floor.

Bronwyn's grin matched Matthew's as her cousin swung her hand up and around. He turned her neatly under his arm, and Bronwyn wondered when he'd grown so tall.

But moments later, as they entered an allemande, the air in the room shifted. The low murmur of whispers was heard beneath the music, and heads turned toward the entrance.

And there was Captain Marsh, whom she'd not seen in some days.

Captain Marsh, who did not attend dances.

Bronwyn missed a step and nearly tripped over Matthew's overlarge feet. He steadied her, though his brows lifted with poorly concealed amusement for her clumsiness.

"Oh, just mind your own steps." Bronwyn's tone only prompted Matthew's grin to widen, and she ignored him to concentrate on her promenade. But when the figure of the dance allowed it, she couldn't help casting another glance to where the captain bowed his greeting to Wynne. With a remote expression upon his face and his hair brushed in the latest style, he was a swan among pigeons.

When the music ended, she shooed Matthew toward the refreshments table.

"D'you want some punch?" he asked quizzically.

"No, but you do."

"But I'm supposed to escort you from the floor now that the dance is ended. Wynne says 'tis the proper—"

"Our cousin says many things, but I assure you, I'm capable of walking ten feet without masculine supervision. I shan't swoon from the exertion. Now, go."

When Matthew left her, giving one last, puzzled look over his shoulder, she made her way to where Wynne greeted the assembly's newest arrival.

"Miss Kimbrell," Captain Marsh said with a tip of his head.

Before Bronwyn could return the greeting, one of the Feather's maids appeared in the doorway, her cap askew as she hissed urgently at Wynne.

"Oh, bother," Wynne said. "Captain, may I leave you in the capable care of my cousin?"

"I would be honored to have Miss Kimbrell's escort for a turn about the room."

Wynne left them, and Bronwyn accepted the captain's arm when he offered it. "You came," she said stupidly.

"I did."

She allowed him to guide her past the press of

dancers. His cologne smelled of sandalwood and surliness. The combination caused her stomach to dip. "D'you know, you've a rare talent for making an entrance."

"I assure you, that was not my intention."

His mouth quirked slightly, and there was that slight note of irony in his voice she was beginning to recognize. The angles of his face appeared sharper than usual. It must be a trick of the light, she thought, or perhaps something else.

She tilted her head, considering him. "You're here…" she mused, "though you don't seem pleased by the fact. Which leaves me to wonder what, precisely, encouraged you to leave the comfort of your lair."

He snorted softly. "My lair, Miss Kimbrell?"

She waved a hand between them. "Or whatever vampires call home."

Leaning close, he said, "Would you believe it's something more than a craving for blood that's drawn me out tonight?"

Bronwyn couldn't help the shiver that tripped down her spine, clear to her toes. Whether it was driven there by the captain's deep voice in her ear or the words themselves, she couldn't say, but she thought the whole business rather… delicious.

Somewhat breathlessly, she said, "What, Captain? What has brought you here tonight?"

"A meddlesome baggage," he said, his jaw tensing visibly.

"A meddlesome—d'you mean *me*?" For the first time, she perceived his irritation was directed at *her*! What had she ever done but try to help him? Her cheeks swiftly heated, but she sensed eyes on them, so she strove to maintain her countenance. "To what, specifically, d'you refer?" she asked through her teeth.

"I refer, *specifically*, to the gossip and speculation you've been exchanging with my temporary servants."

Bronwyn tilted her head, matching his gaze. "With your servants? I've had many conversations with them—they're my neighbors, you'll recall. I'm afraid you'll have to be more specific with your, er, specificity."

His jaw shifted and his nostrils flared. She felt a small degree of victory—however unbecoming—that she'd nettled him. "I refer," he said evenly, "to your assurances that I am considering them for permanent situations, when I am doing nothing of the sort!"

"But I never said any such thing!"

"Did you tell them I am not the sort of employer to overlook hard work?"

This was the cause of his ire? She'd encountered John and Mrs. Davies in Newford the previous week, and they'd seemed so eager to keep their posts, and so uncertain about the captain's plans. It had only been natural to reassure them.

"Oh, well, that. 'Tis true, is it not? You've an appreciation for efficiency and competence—I've seen it myself in the way you move and speak."

"How I move and… speak?"

"Aye! When you walk or ride, there's not a muscle that moves that doesn't need to, and I've never known a man more economical with his words, except per'aps my brother Merryn. Though I'll deny it if you say I paid him such a compliment. 'Tis not *my* style, of course, to be so short with my speech, but that doesn't mean I can't appreciate the trait in others. But per'aps you ought to consider—"

"Miss Kimbrell," he said, rubbing his forehead with one hand. "Permit me to be clear. I've commanded men who've risked their lives for one another, and I know the damage even small misunderstandings can cause. I do not appreciate others speaking about my household, much less presuming to know my intentions, particularly when they convey those presumptions to others as fact."

"I did not, as you unjustly accuse, give it as fact," she said, though a faint flicker of doubt rose as the words left her mouth.

Had she overstepped? The thought itched at her, but it was too late to take her words back now. If she had crossed a line, it was only out of a desire to help. That couldn't be wrong… could it? She lifted her chin to hide her unease.

"When asked for my opinion, I simply said I did not believe a man of your character would make a rash decision. That you were sure to value good work and a reliable nature. I think 'tis not such an outrageous statement, but clearly, I was mistaken." She paused, studying his clenched jaw. "Or is't only that you *enjoy* being angry?"

Gabriel's brows drew together over the imposing line of his nose. "You didn't consider how your words might have given them false hopes?"

They'd reached the refreshments table and Bronwyn turned to him, hands clasped before her. "Well, I did consider it. And I concluded there's nothing wrong with offering a bit of encouragement, if it helps them perform their best until you've reached a decision. However long *that* may be."

And with those parting words, Bronwyn turned with a satisfying flutter of her skirts and left him at the punch bowl.

———

GABRIEL FELT THE eyes of the assembly room upon him, and the old, familiar heat of humiliation washed his face. Miss Kimbrell had left him standing like a fool in a sea of unknown people—*her* people. His breathing felt shallow, and his stomach roiled.

He set his jaw. Then, placing one foot before the other, he strode for the doors. When he reached for the handle, though, some inner voice made him look back. The musicians still played, and dancers still turned in the movements of a quadrille. But Miss Kimbrell's petite form stood rigidly next to her innkeeper cousin. Her shoulders were back, her eyes bright, but he detected the merest uncertainty to the set of her chin.

He'd hurt her. His words had been harsh, he knew. Some might even argue he'd been unreasonable, given the trifling degree of her offense. *Is it that you* enjoy *being angry?* He ignored the niggle of doubt her question caused.

But while no one could argue Miss Kimbrell's concern for his servants was admirable, his own position was equally sound.

He supposed he could have told her he'd already written the agency in London to cancel his contract. They'd bungled it horribly, but to have yielded even this small detail would have felt like he was handing her the war.

Still, the knowledge that he'd upset her struck more deeply than he expected. More acutely, even, than his own discomfort. It was enough to turn his feet away from the door.

"Miss Kimbrell," he said when he was standing before her once more.

She looked at him from the corner of her eye. "Captain Marsh." Her cousin, he was gratified to see, was quick to absent herself.

"I owe you an apology. My words were unnecessarily harsh when it's clear you only meant to help."

Her eyes widened the merest fraction but, curiously, she remained silent.

"As for my objections… please understand, I do not doubt your intentions. But the less said about my household, the better. I hope you will accept my caution, as well as my regret for speaking so precipitously."

A bit of starch left her shoulders. "You do not owe me an apology, Captain Marsh," she said softly, "though I appreciate the sentiment. And I will grant 'tis *possible* you make a valid point."

"Possible?"

"Probable. Per'aps." She frowned and amended, "Nearly certain, rather."

He was surprised to feel the faintest tug of amusement. Miss Kimbrell, it seemed, was not one to toss out apologies lightly—if, indeed, that was what she was doing.

"You are a man accustomed to leading others," she continued, "and I see now that I should have directed your staff's questions to you. 'Tis I who must beg forgiveness." A brief silence passed before she tilted her head to add, "Though I daresay you might have managed things a bit differently if you'd only—"

"Miss Kimbrell," he cut in with a disbelieving laugh. "Perhaps it's time to leave it there, before you risk soiling your pretty apology."

She blinked. "Oh, I *am* meddlesome, 'tis true. Are you terribly angry with me?"

"I'm not… angry." He was surprised to realize it was true. There was something about Miss Kimbrell's earnestness that made it difficult to hold onto his ire. "I confess to feeling baffled, certainly, over your concern for my household. And, perhaps, a little intrigued."

"Well! I don't believe anyone's ever found me intriguing before."

"I didn't say you were intriguing. I said I was intrigued. There is a difference."

She huffed a laugh. "Well, I hardly think 'tis a difference worth mentioning."

The quadrille had finished, and the musicians adjusted their music sheets. To Gabriel's surprise, he heard himself asking if she was promised for the next set.

She made a show of checking the card at her wrist before saying, "Why, no, Captain. 'Twould seem I'm unengaged."

"Then will you do me the honor of standing up with me?"

"D'you know the waltz?"

"I shall contrive not to disgrace myself," he said dryly. "But I wonder that *you* know the waltz. I would not have thought it favored so far from London."

"Oh, we've been dancing the waltz in Newford for ages. The matrons fear we'll devolve into a morass of debauchery and ruin, but alas, 'tis yet to happen."

Gabriel couldn't help his smile at her obvious disappointment. "Well then, Miss Kimbrell, shall we set your matrons aflutter?"

They took their places among the couples, and Gabriel felt the gazes of several dour-faced matrons at the edge of the floor. The fiddler changed his instrument for a violin, and the musicians struck up the first notes.

Bronwyn's cheeks were flushed and her hand was warm in his, even through the fabric of their gloves. She smelled pleasantly of soap and lemon. As they went through the first turn, he was distracted by her elegant posture and graceful movements. Given the exuberance of her conversation, he'd expected her to be all energy and less poise, but her steps were light and fluid.

It didn't take long, however, before she tried to take the lead from him. A light pressure on her hand guided her back into place, and she met his eyes with wry self-humor.

"Perhaps you might permit me to lead," he murmured.

"Per'aps."

Gabriel swallowed his smile and sought a topic of conversation. "Tell me, Miss Kimbrell: I hear you're tasked with managing this year's fair. How do your preparations go?"

"Splendidly! Don't mistake me—there's much to do, what with the stalls and the games, and then there's Mr. Clifton's feud with the butcher—but 'twill be an excellent fair. Oh! Will you join us in setting up the booths next week? Nearly every able-bodied person will be there. I imagine a man of your experience and… and *ableness* must excel at making order out of chaos."

He smiled. She was being deliberately provoking. "Your flattery is wasted, Miss Kimbrell. I shall consider it, but I make no promises."

"Ah! Then I shall count myself fortunate to have secured your consideration."

"Impudent baggage," he murmured as he turned them.

―――

LATE THAT NIGHT, Bronwyn sat at the writing desk in her mother's parlor, reviewing her lists for the fair. Her mother had long since retired, but Bronwyn couldn't sleep.

The house creaked and settled around her as she adjusted her lists—adding a line here and striking a note there. But her thoughts kept returning to the evening's assembly. To the waltz she'd shared with Gabriel, and the way his hand had felt wrapped around hers.

A warm flutter stirred in her belly, and she jumped when the door opened. Dipping her pen, she endeavored to look unaffected as her brother entered, holding a mug of ale.

"Still at your lists?" he asked, settling into their father's old chair.

"Aye. Mrs. P's fair won't organize itself. I thought you'd gone up."

"Not yet." Merryn stretched his legs before him. "I met some of our cousins in the Feather's coffee room. They say Captain Marsh made quite an impression tonight."

Bronwyn paused, her quill hovering above the paper. "Did he?"

"According to the stories, the captain arrived fashionably late, had words with you, then sent half the matrons reaching for their vinaigrettes when you danced the waltz. I suppose 'tis not a surprise, given his reputation with the Foreign Office. The man has many accomplishments, it would seem."

"He dances very well," she agreed before the rest of Merryn's words caught her attention. "Wait… the Foreign Office?" Lowering her voice, she said, "Merryn, have you been making inquiries?"

He shrugged. "I posted a few letters to my contacts in London." At her horrified look, he added, "I'd be a poor brother if I didn't learn more about the man who fixed my sister's wheel, invited her to go riding with him, and accepted her help with his household." She didn't miss how his voice rose a bit on the last words.

"All of which has been very properly consented to by our grandfather," she hastily clarified. "Well, except for the wheel, but that couldn't be helped. You wouldn't have me walk all the way back to Oak Hill, when Penhale was so close, would you?"

"Perish the thought."

Bronwyn disregarded his dry tone to return them to the matter at hand—namely, her brother's interference. "If you wish to know more about the man, you should have simply asked him."

"I inquired about his origins when I first made his acquaintance, but I found his responses too guarded and aloof. Who knows what thoughts or intentions lie behind such a reserved demeanor?"

"Too guarded—? The fact that a gentleman wishes to keep himself to himself, doesn't give others the right to—" Any plan she had of developing this argument was stopped by the wry glint in her brother's eye, and she recalled her own meddling tendencies. "Oh! Never mind that."

"Has he told you that his wife—"

"Oh, please don't," Bronwyn said, though her curiosity stirred at the mention of Gabriel's wife. And yet, as much as she wished to know more, she had a curious aversion to hearing the tale from another. Somewhere along the way, the captain had moved himself from the column of a project to manage or a puzzle to solve to... a person worth befriending.

"The captain's business is his to share."

"You don't wish to know what I've learned?"

Bronwyn swallowed, but she held her brother's eye. "I do not."

Merryn gave her a searching look. Even as children, he'd always been able to tell when she'd given him a Banbury tale. Now, he was silent for a long, scrutinizing moment before he said, "You're not one to turn your back on an intriguing tale. I have to say, I should like this new discretion of yours, but I don't. 'Tis worrisome."

Bronwyn reminded him she was no green miss any longer. She was four and twenty and quite capable of managing her own affairs without his interference.

Merryn ran a hand through his hair, disordering it. "You will always be my sister, but sometimes I forget you're out of pinafores."

Bronwyn's heart twisted a little at the affection in his voice. "I have been out of pinafores for years," she reminded him.

"I know." He set his mug aside and leaned forward, elbows on his knees. He surprised her further when he said quietly, "Do you like him?"

Her breath caught, and heat crept up her neck. "I do," she admitted.

CHAPTER 16

GABRIEL WAS NUDGING a jasmine shoot with the toe of his boot when he heard footsteps. He turned to find Merryn Kimbrell coming toward him with an unreadable expression and purpose in his step. Bronwyn's brother was dressed for business in a simple, well-cut coat and a clean neckcloth, but his boots showed signs of Cornish mud.

"Captain Marsh. I hope I don't intrude. Your man said I'd find you here."

"Not at all. I was merely seeing how my garden grows." His tone was dry as he indicated the jasmine.

Kimbrell tilted his head to examine the vine with a doubtful eye. "I can't claim much knowledge of plants, but this one seems a bit weedy."

"Patterson assures me it will thrive in time," Gabriel said, "but I'm afraid patience isn't my strength."

Kimbrell's mouth twisted with the beginnings of

a smile before he mastered it. "If Patterson says 'tis so, then your plant will live."

He stepped forward, his gaze taking in more of Penhale's garden. Gabriel and Hadley had finally finished clearing the beds and paths. With Patterson's guidance, they'd installed a number of specimens to bring the garden back to life.

An exhausting number, he admitted, particularly for a man not yet decided to remain in Cornwall. But the brightness of Emilia's gaze when he'd shown her the jasmine plants had been worth the blisters on his hands and the ache in his back.

"My sister said you desired to make some improvements," Kimbrell remarked, "but I see she rather understated the matter."

His tone was mild, but Gabriel detected a note of inquiry beneath it. He couldn't say Kimbrell's arrival was a surprise; this meeting had been inevitable since Gabriel's tense exchange with Bronwyn at the assembly. The man was her brother, her closest male relation—he had every right to protect his sister.

"Shall we speak plainly?" Gabriel said. "I doubt you've come to inquire after my landscapings."

Kimbrell's gaze sharpened. "You favor a blunt style."

"The battlefield is no place for subtlety."

"An interesting choice of words, Captain."

"Force of habit, I suppose. Ask your questions, Kimbrell. I'll entertain them, to a point."

Kimbrell gave a curt nod, clasping his hands behind his back as he followed the path away from the house. "Fair enough," he said. "'Twas brought to my notice that you and my sister engaged in a disagreement of sorts at the assembly. May I ask the nature of your conversation?"

Resigned, Gabriel said, "Our discussion concerned the management of my household."

"Her management, or yours?"

"That was about the crux of it."

Kimbrell exhaled an amused breath. Stepping off the path, he bent to inspect a loose stone in the garden wall, running his fingers over the rough surface before giving it a testing tap.

"I've no illusions where my sister is concerned. She means well—there's not a person in Newford with a truer heart—but that makes her more inclined to overstep." Dusting his hands, he straightened and returned to the path.

"Your sister's intentions *are* well-meaning," Gabriel said. "We've since resolved our misunderstanding. There's no quarrel between us." He was surprised by how easily his defense of Bronwyn fell from his lips.

"I heard that as well. I'm told you made a fine pair for the waltz."

Gabriel's brow lifted. "You're remarkably well informed."

"I aim to be. But on that matter, my sister has instructed me that if I wish to know more, I should appeal to you directly rather than continue my inquiries in London."

Gabriel's pulse quickened. "You've been investigating me."

They'd reached the stone bench where Emilia liked to sit. Beyond the cliffs, the sea churned grey and restless beneath a shifting sky. Rain would come soon.

"You can hardly blame a man for making inquiries into the stranger who's captured his sister's interest."

Gabriel ignored the frisson sparked by the other man's words. "I'm certain you overstate the matter."

"Per'aps." Kimbrell folded his arms. "I can't prevent my sister's association with you—she's of age, and 'twould be a waste of breath to tell her no—but I must ask… are you married?"

"If you've been making inquiries in London, then you know I'm recently widowed."

Kimbrell's gaze went briefly to Gabriel's sleeve. "I heard as much, but you don't wear an armband."

"No. My wife and I were estranged, which I'm

sure you've also learned. I mourned her loss years ago."

Understanding flickered in Kimbrell's eyes. "I see. You've my condolences, nonetheless."

"And before you ask," Gabriel added tightly, "I had nothing to do with her death."

The ghost of a smile crossed Kimbrell's lips. "You were in England at the time, were you not? Though I don't suppose that prevents you from hiring another to do the deed."

Gabriel couldn't help his laugh, though it sounded harsh to his own ears. "I said I would entertain your questions to a point. I think we've reached that and more."

Kimbrell's smile escaped this time. "My inquiries have satisfied me, though I do wish to say something before I go."

Gabriel lifted an expectant brow.

Bronwyn's brother released a breath through his nose, setting his mouth in the manner of one resigned to his task. "My sister is a female comfortable in her own mind and firm in her opinions," he said.

"You'll hear no disagreement from me."

Kimbrell clasped his hands behind him once more as they started back toward the house. "What I mean to say is that, while she gives every appearance of confidence and capability, there's a sensitivity about her which others don't readily see. You cannot know this, but she spoke little in the weeks following our father's death."

That was unexpected. Gabriel struggled to reconcile the lively, sharp-witted female he was coming to know with the quiet figure Kimbrell described.

"She came back to herself, of course," Kimbrell went on, "though I've often wondered if she doesn't use her high spirits to fill the silence he left behind." He paused. "The point is, Captain, for all her self-command, my sister can still be hurt."

"I would not presume to speak for your sister," Gabriel said, "nor can I say where our acquaintance may lead. But I assure you, it is not my intention to cause her any distress."

The first fat drops of rain pattered softly on the leaves, misting the air with the scent of dampened stone and earth. As they reached the gate at the head of the garden, Kimbrell turned up his collar.

"'Tis a shame you had to give up your post at the Foreign Office," he said.

Gabriel kicked a stray stone from the path. "It was a profession, nothing more."

"My grandfather and I have acquaintances in Town who could prove useful, should you wish to reclaim your place." Kimbrell's tone was casual, but his meaning was clear. The Kimbrells were not without influence.

"I've acquaintances of my own," Gabriel said coolly. "At any rate, I've no intention of resuming my post. I've a stable of Portuguese mounts I mean to breed, and now I've the time to do it."

Kimbrell arched a brow. "Fine beasts I hear. But a breeding operation's no small endeavor. You'll need land." He hesitated before adding, "You're aware Penhale has some hundred acres of pastureland to the north of the cliff road?"

Gabriel nodded. "I've ridden it several times. There's good grazing and sound footing, though the paddocks need expanding." He paused. "If I decide to remain, that is."

Kimbrell was silent as he appeared to consider this, then he inclined his head toward the garden wall. "Now, about these stones—my uncle's a mason. Shall I ask him what's to be done?"

CHAPTER 17

A WEEK LATER, Bronwyn looked up from her notes just in time to avert disaster. "Dr. Rowe," she called, "the draper's tent must be placed closer to Morwenna's shop, I think, not the apothecary's table."

"But Mrs. Pentreath always puts it here—"

"Sir, think of the ladies' convenience—they'll wish to take their new purchases d'rectly to be made into dresses. You'd not have them carry their parcels the length of the high street, would you?"

Newford's surgeon lifted his hat to scratch his head. Then, with a sigh, he said, "Aye, you've the right of't," before taking up the tent poles he'd just set down.

Bronwyn drew a line through another item on her list, well satisfied with the bustling industry all around her. On an ordinary day, Newford's high street saw the usual activity for a small village with two coaching inns and a tidy but unremarkable harbor. But once a year, the village burst its seams with the fair that traveled from Penzance to Helston to Falmouth, grazing Newford on its way to Truro's High Cross market.

Now, the air smelled of fresh-sawn wood, and hammers echoed along the street. Buntings fluttered from shop fronts, and soon strings of pennants would brighten the green.

Merryn led several men in assembling the puppet booth before the theater, while more stalls lined the high street. Newford's shopkeepers were eager to secure their places before vendors and performers began arriving by boat or wagon.

Even Mrs. Pentreath, newly returned from her sister's bedside, could hardly find fault with the progress. It promised to be a week of high activity, and Newford positively *thrummed*.

Alfie appeared at her elbow, cheeks ruddy from his exertions. His dark hair, which wore the impression where his hat had been, lifted with the breeze. He nodded to indicate Mrs. Pentreath, who pointed her cane at a knot of workers.

"Mrs. P must be worried for her position, given how well you've managed the preparations. Why, 'tis almost as if you're a matron yourself!"

"Ha! That is a compliment wrapped in an insult, Alfie Kimbrell. But what has happened to your neckcloth? You look as if you've been wrestling one of Mr. Evans's sheep."

"Aye," he said with a wink. "One might have escaped the pen."

Bronwyn snorted and returned her attention to her list, listening with one ear as Alfie described the feats he'd been obliged to perform to return the fugitive to her confinement. He'd clearly found far more enjoyment in the activity than he should have, given how much work remained to be done.

Then, thinking the pennant poles should have been installed by now, she said, "If you've time to wrestle the livestock, cousin, you've time to help Mr. Clifton on the green."

Alfie's sigh was dramatic. "I sometimes wonder why I couldn't have been born a gentleman of leisure."

"Leisure! How dull that sounds when you could be *useful* instead. Now, stop dithering and—" She stopped as two figures approached from the lane behind the post office.

The Marshes had come.

Emilia walked beside her father in a soft grey dress with a crisp pinafore tied at the waist. Bronwyn smiled to see her dark hair twisted in a smooth braid—no doubt the handiwork of Mrs. Forsyth.

And Captain Marsh... Gabriel's military bearing was unmistakable, his stride confident and squared shoulders set off by the cut of his dark frock coat. He'd slowed his pace to match his daughter's, but his steps were no less purposeful. She wondered how he must have appeared in his captain's uniform, with its braid and epaulets and shako hat.

Her thoughts, despite repeated admonishments, returned often to their encounter at the assembly. To his ire, of course, and her part in it. But also to his teasing. Even now, the memory of his wry smile as he'd turned them in the waltz brought an uncomfortable warmth to her face.

It was an inconvenient distraction, especially with so many things to be readied for the fair. And if her cousins suspected how Gabriel's nearness left her with a curious twist in her stomach… Ack!

The thought of their teasing remarks had her gripping her pencil more tightly. She feared she'd already revealed too much, though, when she caught Alfie's speculative gaze on her.

"Is that how the wind blows then?"

"There is no wind," she said, fastening her gaze to her paper and giving it a thorough scrutiny. It was one thing to confess her appreciation for the captain to her brother. Quite another to announce it to all her relations.

"To be sure," Alfie said, "there is wind."

Lifting her chin and borrowing a phrase from her young cousins, she said, "'Tis a bag of moonshine."

Alfie shrugged. "Per'aps, though I can't imagine what's motivated the good captain to leave Penhale for our assembly—and now this—when he's kept to himself since his arrival."

Gabriel's solitary ways certainly hadn't made it easy for Newford to warm to him. Still, she leapt to his defense. "'Tis so hard to believe the man desires to know his neighbors?"

At her cousin's lifted brow, she added, with a mental cross of her fingers, "I had only to mention a few more hands were needed, and he readily offered his aid."

"Indeed?"

"'Tis more than I can say for some of my cousins, whose attendance today had to be won with bribes and threats."

"Threats… plural?" Alfie grinned. "D'you mean I'm not the only one to suffer your blackmail?"

Bronwyn breathed easier, relieved to have finally moved Alfie from his course. With a brisk wave of her hand, she shooed him away. "Aren't you supposed to be setting poles with Mr. Clifton?"

"Aye, I'm going." Then, leaning close, he whispered, "But you might wish to straighten your bonnet."

Bronwyn resisted the urge to touch her hat—or throw her pencil at her cousin's retreating form. She checked her irritation as the Marshes reached her.

"Miss Kimbrell." Gabriel said with a polite dip of his head.

"Captain Marsh, Miss Marsh, how kind of you both to come." She ignored the slight lift of Gabriel's eyebrow at this overly formal greeting and cleared her throat. With a smile for Emilia, she added, "I hope you're prepared to lend a hand. We've tasks enough for everyone, I assure you."

"We are at your disposal," Gabriel said. "Where would you have us begin?"

Before Bronwyn could reply, Alfie lumbered past beneath the burden of several tent poles. "Captain Marsh," he called, "have you come to supervise the troops or join the ranks?"

The hammers along the street stilled as all of Newford awaited the captain's reply. Bronwyn held her breath and her tongue, though it went against her natural tendency—it was her habit to fill silences and mend awkward moments with words, but she knew Gabriel would not welcome her interference. He was the incomer among them; their good opinion was his to earn—or squander.

He glanced at his daughter, his reluctance to leave her side clear. Bronwyn assured him, "I would be happy for Miss Marsh's company, if she's agreeable."

At Emilia's tiny nod, Gabriel shrugged out of his coat and draped it over a bench. "I've always found leading from the front yields the best results," he called to Alfie. "Shall I lend a hand with those timbers? They seem to have got the better of you."

There were chuckles at this elegant jab, and Bronwyn's heart gave a peculiar flutter as the captain strode purposefully toward her cousin.

She turned to her young companion. "Well, Miss Marsh! If you think Newford is lively now, you should have seen the bustle this morning!" She took up a box of carpenter's tools, and Emilia fell into step beside her as they walked toward the green.

"Newford was a proper hive—everyone scurrying about like bees in a clover patch. Mr. Pengilley howled when he dropped a hammer on his toe, but Mr. Evans told him he was making a meal of it. And Mr. Clifton—he's our baker, you know—he's in a state because someone nearly placed the confectioner's table just outside his shop." Leaning closer, she confided, "I think he's right to be concerned. The confectioner brings the most delicious sugared almonds. D'you enjoy sweets?"

Emilia smiled shyly, her small hands clasped at her waist. "Yes."

"Then we shall persuade your papa to purchase a treat for you before my cousins take everything for themselves." Switching to Portuguese, she said inexpertly, "Now, I promise you, I have been practicing my Portuguese, but how does your garden come?"

Emilia smiled at her pronunciation before replying in English. "My father sent Hadley to Falmouth for the jasmine. It's small now, but he says it will grow if we're patient."

"How splendid! I cannot wait to see it in your garden."

They reached the green, and Bronwyn passed the box to one of the workers before giving Emilia a serious look. "Now, then, Miss Marsh. Are you ready for a task? 'Tis an important one, mind you—not for the faint of heart."

Emilia lifted her chin. "I do not faint," she said with quiet dignity.

"Oh, no, of course you do not! 'Faint of heart' simply means… well, I suppose it means timid. The task I have in mind is not for the *timid*, and you are clearly not a timid girl. I suspect you and I are cut from the same bolt, though per'aps I've a few more loose threads."

Emilia's smile widened into a grin, and her eyes sparked with the hint of a laugh. "Tell me your task," she said gamely, "and I will do it."

Bronwyn nodded toward a group of children with paintbrushes and wooden signs. "My cousins, Matthew and Daniel, are leading the charge with signs for the booths. I don't suppose you've any skill with a brush?"

Emilia's smile vanished. "My mother liked to paint."

Bronwyn slowed her steps. She'd often sensed Emilia's longing for her home in Portugal, but the girl rarely spoke of her mother. Bronwyn wondered how long it had been since her passing. She recalled her own pain after losing her father and knew better than to press too firmly.

"I imagine your mother was very good at painting," she said gently.

Emilia looked up, a shadow in her dark eyes. When she said nothing, Bronwyn offered, "D'you know, I was twelve when my father died."

Emilia blinked. "Do you miss him?"

"Of course. 'Tis natural to miss a person when they're gone. You must long for your mother."

The girl looked as if she might say more, but then, with a firm set to her chin, she shook her head. "Mourning what's lost is for the weak-hearted. Tears are unbecoming, and they won't bring my mother back."

Bronwyn started at the unexpectedly harsh sentiment. She hesitated, uncertain of the correct response but knowing she couldn't let such a belief go unchallenged. Careful to keep censure from her voice, she said, "I do not believe that to be true."

Emilia's eyes widened the merest bit, but she remained stubbornly silent.

In an effort to bring them back onto safer ground, Bronwyn said, "Your mother enjoyed painting, but what of you? Do *you* enjoy it?"

"I… I do paint sometimes."

"Sometimes is more than sufficient. You are hereby appointed to the office of apprentice sign-maker. Come with me, and I will introduce you."

Bronwyn guided a quiet Emilia to the group, making quick introductions to several children before showing her the required signs.

"Daniel has already written the words for you, but 'tis good to check his letters before you paint. Last year, our chandler was surprised to learn he was peddling *potions* instead of *lotions*."

"It looked like a P!" Daniel protested.

With careful fingers, Emilia accepted a dripping brush from another girl and set to her task. Bronwyn remained for a time, checking the children's work and painting a few signs herself. She only left when she caught Emilia smiling at Daniel and Matthew's jests.

She couldn't escape the feeling that Gabriel ought to know what troubled his daughter—how she hid her grief. But then, as Emilia's father and guardian, he was the most likely person to have put such notions into her head. Had he, in his own grief, convinced himself that mourning was a weakness?

Even as the thought occurred to her, she dismissed it. He could be gruff—surly, even—but she'd seen his efforts to make a home for Emilia. She couldn't believe he was so lost to feeling that he would discourage her memories of her mother.

She searched the workers, and her eyes found him easily, setting posts alongside Alfie. Bronwyn wasn't the only one who noticed him. Several curious glances followed him, though whether they carried approval or speculation, she couldn't say. She would wait for a quiet moment, away from the others, when she might speak with him.

Over the next hour, Bronwyn moved among the workers, directing the placement of stalls, ensuring the pennants were strung properly, and gathering women to hang the paper lanterns.

All the while, she kept a careful eye on Emilia. The girl seemed no worse for their earlier conversation, but her words, and the sadness she endeavored to hide, had settled heavily in Bronwyn's stomach.

CHAPTER 18

GABRIEL STEADIED ANOTHER post, his shoulders burning from the strain. The sensation wasn't wholly unpleasant, and it reminded him of training exercises with his regiment, though the stakes here were considerably lower. Unless one considered the point of Mrs. Pentreath's cane—the lady wielded it with great effect whenever she spied something that didn't meet her exacting standards.

When the last post was set, Alfie removed his hat and wiped his brow with his sleeve. "That should finish this section—unless Bronwyn's got some fresh scheme in mind."

Another Kimbrell groaned good-naturedly. "I do not doubt that she has. Heaven help us if she ever acquires a cane."

Gabriel hid his smile. Their friendly banter continued as he was hailed by the local squire.

"Marsh! Carew of Trevelyan Abbey. I hear you've some fine Portuguese blood in your stable."

Gabriel shook the man's hand. "I may be partial," he said, "but I don't think there's any finer."

The squire's chest swelled. "Got a considerable stable myself," he said. "Been meaning to expand. Call at the Abbey; I want to hear your breeding plans."

Gabriel nodded, masking his surprise. The squire's custom would be a boon to his fledgling operation, whether he remained in Cornwall or not. This had Merryn Kimbrell's hand in it, he was certain.

A short distance away, Bronwyn's brother wielded a hammer at one of the fair's many booths. Sensing Gabriel's gaze, he looked up and spied him with the squire.

From their last meeting, Gabriel gathered the man would be happy to lend his support if it meant removing Gabriel from Newford, but this felt like more. It felt like one neighbor lending aid to another. Gabriel tipped his head in acknowledgment, and Kimbrell returned the gesture.

Carew lingered some moments more, discussing the latest hunter he'd acquired from the market near Bodmin.

When the squire had gone, Gabriel searched the green for Emilia. She sat amidst a scatter of painted signs, her dark head bent close to that of another child. A streak of blue paint marked her cheek, and the sun caught in her hair, highlighting the same raven sheen she shared with her mother. She giggled, her laughter floating across to him before she covered it with her hand.

In the weeks since Brightwell had delivered her to his door, Emilia had been wary and silent. Gabriel had caught the occasional smile—usually in Bronwyn's company—but never had he heard his daughter *laugh*. The sound caused a peculiar twist in his belly.

"I'd say you've earned a bit of refreshment, Captain."

Turning, he found Bronwyn beside him with sawdust clinging to her hem and a mug of cider in her hand. He accepted the cider gratefully.

"I expect you're accustomed to far more taxing labor," she added, "what with leading troops and routing the French."

"I submit that my troops were easier to manage than your cousins."

"And the French?"

"Far less fearsome than your matrons."

Her laugh was unaffected, her energy unflagging. She'd been working tirelessly—managing her list and the efforts of others, lending a hand where one was needed, all to ensure the fair's success. But when Gabriel looked more closely, he detected the merest hint of tension in her frame.

He motioned to a wooden bench on the other side of the green. "Would you care to sit a moment? There's a patch of shade there beneath the ash tree, and I could use the respite."

Her eyes narrowed in suspicion. "*You* require a respite? 'Tis surely a bit of flummery, sir, but I'll allow it suits my purpose as I particularly wish to speak with you."

"I'm on tenterhooks," he said, stepping to the small table where one of the inn's maids served cups of lemonade. He procured one for Bronwyn. As they walked together across the green, more laughter from the children drew his eyes back to Emilia.

"You've found the perfect task for my daughter," he said.

"She's more talented with a brush than she led me to believe." Bronwyn paused, her brow furrowing with a rare touch of uncertainty. Lowering her voice, she added, "She is also determined not to think overmuch on her mother."

Gabriel's stride faltered. "She misses Mariana."

"'Tis understandable, though she believes it unbecoming to mourn those we've lost."

Gabriel frowned. "Unbecoming? Whatever gave her such a notion?"

The furrow between Bronwyn's brows smoothed.

With a small smile, she said, "I confess, Captain, I wondered if she had it from you. But while your manner may be a bit fearsome at times, you are not, I think, an insensitive brute."

"Thank you," he said dryly. Then, "I will speak with Emilia, and I will endeavor not to be fearsome."

Bronwyn settled onto the bench, smoothing her skirts. When he remained standing, she gave the place next to her a meaningful glance.

"Recall, Captain, 'tis *you* who requires a respite. I promise not to compromise your virtue. Even if I wished to, we've a dozen or more chaperones just there across the green."

The jest startled him into a laugh and he sat, though he maintained a proper distance between them. They remained in view of the others preparing for the fair, and though some heads turned in their direction, few paid them any heed.

"You're very direct, Miss Kimbrell."

"Too much so, per'aps," she admitted. "I've been told 'tis one of my worst faults."

"*One* of the worst? Do you have others?"

"My faults are legion, Captain."

He smiled. "I submit you must have a few virtues as well."

"Oh?"

On another female, her side-eyed glance would

have been flirtatious. On Bronwyn, it was simple curiosity to know his opinion. Still, he couldn't resist teasing her. "Are you fishing for compliments?"

A frown darkened her countenance. "If I have to fish for them, then I hardly think they are compliments."

He laughed. "Perhaps I ought to hold my tongue, for anything I say now will be cast in suspicion."

"Captain, *you* were the one who said I have virtues. I am merely curious to know what you think they are."

"Very well." He made a show of studying her, thinking overlong on the matter just to be irksome. Finally, when her finger began tapping with impatience, he offered, "Some might say you've an efficient manner about you—"

"I believe the word others use is *managing*," she corrected.

"Perhaps. How about this, then? The way you wear that straw bonnet is very fetching."

"The way I wear my bonnet? What, tied beneath my chin like *every other female*?"

"Yes, well, the angle has a certain rakishness to it."

She sniffed and looked away, and he decided he rather liked her pique. Still, it would be ungentlemanly to go on teasing her.

"No one can dispute your kindness to my daughter," he said.

"She's a child! Anyone would be as kind."

"Then no one can dispute your kindness to *me*," he added softly.

She turned back to face him. Her irritation was gone, evaporated with a few mere words. "You do not make it easy."

"I expect not."

A long beat settled between them. Across the green, his daughter lifted a sign for Matthew Kimbrell's inspection, her smile shy as he exclaimed over it. The sight made his chest ache. He still couldn't believe—after all that had passed between him and Mariana—that he had a child.

Bronwyn cleared her throat gently. As if she could hear his thoughts, she asked, "Has your wife been gone for very long?"

His fingers tightened around his cider. Such a simple question ought to have a simple answer, but his life seemed tangled with knots and riddles.

"Too long for a child to be without her mother."

"I imagine it must be difficult for Emilia." She hesitated, then added, "And for you."

"I do not dwell upon it."

She opened her mouth then closed it again in a charming imitation of a fish. After a moment's thought, she said, "I understand if you prefer to keep your own counsel."

It was Gabriel's turn for his speech to desert him.

This woman had an unending desire to make herself useful, to lend her aid wherever it was needed (however unwanted it might be), but now she was allowing him his silence. The unexpectedness of it disarmed him. He forced his fingers to unclench and decided then he'd grown tired of riddles.

"I lost my wife years ago," he said, "but for Emilia, it's only been a matter of months."

"I—I don't understand."

"My wife and I—we were estranged for some time." The words landed heavily, weighted with the all-too-familiar shame. That Mariana had abandoned their marriage within a year—that her lover's influence had prevented Gabriel's pursuit—he didn't say. He'd said too much already. Gentlemen did not speak of their wives' indiscretions, and certainly not with gently bred females.

Bronwyn's frown deepened, her brows drawing to a point above the bridge of her nose. Her eyes—dark and bottomless like Portuguese coffee—searched his face.

"But what of Emilia…?"

Gabriel's jaw tensed, and he forced it to ease. His gaze returned to his daughter, whose pinafore now sported a swipe of green.

"It was shortly before I arrived in Cornwall that I learned I have a daughter," he said. "After Mariana's death, her maid delivered Emilia to the embassy in Lisbon. A colleague brought her to me in London—along with the news that my wife had died."

"But that is dreadful! And how frightened Emilia must have been." Bronwyn's expression turned inward until, with an audible inhale, she said, "Such a short time… you're in mourning." Her eyes went to his arm, where the crepe armband he'd never worn should have been, before returning to his face.

"I grieved Mariana's loss years ago when she left," Gabriel said. "I've no need to mourn again."

"But mourning her absence is not the same as mourning her death. And Emilia…" Her gaze drifted to his daughter. "The poor lamb. She's lost one parent and barely knows the other. How difficult this must be for her."

The observation struck uncomfortably close to his own fears.

"And for you," she added. "Despite the circumstances, you must grieve the loss of your wife. You never had the chance to make a proper farewell, or to understand why… she stayed away."

"The reason doesn't signify."

"But d'you think—"

"Miss Kimbrell," he said, his tone firm. Fearsome, she would have said. "The reason matters not. If my wife was unhappy, then I failed her. I was her husband. It was my duty to care for her."

"And hers to care for you." Her own voice was just as fearsome—gratifyingly so.

Gabriel cast her a sideways glance, unsurprised she'd cut so quickly to the heart of his anger. That Mariana had so easily abandoned her vows and her duty was a betrayal he'd not yet reconciled himself to.

But he'd confided too much. This was hardly an appropriate conversation, and he told her so.

"Pish! Don't turn missish on me, Captain."

Gabriel set his jaw. His thoughts were in a spin, his legs restless, as if he were standing on the eve of a long march. He drained his cider, which he'd forgotten, and made to rise.

But then the edge of Bronwyn's hand brushed his on the bench. He allowed the contact to linger— one second, then another. He was surprised to find that, at thirty, he could take comfort from such a small thing.

It wasn't pity he felt from her—had it been, he'd have withdrawn at once. But there seemed a quiet understanding in her touch, though how she could know his heart when *he* barely understood it was beyond him.

He feared he'd do something foolish. Confess his anger, perhaps, or his grief—not for Mariana but for the loss of his naïve dreams. He might have done so, had a commotion not arisen near the church.

Mrs. Pentreath brandished her cane, and her voice carried across the green. "This bunting is shamefully crooked!"

Bronwyn pulled her hand back to her lap, and he felt the loss keenly.

"I think you're being summoned, Miss Kimbrell."

With a sigh, she rose and smoothed her skirts. "I must say, Captain, you've made quite a muddle of the day."

He stood as well. "How so?"

"Why, you've gone and shown yourself to be mortal like the rest of us." Her smile held a hint of mischief. "I fear there's no recovering from that."

"Does this mean I'm no longer suspected of vampirism?"

"Alas, no."

She turned to go, but he stopped her. "Miss Kimbrell."

She paused and glanced back.

"Thank you."

"For what?"

"For not offering empty platitudes or hollow consolation."

"Ah, well." She gave a rueful smile. "I've never been good with platitudes, empty or otherwise."

CHAPTER 19

Bronwyn's hand trembled as she adjusted Mrs. Pentreath's bunting, and she silently cursed her fingers for betraying her. It was the most curious thing—only moments before, she'd been perfectly composed, directing the fair preparations with laudable efficiency. But now, she was unsettled, her thoughts in a tangle and a fizzy queasiness in her belly.

"There now," she said, leaning back. "What d'you think of this?"

Mrs. Pentreath pursed her lips, examining the correction with her shrewd gaze. After what felt an age, she gave a brisk nod.

"It will do," she declared, "though I cannot think why you thought it prudent to assign such an important task to the Polwhele boys. Between them, they haven't the sense of a turnip."

"Aye, but they're keen to help," Bronwyn said diplomatically. And applying them to the bunting kept them from the handsaws.

Mrs. Pentreath harrumphed, already moving on to her next inspection.

Bronwyn climbed down from the ladder and pressed her hands to her middle, willing her nerves to steady. A glance toward the ash tree showed the bench stood empty. Nearby, the children's signs were neatly stacked, the painters dispersed. The Marshes had gone.

She recalled Gabriel's quietly spoken words, and her throat tightened. Was it any wonder he kept to himself? She'd assumed his reserve was simply part of his nature, but now she understood it was more than that.

He'd been learning to be a father to a grieving child while managing his own grief—feelings that could only be complicated by the circumstances of his marriage.

Added to that, she suspected his pride must have suffered, given his wife's shabby treatment of their marriage vows. Bronwyn had enough male relations to know her leaving couldn't have been an easy thing for him to admit.

Not that he'd admitted to it, *per se*, but she'd read enough between the lines of what he *had* said to gather their estrangement was his wife's doing.

"You're wool-gathering."

Bronwyn started at Wynne's voice. "I was thinking about my list," she fibbed. "There's still much to be done."

Wynne's gaze went to the bench across the green before coming back to Bronwyn's. "You and the captain were having quite the conversation."

Warmth rushed to Bronwyn's cheeks. "We were discussing his daughter."

"Oh?" Wynne's tone remained light, but something in Bronwyn's expression must have given her pause. Her teasing smile was replaced with an expression of concerned inquiry.

Bronwyn lifted her chin. "I won't say anything more about what was given to me in confidence."

Wynne studied her for a long moment, then nodded in quiet understanding. "And so they begin..."

"What begins?"

"The languishing sighs."

"Oh, pish," Bronwyn scoffed with a wave of her hand. "Now, d'you have the cloths for the refreshment tables?"

"I will send Daniel for them," Wynne promised before moving away.

Bronwyn was relieved to see her cousin go. Her thoughts were too muddled now for clever responses.

Languishing sighs, indeed.

She'd wanted to hear the captain's story from the man himself. Now that she had, she wasn't sure what to make of it. She could only imagine in the vaguest sense what the loss of a spouse must feel like, but to have that loss clouded by his wife's betrayal… How his heart must ache.

She released a slow breath, then caught herself before it ventured into a sigh.

———

GABRIEL KEPT A careful hand on the reins as he guided the horses up the winding lane. Penhale's job-wagon creaked and swayed, its wheels finding every rut in the packed earth. The late afternoon sun filtered through the beech leaves overhead, dappling the path ahead with light and shadow. Dusk was falling, and soon it would be time for Emilia's supper.

They'd remained in Newford longer than he'd intended, but as he recalled Bronwyn's parting smile, he couldn't regret it. Although, he couldn't delay his conversation with Emilia any longer.

She sat quietly beside him on the wooden seat. Blue and green paint stained her fingers, and despite his efforts with a damp cloth, a smudge still marked her cheek. With a determined set to her pointed chin, she looked like a younger version of her mother.

He was surprised—and relieved—when the memory of his wife's countenance failed to send a flush of anger through him as it usually did.

But that his daughter believed her tears were a weakness troubled him. Had his own reluctance to speak of Mariana given her the notion?

He cleared his throat, the sound loud in the dusky stillness. "You seemed to enjoy painting with the other children."

She nodded, and a strand of hair escaped her plait to flutter against her cheek in the evening breeze.

"Did they have amusing stories?"

A faint smile appeared. "Daniel said last year's puppet show was"—she wrinkled her nose in con-centration—"some rumbustious."

"Did he?"

"He said the puppet man's strings tangled, leav-ing the villain to rescue the king while the prince fell into the moat."

"That does sound… rumbustious."

With a sidelong glance, he considered his next words and wished Bronwyn were there. He was abysmal at this.

Finally, he said, "And what of you? Did you tell stories of your mother, perhaps?"

The smile faded, and her shoulders inched up. The wagon wheel struck a stone, jolting them both, and she used the movement to turn her face away.

He switched to Portuguese. "I know you miss her. It is acceptable—it's natural—to do so."

She turned to him in surprise. "But Tio says—" She stopped, her lips pressing into a frown.

Tio. He didn't remind her again that Vasco Ribeiro was not her uncle. "What does he say?"

Her voice was small but determined. "He says she is gone, and crying is cowardly. I must be strong like a Braganza."

A Braganza. His wife had been a second or third cousin to Portugal's royal family. She'd enjoyed all the benefits of such a connection, though she'd never gone so far to claim herself a Braganza.

But it seemed Ribeiro—who already wielded influence within the Portuguese regency—desired more. Did he mean to use Emilia's connection to the Braganza to further his own ends? Nothing, he thought, could be more contemptible than the use of a child.

"He is wrong."

Emilia's head came up sharply, her dark eyes widening at his tone.

He gentled it, choosing his words carefully. "Being sad when we lose someone we love isn't a weakness. It means we loved them well."

"Are *you* sad?"

His hands tightened on the reins, and the horses

shifted under his grip. Bronwyn had suggested he was grieving Mariana's loss. He'd denied it then, and would have again—were it not for the elfin face turned up at him.

"Yes," he admitted, his throat tight. "I am sad."

The words sat between them for a moment, heavy but not unbearable. He released a slow breath until the weight of them lifted, costing him less than he'd expected.

"But," he confided, "I am also very happy to have you with me."

She studied him, her dark brows drawing together in that way she had, making her look older than her seven years. "Can we be both?"

"Indeed, we can." At her skepticism, he reminded her, "You enjoyed painting, but you didn't stop missing your mother, did you?"

She gave a tiny shake of her head.

Clearing his throat, he said, "Mariana... your mother... I remember she loved to sing, did she not?"

Emilia nodded, her expression softening. "She sang while she painted. Old songs about the sea and the mountains."

"Tell me about them."

As the horses plodded between the moss-covered stone hedges lining the lane, Emilia described how Mariana used to set up her easel by the windows, humming Portuguese ballads while she painted.

His daughter's voice grew drowsy, and soon she was leaning against his arm. He liked the weight of her small body against his side. Soon, her breaths fell into the easy rhythm of sleep, and he settled her more securely, one arm holding her steady as he turned them onto Penhale's drive.

The trees lining either side cast long shadows across the forecourt. As he entered the stable yard, Hadley emerged from the tack room. Gabriel had given his groom the day off—he understood Hadley meant to ride down to Falmouth, where he'd made the acquaintance of an agreeable tavern maid. Now, though, his face was lined with concern.

Gabriel came fully alert. Something was wrong.

Emilia woke when he lifted her down. She blinked sleepily up at him as he set her on her feet. Only when she was safely inside with Mrs. Forsyth did he turn back to Hadley.

"What is it?"

Hadley tugged his ear. "May be nothing, sir, but I encountered a man in Falmouth."

Gabriel studied him as he removed his gloves. "Go on."

Hadley glanced toward the house before lowering his voice. "Didn't know him, but he weren't English—not with that dark coloring. He's from the Peninsula, sure as I'm standing here."

Gabriel suppressed a flicker of unease. Packets

regularly sailed into Falmouth's bustling harbor. A foreigner was no cause for alarm. "A sailor perhaps?"

Hadley shook his head. "He carried himself like a soldier, sir—watchful-like. I had the sense he was following me. Not outright—never too close—but I'd see him now and then, lingering by a shop, loitering near the tavern. Always watchful."

Gabriel's grip tightened around his gloves. "You're certain?"

"As certain as I can be without asking him outright," Hadley said. "Thought it best not to let on I knew he was there. Took my time winding through the back streets, made a few unnecessary stops. Finally lost him in the alleys near the harbor. If he meant to follow me back to Newford, he didn't manage it." He hesitated. "Could be nothing, sir, or just a man bent on some idle mischief. But I thought you'd want to know."

Gabriel nodded and pushed aside his unease. It was probably nothing—a rival for Hadley's maid's affections, perhaps, or a pickpocket. But instincts honed by years of war wouldn't stay silent.

"Keep your ears to the ground," he ordered.

Hadley grunted. "Should we alert the constable? He's said to be capable—a cousin or relation of some sort to Miss Kimbrell."

"There's little enough to report yet. But let me know if anything else seems amiss. And Hadley—"

He waited until the groom's gaze met his. "Ensure the doors and windows are secured. I'll check them again before the house settles in."

Hadley gave a sharp nod, but as they strode toward the house, he ventured, "Do you think Ribeiro will follow the girl all the way from Portugal?"

Gabriel studied the shadows. It had been too long since he'd heard from Brightwell. He'd taken silence as a sign Ribeiro had abandoned whatever plans he had for Emilia. Had he been too complacent or was he making something out of nothing?

Ribeiro wouldn't come to England without first confirming his quarry was in sight, but he had men to do his business for him. Was Hadley's follower one of them?

He drew a measured breath. He'd not leap to conclusions—no campaign was won on faulty supposition—but neither would he lower his guard.

"I'd be a fool to underestimate Ribeiro," he said.

CHAPTER 20

THE FAIR ARRIVED in Newford without further incident, and Gabriel's tension began to ease. The morning unfolded with the delays he was coming to expect when taking his child out—despite Mrs. Forsyth's capable attentions, his daughter's toilette was not to be taken lightly.

First, there'd been a studied debate over hair ribbons.

Then, the discovery of an unaccountably loose hem that demanded attention. How the thing had come unstitched in the first place was a mystery.

Finally, as John held the door for them, Emilia realized she'd left her handkerchief in the nursery.

The sum of these delays might have tested Gabriel's patience, were his thoughts not otherwise occupied with Hadley's follower in Falmouth and the weight of the small knife now concealed in his boot.

By the time they descended the hill to Newford, the high street was already bustling. The warm scent of roasted chestnuts mingled with that of fresh bread from Clifton's shop, and tradesmen called out to fairgoers from their stalls.

Nearby, a gypsy woman in a colorful shawl unpacked a litter of puppies from a large wicker basket. Catching Emilia's interested gaze, she winked.

"Captain Marsh!" Bronwyn's voice rose above the din from where she stood a few stalls away, dressed in a pretty orange dress that matched the day's liveliness. It wasn't the pale blush of a peach nor the jarring, over-bright hue of tangerines, but the rich saffron of a butterfly. It suited her.

She wove through the fairgoers to reach them. "I'd begun to think you'd lost your way," she teased.

"We were unexpectedly delayed," Gabriel replied dryly. "A discussion of some length was had regarding the hair ribbons suitable for such an occasion."

Bending to examine the ribbons woven into his daughter's hair, Bronwyn replied, "Ah, a weighty matter, for I see Miss Marsh has chosen *two* ribbons for her plaits."

"Blue *and* green," Emilia volunteered.

"An excellent choice! They look very fine together, and now you needn't offend one by choosing her sister." Emilia smiled at this nonsense and Bronwyn straightened.

"Oh, look!" she said in a lowered voice. "Mrs. Pentreath is coming this way."

Indeed, the woman was making straight for them, wielding her cane like a sword to make a path through the crowd.

"Why does she seem displeased?" Gabriel asked.

"She is always displeased, but I suspect she is seeing the adjustments—the tiniest of changes, really—that I made to the fair's arrangement."

"But she was here during the preparations."

"Well, 'tis true," Bronwyn said with an eye for the advancing matron. "But we didn't fix *all* the signs to the booths until late last night, you see."

"Ah. A surprise attack."

"Just so."

Emilia's tug on Gabriel's sleeve drew his attention. "May we please see the puppies?"

Across the way, the gypsy woman had emptied her basket. She cradled a sleepy ball of fur against her breast, its paws kneading the folds of her shawl.

"Oh, you should," Bronwyn encouraged. "Zilka comes every year with a new litter, and every year she leaves with an empty basket."

The woman beckoned Emilia with a braceleted arm, but Gabriel hesitated. He was loath to leave Bronwyn to the matron's displeasure, and judging by Mrs. Pentreath's deepening frown as she neared, it was high indeed.

Bronwyn must have sensed his reluctance, for she whispered, "Go. You needn't suffer Mrs. P's ire on my account."

That settled it.

"You may see the puppies," he said to Emilia, "but you are to go no farther than the gypsy's wagon."

Her eyes brightened and she turned eagerly, but he stayed her with a hand on her shoulder. "I'll have your promise, if you please."

"I promise."

Gabriel watched her go until the gypsy woman held the puppy out for her to pet.

"Miss Kimbrell." Mrs. Pentreath's voice preceded her like a cold Atlantic wind. "Under whose authority did you rearrange the booths in such a ramshackle manner?"

Gabriel stepped forward. "Mrs. Pentreath." He was ready to come to Bronwyn's defense, but there was no need.

With a bright smile, she said, "How kind of you to notice, ma'am! As you instructed, I took particular care with the placement this year, though I did make the tiniest of alterations to the previous scheme. You see, now the confectioner's stall, with its tempting smells, draws people through to the other end of the street, while the draper's position allows ladies to select their fabrics before visiting

Morwenna's establishment."

She explained a few more of her "tiny" changes, concluding her report with, "'Tis all much the same as you left it, only better."

Mrs. Pentreath blinked, momentarily stymied by this enthusiastic response to her criticism. Then, tapping her cane against the cobbles, she found her argument again. "But tradition Must Be Upheld. Change for the sake of novelty is rarely wise, my dear. Our usual arrangement is pleasing to the eye, and no one need wonder where to find the tinker's booth. I suppose, given your inexperience with such things, we must be grateful you've not set Mr. Hornsby's dancing hounds beside the butcher's shop."

"Oh, no, ma'am—'tis not as if I've learned nothing from you all these years!"

Gabriel pressed his lips against a smile, but Bronwyn's arrow had gone wide. The low pitch of Mrs. Pentreath's brows suggested she detected an insult but couldn't quite locate it.

"Fear not, ma'am," Bronwyn added more gently. "I'm not such a goose to think I have the right of everything. I obtained Mrs. Clifton's approval before any changes were made."

Mrs. Pentreath sucked in a breath. "Agnes! She would not have sanctioned such a scheme without speaking with me first!"

"I'm sure she only wished to lighten your burden, when you've had so much upon you with your sister's illness. I'm relieved to know she's much improved, by the by."

With a sniff, Mrs. Pentreath pivoted on her cane and tapped away.

"That was an expert flanking maneuver," Gabriel murmured, "but ought we to fear for Mrs. Clifton?"

"Oh, she's had the handling of Mrs. P far longer than I have. I daresay she's been waiting years to launch her rebellion." Then, turning to him, she said briskly, "Now, what d'you say to a game?"

"I'm not overly fond of games, Miss Kimbrell."

"But all the gentlemen try their hand at the quoits pitch, or… per'aps you fear a poor showing against our Cornish throwers?"

"Of course not, minx. I'll have you know I've an excellent aim."

"Then you'll do it?"

There was no mistaking the challenge in her eyes. He recognized her tactic for what it was, but he found himself rising to it anyway.

"I suppose I must," he said, "if only to defend my abused honor."

He looked toward the gypsy wagon to summon Emilia, but she wasn't there.

His heart jolted, and his eyes swept the crowd.

"Emilia!" His voice was sharper than he intended, but there was no answer.

A hand settled on his sleeve—Bronwyn's—but he barely noticed it. He turned in a full circle, certain he'd find Vasco Ribeiro among the crowd, but he didn't. His pulse quickened as he strode toward the gypsy's wagon.

"Emilia!" he called again.

Then he saw her, hidden behind the woman's full skirts, a puppy cradled in both hands. His relief was swift and strong.

"I am here," she said, her small face innocently bright, as if she'd not just stripped a decade from his life.

"Captain Marsh?" Bronwyn asked tentatively.

His heart slowed, relief yielding to acute embarrassment. He'd overreacted. Vasco Ribeiro was not in Cornwall. No one was coming to take his daughter. He'd feared the worst, only to make a fool of himself, yelling for Emilia like an overwrought fishwife.

"My apologies," he said stiffly to Emilia. "I... I thought you had ventured off." His hands still shook, so he set them on his hips.

Emilia tilted her head. "But I was just there, beside the wagon like I promised."

He nodded to himself as much as to her. "Return the woman's puppy."

"But—"

Forcing the harshness from his voice, he added, "Miss Kimbrell has invited me to demonstrate my skill at the quoits pitch."

Bronwyn's questioning gaze lingered on him, a small furrow between her brows, and he gave her a faint smile.

Reluctantly, Emilia did as she was bid, and they walked to where several men threw rings at an iron stake in the ground.

———

BRONWYN LOOKED OVER her shoulder to be sure Gabriel followed. His shoulders were more rigid than usual, and though the stricken look was gone from his face, he still looked a trifle pale. And Emilia... she seemed confused over the upset she'd caused, and rightfully so.

There was nothing to fear in Newford.

A distraction was clearly needed, and what better way to distract a gentleman than with a test of his skill?

"I don't know this game," Emilia said when they reached the quoits pitch—a patch of well-packed earth at the edge of the green, worn smooth by years of play.

"Oh, quoits are quite simple," Bronwyn said,

putting a bit more enthusiasm into her voice than necessary. "The aim is to cast one of those metal rings—the quoits—to land as near to the pin as you can. And if a quoit encircles the pin, the gentlemen call it a ringer. I imagine it must be some satisfying to accomplish."

"It's similar to the game of *argolas*," Gabriel explained. "Did you play that in Portugal?"

Emilia's eyes brightened. "Yes, one of the grooms taught me, but we used rings made of rope, and the pin wasn't so far as this."

"Well," Bronwyn said, "I imagine all one needs is a steady hand, a keen spirit and a proper intuition."

The corner of Gabriel's mouth lifted at her theory. "I'm sorry, Miss Kimbrell, but I believe you've overlooked a few variables in your calculation."

Bronwyn crossed her arms and lifted her brows. "I suppose you're one of those gentlemen who worries over angles and velocity or some such nonsense."

"There are sound mathematics behind the science of a proper aim. There's rather more to it than *spirit* and *intuition*."

Bronwyn bit her tongue against a reply as a few chuckles rose from the men gathered round the pitch. By now, the field had cleared, and a growing crowd gathered to take the incomer's measure. The gamekeeper called for anyone willing to take on the captain, but no one stepped forward.

Bronwyn thought a lesser man might have taken offense, but Gabriel merely rolled his shoulder, paid his fee and accepted a ring, testing its weight on his palm.

Placing his feet, he took aim. His first throw struck the packed earth with a dull *thunk*, skidding a few inches before coming to rest impressively close to the pin.

"Nicely done!" Bronwyn declared. "Though per'aps 'twas only beginner's luck." This earned her several dissenting murmurs from the crowd and an arched brow from Gabriel.

Mr. Pengilley, a loud and weathered sailor, called out from across the pitch. "D'ye think ye can do better, lass?"

Emilia turned an anxious gaze up at Bronwyn. She laid a reassuring hand on the girl's shoulder and called to Mr. Pengilley, "There's no need, sir. The captain's mathematics seem to have things well in hand."

Pengilley barked a laugh, but his neighbor, Mr. Evans, jumped into the fray. "If the lady thinks 'er intuition can best the captain's science, I say she oughta put a few coins behind 'er words."

Gabriel, who'd been preparing to toss his next quoit, straightened. "Now, gentlemen—"

"Oh, but they've the right of it," Bronwyn said. "'Tis only proper, I think, that I have an opportunity to test my claim."

More laughter rippled through the crowd as bets were swiftly placed.

Gabriel stepped toward her, leaning so close she could smell the spicy scent of his shaving lotion. "You needn't do this if you'd rather not," he murmured. Then, more loudly, "They shouldn't tease a lady—it's ungentlemanly."

She smiled. "I appreciate your consideration, Captain, but I'd hardly be a Kimbrell if I couldn't endure a bit of quizzing."

He regarded her for a long moment before dipping his head in agreement. "I've already had a turn. One toss from you declares the winner?"

"Oh, I think I'll need a few to accustom myself to the pitch. What d'you say to the best of three?"

His eyes narrowed slightly, but he agreed.

"And the stakes?" she prompted.

"The stakes are an end to this spectacle. Either way, we both win."

She laughed. "I think we must do better than that. If, by some miracle of divine providence, *I* should win..." She tapped a finger against her chin before inspiration struck. "If I win, you must acquire a puppy for Miss Marsh."

Emilia gasped, twisting to look up at her, her expression a charming mix of shock and admiration.

Gabriel, to Bronwyn's relief, was smiling, the tension from before nearly gone from his frame. "And when I win, Miss Kimbrell?" His tone was warm and teasing, though she didn't miss the confidence in his choice of words. "What will you grant me?"

A kiss.

The thought swooped in and left her breathless, her heart fluttering like a trapped bird. "I—" She swallowed and licked her lips. "A puppy," she blurted.

His brows fell. "You wish to give me a puppy?"

"If you win, *I* will acquire a puppy for your daughter. Either way, Emilia wins."

"Either way, I'm left with a mongrel in my stable."

"Well, 'tis certainly one way of looking at it."

He was silent for a moment, and she thought she detected a hint of disappointment in the rueful twist of his lips. Had his thoughts traveled the same path as hers? Was he even now wishing for something more from their contest than a dog?

Warmth flooded her insides. She wished she were bold enough to set out real stakes, but then she spied Merryn at the edge of the green and sighed.

No kiss, then.

Without taking his eyes from hers, Gabriel said loud enough for the crowd to hear, "We play for a puppy."

There was laughter as he returned to the game-keeper for more rings. Bronwyn, released from his gaze, breathed more easily. She removed her gloves and gave them to Emilia for safekeeping before stepping onto the pitch.

Accepting a ring from Gabriel, she considered the target some yards away. Then, closing her eyes, she let the iron sail.

It struck the pin with a satisfying *clink*, spun and dropped neatly around it.

"A ringer!" Mr. Pengilley crowed as more wagers were hastily made.

Gabriel stood, arms crossed and one hand bracketing his jaw as he stared at her toss. He looked then to Pengilley and Evans, and she perceived the moment he realized the depth of their play. It was there in the narrowing of his eyes and the muscle that hardened his jaw.

She hoped he wasn't *too* angry, but he really was too serious.

Leaving the pitch, she took her place at his side again and offered innocently, "Goodness, 'tis a shame I suggested the best of three."

"Miss Kimbrell," he growled in her ear, "why do I have the sense I've been swindled by the entire *village*?"

"Heavens, Captain! *Swindled* is a bit dramatic, when 'tis no secret I have been playing quoits for *ages*."

To his credit, Gabriel's answering scowl, though

fierce, didn't last long. He gamely made his next toss, which was also a ringer and earned Emilia's applause.

By the end of their allotted three tosses, though, they found themselves at a draw.

"A draw?" Emilia asked. "What does that mean? May I still have a puppy?"

"It means Miss Kimbrell is a cunning sharp, and unsuspecting little girls should never agree to any of her schemes. But yes, you may have your puppy."

Emilia wasn't certain how to take her father's curt reply, but a smile lurked in Gabriel's eyes as he spoke, so she chose to focus on the most favorable aspect of his words.

To Bronwyn she said, "Do you think my new puppy will like to play with Brioc?"

"We can certainly ask him. Or her," Bronwyn said. As she escaped with the girl back toward the gypsy wagon, she was pleased to see several men offering Gabriel congratulatory handshakes.

CHAPTER 21

GABRIEL LINGERED AT the quoits pitch as the crowd dispersed. His gaze followed Bronwyn as she led Emilia back toward the gypsy wagon, her head bent low to hear whatever his daughter was saying. For a moment, he felt disoriented—as though up was down and black was white. Nothing was as it should be.

Pengilley approached, jingling a purse Gabriel suspected was heavier than it had been moments before. "Proper job, Cap'n. Ye held yer own, and I thank ye for't. The lass 'as bested ev'ry man 'ere one time or t'other."

Evans, muscling Pengilley aside, added, "Yer last toss had us worrit. Looked short for certain."

It dawned on Gabriel then: in drawing him into her ridiculous wager, Bronwyn had made it possible for the men of her town to accept him. Her clever management of the situation had given them common ground—a common enemy, as it were.

"I gather Miss Kimbrell's reputation as a quoits player is well known," he remarked dryly, the corner of his mouth twitching upward.

Pengilley chuckled. "Oh aye, she's got the *in-tew-ishun*, that one. Been playin' since she was no bigger'n a midge."

"And, of course, no one thought to warn the incomer."

Evans grinned. "Where's the sport in that? 'Sides, ye seemed capable enough."

"*Ye* said he'd never hit the pin!" Pengilley argued.

"Only so ye'd up yer measly wager. Nev'r saw a man so tight-fisted."

Their conversation fell into what seemed an age-old argument from there, and Gabriel took his leave with a tip of his head.

As he went, Pengilley nodded toward the gypsy wagon. "Ye'll be wanting to catch 'em afore Miss Kimbrell lets yer girl pick the puniest pup o' the litter."

"Saints preserve me."

He crossed the green, and his thoughts lingered on Bronwyn and how different she was from Mariana. She'd tricked him, yes, but there'd been no malice in it. His late wife, though, had wielded social occasions like weapons. She'd delighted in creating situations designed to wound others.

Mere weeks after their vows had been spoken, Mariana had confided in a young Vasco Ribeiro the details of their latest argument. It had been a trifling matter—he couldn't even recall the cause of their quarrel now—but her embellishment had painted him as a cold, unfeeling brute.

Ribeiro had the audacity to call him out for his poor treatment of his wife, and Mariana had basked in the attention. Gabriel had bested Ribeiro that time, delivering grave injury to the man's arm, but he'd not escaped unscathed. He'd left the encounter with a saber wound both to his face and his pride.

But Bronwyn... She had no interest in such games. When Gabriel realized her scheme, she hadn't gloated or taken pleasure in his discomfort. Instead, she'd drawn him into her jest with a teasing sparkle in her dark eyes and a playful lift of her chin. She'd invited him to join the fun, and heaven help him, he liked her for it.

———

ZILKA'S SMILE WAS one of amusement when Bronwyn and Emilia returned to the gypsy's wagon. "The miss has come to choose her pup, has she?" Her wooden pen was lively with tiny canine bodies tumbling over one another, tails wagging and pink tongues darting out.

The gypsy woman's bracelets jingled as she reached for a black bundle of fur with white feet. "This one has spirit," she said, setting the pup into Emilia's arms. "Or perhaps you'd prefer his brother?" She reached into the pen again and placed a grey puppy with floppy ears onto the cobbles at Emilia's feet. He assessed his surroundings before toddling forward to sniff at her skirts.

Emilia's eyes widened at the choice before her. "They're both very nice," she whispered, crouching to let both animals snuffle at her fingers.

Zilka took out a tin of biscuits and passed some to Emilia to give to the puppies. "Take your time, love. The right one will choose you."

Bronwyn smiled at Emilia's obvious indecision. The girl had a dilemma of heroic proportions before her, but a low-voiced murmur nearby soon caught Bronwyn's attention.

"… a dreadful match… I hear the wife fled afore the year was out… and he—why, he lifted not a finger to fetch her back…" These whispered confidences were delivered by Mrs. Tretheway into Mrs. Pentreath's eager ears.

"… what else could he do but claim the girl as his own—"

It was easy enough to guess the subject of their gossip. Bronwyn aimed a swift glance at Emilia, relieved to see her wholly absorbed in the puppies.

As she and Zilka tempted the dogs with biscuits, Bronwyn took a step closer to Mrs. Tretheway.

That was when she noticed a lone man lingering near Mr. Clifton's bakery. With dark hair and eyes, his gaze remained fixed on the matrons. Unlike the other fairgoers, he neither browsed the stalls nor chatted with neighbors. Instead, he seemed intent on the ladies' gossip, though they were oblivious to his interest.

Bronwyn bumped the basket on Mrs. Tretheway's arm. "Oh, forgive me!" she exclaimed with feigned surprise.

The lady gave an indignant huff. "Really, Miss Kimbrell."

"Oh, but Mrs. Tretheway—you're just the person I wished to see."

The ladies cast her a look of joint suspicion, and Mrs. Tretheway's nod was curt. "What is it you require?"

"Why, I wished to tell you the herbalist from Penzance has brought more of that tonic you like— the one for chin hairs."

Mrs. Tretheway's face flushed and her lips puckered. "Mrs. Tolliver's Tonic is an invigorating elixir for the nerves," she said haughtily.

"Is it? I'm afraid you'll have to forgive my ignorance, but I suppose that explains—" She stopped and waved vaguely at her chin. "At any rate you'll wish to hurry. With this crowd, the herbalist won't have your tonic for long."

With another huff, Mrs. Tretheway lifted her chin hairs. "Let us go, Edith."

Mrs. P led the way, but before Mrs. Tretheway could make her escape, Bronwyn placed a hand on her arm. Assuring herself Emilia remained occupied with the puppies, she lowered her voice. "I recall hearing a tale about your sister some years ago. I cannot speak to its truth—you know how gossip is—but 'tis best to let sleeping tales lie, don't you think?"

Mrs. Tretheway jerked her arm away and hastened to follow her colleague. With any luck, their talk would turn to the Kimbrell hoyden's poor manners—to be sure, there was enough fodder there to keep them entertained for a good while.

Bronwyn smoothed her skirts and glanced toward the bakery, but the lone man was gone. She returned to Zilka's wagon, a vague unease prickling the back of her neck, but she dismissed it as Gabriel approached with his measured stride.

She was glad to see he wasn't angry over their game of quoits. In fact, there was even the suspicion of a smile in his eyes when he reached them and quickly assessed the situation at Zilka's wagon.

"I see we've not yet settled on a victory prize," he said, his voice as dry as autumn leaves.

"Your daughter possesses a remarkable discernment, but alas, we have not."

Emilia looked up at her father, her small face earnest. "The black one is very lively," she said. "But the grey one seems shy. And their ears are soft, like velvet ribbons."

"A quandary indeed, but you must choose one."

"Or per'aps…" Bronwyn began, but she was overridden by Emilia's parent.

"One," he said firmly.

"I choose this one." Emilia gathered the grey puppy into her arms, and it nestled against her chest. "If… if I may?"

"An excellent choice," Zilka said with a smile. She named her price, and Bronwyn turned expectantly to Gabriel.

His lips twitched. "I don't suppose you've brought funds to cover your half of our wager?"

"Well, of course, I haven't brought my reticule." She lifted her chin, fighting a smile.

"Of course you haven't." But he was already reaching into his coat, and there was a warmth in his voice that belied his stern expression. "I begin to think you are enjoying this far too much."

"Pish! I am enjoying it precisely the right amount."

That startled a laugh from him—brief but genuine—and Bronwyn felt an answering warmth spread through her chest. He handed his coin to Zilka, who winked at Bronwyn.

"You must feed him twice every day," Gabriel said to Emilia. "Not too much at first. A bit of meat, perhaps, and some bread soaked in milk." She nodded solemnly, serious in her new role as caretaker. "And you must teach him his manners if he's to be permitted in the house."

The pup chose that moment to squirm in her arms, nearly tumbling to the ground before Gabriel caught him. He held the wriggling animal away from his coat. "Perhaps we ought to attach his lead."

Bronwyn accepted a handsome lead of braided leather from Zilka and demonstrated for Emilia how to thread it through the small loop at one end. "You simply pass this end through the loop like this, then slip it over the puppy's head…"

Her hands brushed Gabriel's as she settled the lead in place, and a shiver of awareness coursed down her spine. Her eyes met his, and for a moment the bustle of the fair faded, leaving only the warmth in his gaze and the slight curve of his mouth. He had the most curious flecks of gold in his eyes, and a tiny freckle above his right brow.

Emilia's puppy bit her finger then, recalling her attention. "Right," she said to Emilia. "Keep the lead loose like so."

Emilia took the pup from Gabriel and set him

down gently. The animal immediately twisted to chew at the leather, but at a whispered admonishment from his new mistress, he abandoned this endeavor to investigate his surroundings.

"What will you call your new friend?" Bronwyn asked.

Emilia considered the question with the gravity it deserved as the puppy trotted at her side. "I think I shall call him Sombra."

"Sombra," Bronwyn repeated. "It has a lovely sound. What does it mean?"

"Shadow," Emilia translated. "Sombra was my mother's favorite horse." Emilia looked up at her father, her eyes hesitant until he nodded his approval.

"I think 'tis a fine name," Bronwyn said.

They walked toward the puppet booth, passing the draper's stall where Mrs. Tretheway was in fierce negotiation for a length of green-and-puce muslin. Nearby, Mrs. Pentreath gave an imperious nod to none other than the man in the dark suit. They were partially hidden by the crowd, their words obscured by the noise around them, but Bronwyn didn't doubt the subject of their conversation.

She frowned then glanced at Gabriel. Would he wish to know there was talk afoot? It was an inevitable part of village life, but she knew how cautiously he guarded his privacy, and now that she knew a little of his wife's betrayal, she understood more easily the reason for his reserve.

But the day had been far too enjoyable—from their wager on the quoits pitch to that heart- pounding moment their hands had touched over Sombra's lead. No, she decided—why burden him with unpleasantness?

Her decision was made easier when Emilia said softly, "Thank you, Papá, for my puppy."

Surprise played across Gabriel's face, but he quickly mastered it. There was a rasp to his voice when he spoke. "You are welcome, though I believe your thanks ought to go to Miss Kimbrell for her ridiculous scheme."

Emilia performed a hasty curtsy. "Oh, yes! Thank you," she said with a shy smile.

"You are most welcome. Whenever you have need of a ridiculous scheme—"

"Miss Kimbrell," Gabriel said sternly.

"Of course. The pleasure was mine."

When Sombra pulled Emilia ahead of them, Bronwyn leaned toward the captain. "What caused such a look of startlement to cross your face? Has your daughter never had occasion to thank you before?"

He gave her a sidelong glance. "My daughter has never had occasion to call me 'Papa' before."

CHAPTER 22

THE INVITATION FOR supper at Oak Hill came one week later. Gabriel closed his book on breeding principles and leaned back, rubbing his eyes. An evening of food and conversation with his neighbors (and perhaps some music and dancing, Kimbrell warned) didn't sound as ominous as it might have only weeks before. In fact, the more he considered it, the more he found himself desiring the outing. Bronwyn would be there.

Not allowing himself too much time to think, he wrote out his acceptance and handed it to John.

This anticipation was a feeling he'd rarely experienced—not since his early days in Lisbon before his marriage. The city had been a base for British operations, and there'd been frequent gatherings organized by married officers and diplomats. From balls to theater outings and lavish suppers—Lisbon had been a lively place for a young lieutenant with passable looks and tolerable dancing skills.

On the evening of the Oak Hill supper, he instructed Mrs. Forsyth to see his daughter properly scrubbed and re-plaited. The housekeeper got on well with Emilia, but he'd have to renew his search for a governess—one who didn't quail at the thought of teaching foreign children.

Certainly, his daughter required more refinement in her education than the soldier's lessons he provided. But as he taught her English, geography and sums each day, he learned a little more about her. A few more weeks' delay couldn't hurt.

He paused at his dressing mirror, struck by how different his sentiment was now than when he'd first arrived in Cornwall. Though he couldn't have anticipated it then, he owed much of the change to one dark-eyed slip of a lady with a glib tongue.

The cracked door to his chamber inched open as he made a final adjustment to his cravat. "Come in," he called.

Expecting John, he was surprised when the door widened to reveal Emilia. Mrs. Forsyth had dressed her in a pale cream gown with tiny puff sleeves. The hem sat a trifle higher than he thought it was meant to, and he wondered whether it could be let down again or if she would soon require an entirely new wardrobe.

"Papá?"

His hands stilled. She'd not called him that since the fair, and he'd attributed her singular lapse to the excitement over her new puppy. But now, as she stood before him with a furrowed brow, worrying her handkerchief in her small hands, it was clear something was amiss.

He guided her to the chaise and sat so he could better meet her eyes. "What is it?"

After a small hesitation, she blurted in Portuguese, "Must I go to supper?"

This was unexpected. "Do you not wish to?"

Lifting her chin, she shook her head.

"May I ask why?"

Her gaze went to a place beyond his shoulder. With a sniff, she said, "There will be adults—more than Miss Kimbrell and her grandfather."

"Yes, but there will also be other children. You'll take your supper with them in the nursery. What is this objection to adults?" When she remained stubbornly silent, he said, "Emilia. I wish to know so I may help."

Finally, she whispered, "What if they say unkind things?"

Gabriel couldn't help the lift of his brows any more than he could stop the immediate flash of anger that raced through him. "Has someone said something unkind to you?" When she found a sudden interest in the toe of her slipper, Gabriel took one of her hands in his and held it. "Emilia?"

Bringing her eyes back to his, she said hastily, "I heard them at your house in London—the man with the whiskers and his wife. They said my mother was bad, and I am, too."

His stomach soured. The man with the whiskers had been his superior at the Foreign Office. Gabriel had heard them, too, moments before he entered his drawing room. He just hadn't realized Emilia, who'd taken to hiding in the servants' corridor those first weeks, had been listening as well.

They say the child isn't his.

It's as I told you, Charles: nothing good ever comes of marrying a foreigner.

I met the mother once in Lisbon, you know, years ago. For all her airs, Mariana Alves was no better than she ought to be. I can't imagine the daughter will prove any different. Blood will tell.

Moments later, Gabriel had given his notice in terms that left the man's wife gasping in offended outrage. When a report arrived the next day from Brightwell—*Two men have made inquiries regarding your daughter*—it had been easy enough to leave London behind.

Now, he tugged Emilia's hand until she came closer. Choosing his words with care, he said, "Your mother was an intelligent, beautiful lady who loved you, and nothing can change that. People will always find something to prattle on about, and though their words may sting, they hold no true power unless you grant it. You are my daughter—you are a Marsh. Let them whisper if they must, but hold your head high, for no gossip can alter the truth of who you are. You are bold and brave and kind."

Her eyes widened at this speech, but she remained silent.

"I will be at Oak Hill," he continued, "as will Bronwyn. Many of the other guests are her family, and I do not believe them to be mean-spirited. I cannot promise that thoughtless things won't be said—people often speak before they think. But I can promise that I will not tolerate it. Now, what do you say? The choice to stay or go is yours to make."

Emilia's chest rose and fell with her breath before she nodded. "I will go."

———

DESPITE GABRIEL'S ASSURANCES to Emilia, his own nerves were not as steady as he might have wished when their carriage turned down the drive to Oak Hill. Her admission, and the anxiety that accompanied it, had unsettled him. He'd thought to protect her from the gossip in London, but all this time she'd been laboring under its weight.

It was much easier to dispense advice than to heed it, and though he'd counseled her to rise above the whispers, he knew from experience how difficult that could be. He only hoped she'd find the larger Kimbrell family as welcoming as Bronwyn and her grandfather, but as they joined the line of carriages and wagons depositing guests at his neighbor's steps, he was beginning to feel his troops were out-numbered.

"Send for me at any time if you wish to leave," he said to Emilia.

Her face was a small, pale oval reflected in the window, but she turned at his words. "I am bold and brave," she said softly.

His heart twisted for her determination, but he didn't miss the steady motion of her fingers as she pleated her handkerchief. Then, the light from the carriage lamp caught the linen's embroidered edge, and he narrowed his eyes on the thing.

It was one of his.

He thought he'd been careless these last weeks, but no. His daughter was a *handkerchief thief.*

He opened his mouth to ask her about the pur-loined square then stopped. How many times had he seen her clutching a handkerchief like a talisman? When she first arrived in London, she'd carried one of her mother's, but it seemed she'd grown her collection.

How many? he wondered. It was a devilishly odd habit, but if she drew comfort from the linen squares, he wouldn't take that from her. He'd buy an entire case of them if she required it.

When they left the carriage, Kimbrell's housekeeper came to escort Emilia to her supper in the nursery. She had a warm smile and a gentle manner that seemed to put Emilia at her ease.

"Young Master Henry is already in the nursery," she said, "along with Henry's governess. I believe Miss Litton plans a game of charades when the other children arrive. Will you like that, d'you think?"

Emilia nodded and only looked back once as she went off with the woman.

Oak Hill's drawing room was in the same style as the rest of his neighbor's home. Dark beams crossed the ceiling, and thick rugs in rich reds and blues lent warmth to the cold stone floor. A pianoforte—the room's only modernity—had pride of place before leaded windows that reflected the fire within.

Kimbrell's butler announced him, and Gabriel's gaze swept the prodigious Kimbrell clan before finding Bronwyn on a striped settee with her cousin Morwenna. Her eyes met his, and she smiled before excusing herself to her cousin.

"Captain," Alfie Kimbrell said, "I hear you lost a wager to my cousin and gained a dog in the bargain. One of us should have warned you she plays to win."

"A word of caution would have been welcome, though I would like to clarify I did not *lose* to Miss Kimbrell. We reached a draw."

Alfie grinned as Bronwyn joined them. "'Tis not precisely how she tells it," he said.

Gabriel might have offered a retort, but he lost the thread of the conversation somewhere between Bronwyn's dark eyes and her easy smile.

Alfie was summoned by an uncle or cousin, and Bronwyn looked up at Gabriel. "You're not regretting our wager, are you?" she said with an innocence he didn't believe for a moment.

He snorted. "Why would I have regrets when a puppy of questionable breeding sprinkles my carpets at least twice every day? But," he added in a softer voice, "Emilia adores him, so I must endure the pestilence."

"Oh, splendid! That does not sound like regret at all. Sombra is such a clever little dog, sprinkles notwithstanding, and he's sure to be a good companion to her."

"He is an abomination of the worst sort."

The evening flowed from there, as did Kimbrell's wine. One conversation turned easily to another in the natural way of families. Gabriel found himself often enough on the receiving end of the Kimbrells' teasing, though he delivered his share of pithy rejoinders himself.

He enjoyed the family's back-and-forth quizzing that was so different from the stiff formality of London society. Their easy banter put him in mind of his army days, of friendships formed during long marches through endless forests and rugged hills. It was the sort of amity that allowed a man to laugh even when his bones ached with exhaustion. He hadn't realized how much he missed that simple, unpretentious ease until he found himself surrounded by it once more.

After supper, the gentlemen returned to the drawing room to find the children had joined the ladies. Emilia sat between Bronwyn and Morwenna, plying a needle through a small sampler or some such.

The candlelight caught the copper threads in Bronwyn's dark hair as she guided Emilia's stitch. Mariana would never have been content with such a scene of domestic tranquility. She'd always been more interested in entertaining the company with amusing tales. Her flirtation was one of the things that had drawn him to her. She'd had a vibrant, captivating energy that had been alluring in his youth, but now, Gabriel was struck by such an overwhelming feeling of calm that he was rendered momentarily speechless.

The ladies looked up at the gentlemen's return. At a whisper from Bronwyn, Emilia came to him and presented her sampler. He made what he hoped were appropriate sounds of approval.

"Are you enjoying yourself?" he asked and was relieved when she nodded. The tension he'd witnessed in her earlier seemed to have eased.

"Henry is nice, but his brother-in-law is a famous stone carver, so he only wants to talk about rocks." She delivered this pronouncement with a wrinkle of her nose, a hint of childish disdain that made him smile.

"I think you'll find most boys your age have rather dull interests. I, myself, found rocks rather fascinating at one point. And beetles, too, if I recall."

She pulled her head back, clearly appalled by this admission, and he gently tugged the end of her braid.

Presently, someone suggested music and dancing to pass the evening. The gentlemen began moving the furniture aside while the ladies selected sheet music for the pianoforte.

"Bronwyn, my dear," Alan Kimbrell said, "I can't abide an evening with nothing but these modern gallops. Why don't you see if you can find some of Beethoven's sheets in the library? Your grandmother always favored his minuets."

There were good-natured groans at the prospect of an evening spent dancing such old-fashioned figures, but the company resigned themselves to it. But as the minutes passed and Bronwyn still hadn't returned, her grandfather approached Gabriel.

"Marsh," he said, leaning on his cane, "would you mind lending your assistance to Bronwyn's search? I don't recall where I left Evelyn's Beethoven."

Gabriel agreed and found the library two doors along the corridor from the drawing room. The space was lit by a pair of flickering wall lamps, and a candle burned low on the desk.

Nearby, Bronwyn balanced on a ladder, stretching for a box that was just out of reach. Her brow was furrowed, and a stray curl of dark hair had escaped her pins. He hastened to her side. "Allow me."

———

BRONWYN BALANCED ON her toes, reaching for the box that lay stubbornly beyond her grasp. She lacked only an inch or two, but the ladder had reached the end of the rails and wouldn't go any farther. An unladylike groan of frustration escaped her.

"Beethoven, you'd better be in there," she muttered. She shifted on the rung so she might gain her missing inch. The ladder wobbled and she steadied herself.

"Allow me."

Gabriel's low voice sent an unexpected ripple along her spine, and she looked down sharply, not having heard him enter. "'Tis all good, Captain," she assured him, stretching for the box once more.

"Will you please come down from there and allow me to retrieve your box?"

"I've nearly got it."

"Lord preserve me from contrary females,"

"Pardon?"

"I said, mind the ladder doesn't slip the rails."

Bronwyn couldn't help her smile—she was nearly certain that was *not* what he'd said—but her smile fell away when a weight settled on the ladder behind her.

"What—?" Twisting, she was alarmed to see Gabriel on the first rung. He climbed another, then another. "What are you doing?" she squeaked.

Squeaked, like a blasted mouse. Her cheeks flushed with sudden heat, and her breath caught in her throat.

"My arms are longer than yours."

"But—" Her mouth betrayed her, and nothing more came out of it. Another step and she could feel the warmth of his body directly behind her. His nearness was deliciously improper, and her heart thumped a drumbeat.

"Have I finally rendered you speechless?"

She found her tongue. "Of course not. 'Tis only, this is rather… irregular."

With seemingly little effort, he reached past her, his shoulder brushing hers, and liberated the box from its shelf. "Victory," he whispered in her ear.

"I think you must use the same soap as my brother," she said stupidly.

"An interesting fact," he said, "and yet, one I didn't need to know."

Through the open door came the faint strains of music from the drawing room. Gabriel stepped off the ladder and took his warmth with him. Setting the box on the desk, he turned to offer his hand as she descended.

She ignored it, taking a shaky step down on her own. Rifling the contents of the box, she searched for Beethoven's minuet among her grandfather's sheets of music and tried not to notice Gabriel's nearness. She failed miserably.

Glancing up, she was struck by how the lamp-light shone on his dark hair and highlighted the scar on his cheek. Her fingers itched to trace it. She wondered again how he'd come by it. It was a visible reminder of a past he rarely spoke of, a history that seemed to both haunt and define him.

Her image reflected back to her from his hazel eyes. With his dark and light places, Gabriel appeared much like the vampire her cousins had teased her about, only… more.

There was something far more compelling about him than any character she'd ever read. He was vulnerability wrapped in steel. Layer upon layer, twist after twist, like a complicated maze with no solution.

She took a step closer, and his eyes widened before falling to her lips. The air between them cracked with tension, a silent question hanging in the space.

She swallowed. "'Tis not here," she whispered. Her voice was barely audible, even to her own ears.

"I beg your pardon?" He leaned in slightly, his brow furrowed.

"The Beethoven… 'tis not the right box. I'm afraid your victory was for naught."

Her words hung between them until he said, "I disagree."

Her stomach plunged to her toes. He meant to kiss her. What, she wondered, would his lips feel like? Would they be soft or hard? Cool or warm? Would he taste like he smelled—clean and crisp and faintly spicy? Would he be able to tell *this* was her first kiss? She'd read countless novels about passionate embraces, but no words could have prepared her for this heavy, breathless anticipation.

The door opened wider then, admitting more light from the hall and the frowning face of her brother. Bronwyn jumped, moving to put space between her and Gabriel.

Merryn's brow furrowed as he took in the scene before him. "I came to see if the pair of you require assistance," he said wryly.

Bronwyn waved vaguely at the box on the desk as her brother strode into the library. He inspected it briefly before crossing the room to a low cabinet. Removing a sheaf of papers from the top drawer, he fluttered them with a frown.

"Grandmother kept them here," he said before bundling Bronwyn from the room.

——

LATER THAT NIGHT, after Emilia had been tucked into her bed and the house had gone quiet, Gabriel sat in his library, a glass of brandy untouched at his elbow. The fire had burned low, but he made no move to stoke it.

His mind kept returning to the library at Oak Hill, to the scent of old books and leather bindings, and to Bronwyn. The way her eyes had widened when he'd climbed the ladder behind her. The soft catch in her breath when his whisper had brushed her ear. The warmth of her body, so close to his own.

He rubbed a hand over his face, grimacing. What had he been thinking? He didn't go about kissing—*almost* kissing—innocents.

He wasn't some green lieutenant anymore, stealing kisses in darkened corners at embassy balls. He was thirty—a father, for heaven's sake—with responsibilities that went beyond his own desires.

And yet, even as his mind made the argument, his heart sensed the truth.

The memory of Bronwyn looking up at him, her dark eyes reflecting the lamplight, her lips slightly parted… It stirred something in him he'd thought long buried. Not the hot flash of attraction he'd felt for Mariana all those years ago, but something deeper and far more unsettling. Something that made him want to know Bronwyn's thoughts, to understand the mind behind her expressive eyes.

He'd noticed, of course, how she was with Emilia—patient and kind, drawing his daughter out with her gentle persistence. He appreciated her wit, her forthright manner, even her impertinence at times. But he hadn't expected to find himself so thoroughly charmed.

He muttered a curse and reached for the brandy at last. It burned his throat but failed to distract him from his thoughts.

Surely, he was a fool. His marriage to Mariana had taught him the dangers of mistaking attraction for something deeper. That path had led swiftly to bitter disappointment and regret, and it had been long years since he allowed himself to think of anything resembling love or family.

But he had a child now—something he'd not expected since Mariana left—and despite the imprudence of it, hope was taking root again.

Morning, however, brought the post, and with it, new worries.

CHAPTER 23

GABRIEL'S FINGERS CRUMPLED the edges of Brightwell's letter. His colleague had provided a detailed report, but the essential message was clear: *Ribeiro leaves Lisbon soon.*

Outside the library window, a humid southwesterly wind pressed against the glass. A log popped, showering the hearth with ash, but he scarcely noticed. He read Brightwell's report again to be certain, but his colleague's intelligence was sound.

Ribeiro was sailing. That much was clear, but his destination remained uncertain. Brightwell believed he meant to serve as escort for the king's return from Brazil, but he couldn't discount the whispers he'd heard of a journey to London.

The library seemed smaller, Gabriel's heartbeat louder.

London. It wasn't unusual for a diplomat such as Ribeiro to have business in England's capital, but the course from Lisbon would bring him within bowshot of Cornwall. He might even stop at Falmouth for provisions, and from there, it was less than a day's ride to Newford.

And all of this assumed the whispers were even true. Was he making something out of nothing, like when he thought he'd lost Emilia at the fair? Was he worrying when there was no cause?

He dragged a hand through his hair and let out a low growl of frustration for the uncertainty of it all. The weight of the blade he still carried in his boot was faint solace.

His thoughts leapt ahead to precautions and contingencies. His gaze found the drawer where he kept a brace of pistols. Since the war had ended, it had been his fervent hope never to fire one again.

So caught up was he in plans and strategies that it was a long moment before he sensed danger of another sort in the warm, damp scent that filled his library. Spinning, he rounded the desk to find Sombra, eyes bright with mischief as a fresh puddle formed on the Axminster.

Gabriel shouted a stern command, but the idiot dog took it as an invitation to play. The animal bounded over to him with ignorant delight, his stubby tail wagging shamelessly.

Exhaling slowly through his nose, Gabriel pondered a fitting end for unruly beasts. The pup, unaware of the danger he courted, merely fell onto his haunches and cocked his head.

Gabriel pointed. "You are perilously close to finding a new home in a burlap sack."

Sombra lifted a hind leg to scratch his ear.

A muscle ticked in Gabriel's jaw. First, Brightwell's letter and now this.

He'd commanded his troops with authority, executed maneuvers of precision and strategy, and routed the *bloody French*. Now, he was reduced to doing battle with a creature no larger than a round of cheese, and with half as much sense. He'd endured purloined handkerchiefs and debates over hair ribbons without complaint, but this daily offense upon his carpets was the final push that breached the limits of his patience.

Crouching, he scooped the dog in one hand.

Sombra wriggled joyfully, his pink tongue darting out to lick Gabriel's wrist.

"You are a menace."

The pup responded with an indelicate sneeze.

"Saints preserve me," Gabriel muttered, holding the animal at arm's length. His other hand found a handkerchief—one of the few that hadn't been liberated from his chamber—and he wiped his cheek.

"Sombra!" Emilia called from the corridor. "Where are you? I—oh!"

She entered the library but skidded to a stop,

taking the full measure of the scene. Her gaze flicked from the stain on the carpet to Sombra, then up to her father's frown. Her lips parted, the beginnings of a plea forming, but Gabriel was in no mood for negotiation.

"He goes to the stables," he said, his tone allowing no argument.

Emilia's eyes widened. "But—"

"Now."

Her small hands clenched into stubborn fists. "But he is so little," she persisted, her voice edged with urgency. "He does not mean to—"

"He has been in this house for nearly a fortnight," Gabriel said, the thread of his patience fraying. "If he has not yet grasped the basic civilities, I hold little hope for his future enlightenment."

Emilia's chin lifted. "You said I could have a dog," she reminded him, switching to Portuguese as she did whenever emotions overtook her.

"I said you may have a dog," Gabriel bit out in English, "not that the dog may have my *library*."

He deposited a wiggling Sombra into her arms, and she cradled the pup to her chest, her little chin burrowing into his grey fur.

Sombra whined and twisted to lick her cheek.

"You've wounded his sensibilities," Emilia accused. She might as well have said he'd wounded *her*, for the expression in her eyes and the wobble in her voice were just as pained.

The worst thing happened then: a tear slid down her cheek, impossibly slow so he couldn't miss it. He closed his eyes and sighed. "Emilia."

But she had already turned away. With a sniff, head bowed over the bundle of fur in her arms, she closed the door behind her with more noise than such an action warranted.

Gabriel rubbed the back of his neck where a knot was forming. Turning, he found Brightwell's letter once more. He should be wondering at Ribeiro's intent. Instead, all he could think about was the look on his daughter's face as she walked away.

He reached for the bell pull.

When John arrived moments later, he said gruffly, "Send in Hadley. And John, see to the carpet."

———

BRONWYN STIRRED HER tea slowly, her thoughts returning again to Gabriel and the night of her grandfather's supper. There'd been no discussion—much less a recurrence—of the moment she was certain would have become a kiss were it not for her brother's irritating and untimely arrival.

"Wool-gatherin' again?" her grandfather said.

Recalled to the present and Oak Hill's drawing room, she straightened. "Why do you say that?"

"You've been stirring this last minute and more, but your cup is empty."

She looked down to see he was right. She set aside her spoon and sighed. The sound was echoed by Brioc's snores as he stretched, his long body taking up the cold stones of the hearth.

"What do you think love is, Granfer?"

"Love! 'Tis to be that sort of conversation, then."

"You're the most qualified to answer the question. You loved my grandmother for more than fifty years."

"Aye, that I did, though she made it easy. Evelyn was light itself. But love…" His gaze turned distant as he considered the question. Finally, he said, "I imagine 'tis desiring another's happiness over your own. A parent for a child, a brother for his sister, a lady for her gentleman." He gave her a meaningful look as he added, "'Tis far more than a moment stolen in the library."

"Well, as if I didn't know that!" she said, her cheeks uncomfortably warm.

He chuckled, and Bronwyn filled their cups in an effort to occupy her hands. Fortunately, they were interrupted by the arrival of Parsons, announcing Miss Marsh was at the door without a hat.

Bronwyn set down the pot with a clink. "Miss Marsh?"

"She has inquired after you in particular, miss."

"Of course, please show her in!"

Parsons soon returned with their visitor, who entered rather stiffly, hands clasped about her puppy. Though her face was composed, there was a telltale redness about her eyes. Bronwyn immediately stood and went to her.

"Emilia!" she said, placing a hand on the girl's shoulder and guiding her to a place on the settee. "What a delightful surprise, though I confess I'm a bit anxious to think of you walking all this way alone."

Sombra leapt from her arms to yip a greeting at Brioc. On being rudely awakened in this manner, the wolfhound jumped, his feet skittering and sliding on the smooth stones of the hearth until he steadied himself.

Emilia folded her hands in her lap and lifted her chin. "I apologize for calling without an invitation, Miss Kimbrell. Sir."

Bronwyn's grandfather proclaimed this to be a pile of nonsense while Bronwyn said, "Pish! You are always welcome here. And just look how your Sombra goes along with Brioc." Indeed, the wolfhound, having recovered from his sleepy confusion, exchanged courteous sniffs with the tiny pup.

"We were having our tea," her grandfather said. "Will you join us?"

Emilia looked hesitantly toward the tea things, and Bronwyn added, "Of course, you must! My grandfather's cook makes the most delicious lemon cake."

"Yes, I will have some," she said softly.

As her grandfather arranged slices of cake on a fresh plate, Bronwyn poured out a cup of tea. She cast him a look of uncertainty over Emilia's head before asking their guest what new tricks Sombra had learned.

Emilia's answers were brief, though, her mind clearly elsewhere. As she made tiny nibbles to a slice of lemon cake, Bronwyn said gently, "I hope all is well at Penhale."

For a moment, Emilia maintained her formal pose. Then her lower lip trembled, and she twisted her handkerchief. Bronwyn's stomach dropped at the girl's distress, and her palms grew damp. Was someone injured? Ill? "What is it?" she pressed.

"My father was cross with me."

Bronwyn's pulse steadied. No one was injured. That was good, but she knew well the pain of a father's disappointment over some ill-advised lark or another. But how much worse it must be for a young girl not yet confident of her place in her father's home.

Her grandfather, perhaps sensing there were tears ahead, excused himself to send for more cake.

When the door had closed behind him, Bronwyn turned back to Emilia. "D'you know, your father has been cross with me more times than I can count, but I've found his ire to be quick as a flash. Here one moment, then gone before you can blink." Leaning closer, she added conspiratorially, "'Tis easy enough to tease him out of't."

Emilia's only response to this confidence was a forced smile.

"Might I ask," Bronwyn said, "what was the cause of your father's displeasure?"

Soon, she had the whole dreadful story from the girl, from Sombra's unfortunate habits to Gabriel's sharp words. Bronwyn had never heard him raise his voice, even when she'd vexed him with their quoits wager. His habit tended more toward low growls than shouts, but she couldn't deny the girl's distress. And Gabriel, she was certain, must be feeling equally low by now.

"'Tis unfortunate," she said as Emilia sniffed into her handkerchief, "but not such a disaster, I should think. Why, I suspect—" She stopped before she assured the girl how much her father must be regretting his words. Recalling how he disliked it when she presumed to know his thoughts, she offered instead, "I suspect you will feel better if you make your apologies for Sombra."

"Do you think so?"

"I am certain of't."

Emilia considered this for a long moment before

saying, "Do you think my father will send Sombra away?"

Bronwyn had witnessed how earnestly Gabriel desired to make a home for his daughter—from reclaiming Penhale's vast gardens to purchasing a puppy against his own wishes. She couldn't believe he would send Sombra away, but she wouldn't speak for him.

"I think this is a question for your father," she said gently. "'Tis his house, and his rug that suffers, though I have seen him to be a fair and honest man. I suggest you offer an apology and per'aps a solution to the problem."

"Sombra doesn't mean to do it."

"Of course not! He's still learning his manners, but per'aps we might engage John or Hadley to walk him a bit more. And d'you know, there are books and such on how to train dogs. I think we ought to purchase one so you know just what to do when Sombra misbehaves."

Emilia nodded at this plan and, collecting her courage, stood to go. As she gathered her pet, Bronwyn cast a swift glance about the drawing room, relieved to see her grandfather's rug remained free of stains. "Let me fetch my hat," she said, "and I will drive you."

—

GABRIEL'S BOOTS RANG against the parquet as he strode through Penhale's silent corridors. His words to Emilia had been harsh. He expected to find her plotting his demise somewhere in the house, but she was nowhere to be found.

He'd checked the stables first, where he'd sent her with that wretched hound of Hades, but she was not there. Neither was she in the nursery, nor the garden, nor the kitchen sampling Mrs. Davies' biscuits. There was also, he noted, a curious lack of puddles in his house. The dog was gone as well.

"John!"

"Here, sir," John said from where he'd been lurking beyond his elbow.

"Have you seen Miss Marsh?"

"Not since she left your library this morning, sir."

Gabriel's heart gave a peculiar lurch. He summoned Hadley and directed both men to search the grounds and the adjoining wood while he checked the house again.

His mind leapt to Brightwell's letter. Was it merely coincidence that Emilia should disappear the same day he learned Vasco Ribeiro had left Portugal? But if Ribeiro had found them... if he'd taken Emilia while Gabriel was distracted by a blasted puddle on his carpet...

He wouldn't allow himself to think it.

No. Brightwell reported Ribeiro *would* leave, not

that he had left. It was too soon for him to have landed on England's shore, if indeed England was his destination. This rationalization did little to ease his fears, though.

The crunch of wheels on the drive drew him to the window. Bronwyn's pony cart rounded the fountain before the house, and there sat Emilia, quite safe, with that cursed dog in her arms.

He exhaled sharply. He'd made a fuss out of nothing—again. This father business would be the death of him, he was certain. Nevertheless, he was through the door and down the steps before the cart came to a full stop. Without a word, he lifted Emilia down and crushed her to his chest, his heart thundering against his ribs.

For a moment, she remained rigid in his arms. Then, slowly, hesitantly, her arms crept round his neck. "I am sorry," she whispered in Portuguese. "I went to Oak Hill."

"*Nunca mais*," he murmured into her hair. "Never again." Then, switching to English, he added more gently, "You must tell someone where you go."

"Yes, Papá."

His heart slowed, and he simply held her, delighting in the little-girl scent of her cheek and the softness of her hair beneath his hand.

When Mariana had left him, he'd given up on the thought of ever being a father, but how might the last years of his life have been different had he known Emilia?

Certainly, they would have been humbling, for nothing forced a man to confront his shortcomings more than the care of a child. But his life had new purpose since Emilia had come to him, a purpose different from that of a man—a soldier—finding his way in the world alone. No matter how he felt about Mariana's betrayal, he couldn't be anything but grateful for the gift of her child. *Their* child.

He released his daughter and set her on her feet. When he lifted his head, he found Bronwyn watching him from her perch. There was no judgment in her dark eyes, only a curious brightness that she blinked away.

Emilia's fingers twisted one of his handkerchiefs. "Miss Kimbrell says I ought to ask if you're going to send Sombra away?"

"That is," Bronwyn interjected hastily, "Your daughter expressed some concern over the possibility, and I encouraged her to speak with you d'rectly about it."

In their brief but eventful acquaintance, Miss Kimbrell had shown a decided lack of hesitancy in dispensing advice, invariably delivered with unwavering conviction. Yet there she sat, exhibiting a most uncharacteristic restraint. The unexpected novelty of it momentarily discomposed him.

Then, recalling his daughter's question, he replied, "Sombra belongs to you, Emilia. That will not change." He paused to let this sink in before adding firmly, "But he must learn his manners, and you must help him to do so."

Emilia's face brightened at this. "Miss Kimbrell says there are books about training dogs. May I purchase one?"

"We shall see what we can find."

"And I will ask John to walk him more often, and Hadley…"

Emilia bent to collect her errant pup, who'd begun investigating Bronwyn's wheel. "Perhaps you might take Sombra for a walk now," Gabriel said. "Though mind you stay within sight of the house."

Once Emilia had led her pet away, Gabriel approached the cart. "Miss Kimbrell, I find myself in your debt once more. Thank you."

Her lips parted in surprise before curving into a smile. "Why, 'twas naught but a simple kindness."

"I am coming to believe there is nothing 'simple' about you."

"Why, thank you, Captain Marsh." She considered him for a moment before adding, "At the risk of overstepping, I can't help but notice your daughter has a fondness for handkerchiefs. This one she carries today appears to be one of yours."

"I am aware. Should I be concerned or flattered

that you recognize my linens?"

"You may be sure 'tis not flattery."

He heard the rest of her words then. "This one? Do you mean there have been others?"

"Aye…" Bronwyn adjusted her grip on the reins. "'Tis only that I may have dropped one in your drawing room—quite by accident—and Emilia took a liking to it. And then, seeing the square she carries today, it became clear that mine was not the only one…"

"She took a liking to your handkerchief? Do you mean she absconded with it?"

"She has done nothing so criminal! I was the careless one, and it seemed a small thing to quibble over."

Gabriel tucked his chin. "I do apologize. I shall replace it."

"Captain Marsh," she said with some exasperation, "I assure you I am not concerned over a square of linen. I only thought you should know." She paused, then added more quietly, "I believe she takes comfort in them."

He rubbed a hand over his face. "Yes, I have thought the same." Then, throwing caution aside, he admitted, "I am at a loss. What do you think I should do?"

Her expression was a delightful mixture of surprise and confusion. "I'm sure I don't know. I am not her mother."

He glanced to where Emilia tempted Sombra with a stick some distance away. "If you were her mother, what would you do?"

Bronwyn appeared flustered by the question, but she recovered to say, "Why, I suppose I would make certain she knows she's loved and wanted. We can't fault her for seeking comfort wherever she may find it. There's been much to overset her in so short a time, with the loss of her mother and now, the discovery of a father she doesn't know. Show her love, allow her to take comfort where she may, and she will come about."

He sucked his teeth as he considered this. Then, deciding Bronwyn Kimbrell was uncommonly brilliant, he told her so.

She gathered her reins. "'Tis about time you admitted as much."

Gabriel laughed.

All would be well. Ribeiro must be on his way to Brazil by now. Emilia was safe, and this woman… Well, the thought of making his home in Cornwall had begun to hold more appeal for him than it once had done. He was so used to watching for the enemy over his shoulder that he'd failed to see his future ahead of him.

"Miss Kimbrell," he said, before he could overthink the matter. "I should like to court you."

Her brows inched up and her lips parted in surprise. It occurred to him he'd been rather direct, though she must have suspected his feelings from that night in her grandfather's library. Still, he amended his words. "That is to say, I enjoy your company. I suspect you enjoy mine, though I leave it to you to confirm or deny."

The corner of her mouth lifted. "I do not deny it."

"Then we are agreed?"

"We are agreed."

He watched her cart disappear down the drive as Emilia returned to his side. His daughter's small hand slid into his while Sombra investigated his boot with far too much interest.

CHAPTER 24

THE NEXT WEEKS passed too swiftly for Gabriel's liking. He invited Bronwyn to attend a theatrical production at Newford's small theater, where they were properly chaperoned by the entire town, more or less.

Then there was tea. Bronwyn invited him and Emilia to join her mother and cousins for an afternoon that proved more pleasant than he expected. Her mother took an instant liking to Emilia, plying her with biscuits and cakes, which earned the woman his daughter's adoration in return.

Most recently, he'd attended church—an infrequent event for him these past years—followed by luncheon at Oak Hill. Though Emilia enjoyed herself excessively, he found the sheer number of Bronwyn's relations—more, even, than had attended his neighbor's supper—a trifle exhausting.

There'd been no opportunity for a quiet walk with Bronwyn among the hedges of Oak Hill's garden, and certainly no stolen moments in her grandfather's library.

Today, he meant to invite Bronwyn and her mother to supper. He'd already discussed the matter with Mrs. Davies, who assured him she'd see a proper table set for the occasion. With only the four of them to dine, he anticipated a quieter evening. And perhaps, while Emilia entertained Bronwyn's mother, he might show Bronwyn Penhale's library.

The thought quickened his step, and the bell above Morwenna Williamson's door chimed as he stepped inside her shop. Mrs. Tretheway stood near a silk display, deep in conversation with another lady over a bolt of cloth. At the sight of him, though, their voices fell silent. He removed his hat and dipped his head at them, a gesture they returned with pinch-lipped nods.

"Captain Marsh," Morwenna said, coming round the counter. "Your timing is exceptional. I've just this last hour finished letting down the hems on Miss Marsh's garments. Shall I wrap her dresses or would she like to try them first?"

The matrons bustled past him and out of the door. He watched them go before returning his attention to Morwenna. "Emilia is enjoying sweets at the inn with Miss Kimbrell, so you may wrap them."

"Ah, she's discovered Wynne's raspberry tarts then. It won't take me but a moment."

While he waited, his gaze drifted over the displays of ribbons and lace behind the counter. A dark green velvet caught his eye. It was a few shades darker than Bronwyn's riding habit, and he thought it would complement very well. When Morwenna returned, he requested an ell of it to add to his purchase.

His parcels felt oddly significant beneath his arm as the shop door closed behind him, and he anticipated Bronwyn's reaction to his gift. Would she be pleased? Surprised? He waited for a wagon to pass, and then for a small crossing boy to sweep the path ahead of him. He flipped him a coin, which the lad caught with swift fingers.

"Obliged, guv!"

The sun was high, the air clean, and there was a lightness to his step as he strode into the Fin and Feather Inn.

The inn was busy with travelers from the London stage and a few locals who'd come to take their luncheon. Bronwyn's faint voice reached him from the coffee room, and he rounded the corner to find her near the window, smiling up at a tall gentleman in a well-cut coat. The light caught the curve of her cheek and the sheen of her hair. It was an arresting sight, one he might have lingered over, but something was wrong.

Though the stranger's back was to him, his form—and the stiff manner with which he held his left arm—were all-too familiar. A flicker of unease tightened Gabriel's spine.

The man shifted, revealing a blade of a nose and a square chin. Dark hair swept back from a smooth forehead, and a gleam of provocation in his dark eyes when they found Gabriel.

Vasco Ribeiro.

Gabriel's every muscle tensed. The morning's bright warmth vanished, replaced by an icy weight pressing against his ribs. He then spied Emilia on Ribeiro's other side, hands clasped before her and a smile tilting her lips. Seeing Gabriel, she brightened.

"Papá! Tio Vasco has come!"

"Lieutenant Marsh," Ribeiro said smoothly, his Portuguese accent curling around the English words. "Though I understand 'lieutenant' is not correct—you achieved a captaincy, I heard. It has been some years, has it not?"

Gabriel's first instinct was to place himself bodily between Ribeiro and Emilia, to shield his daughter from the man's presence. Instead, he forced himself to remain still. Controlled. Once known, a soldier's weakness became a weapon in his enemy's hands.

"It has not been long enough," he said.

Bronwyn's brows drew together as her gaze moved between them.

Ribeiro's smile didn't falter. "I had hoped we might speak, you and I. There are matters—"

"I'm afraid your travels were in vain," Gabriel interrupted, his voice hard as flint. "There is no business between us."

Bronwyn's lips parted, but something in Gabriel's expression stopped her from speaking her thoughts aloud. Emilia, however, knew no such restraint. "But—"

"Come, Emilia. We are returning home," Gabriel said, his tone allowing no argument. "Now."

He turned to Bronwyn, dipping his head in a curt farewell. "Miss Kimbrell."

She didn't protest, but her frown deepened.

As he strode away with Emilia in tow, his pulse pounded with fury and fear. He'd begun to allow himself to think his past was just that—over and done with. Mariana was gone, and despite Brightwell's reports, there was really no reason he should ever encounter Vasco Ribeiro again. But the man had come.

And though he'd told himself he would not do it, Gabriel had searched the man's face for traces of his daughter. Heaven help him, but he'd seen none. He couldn't find anything of Emilia in Ribeiro's smug countenance.

Was he blind to it? He would not discount the possibility, but if Emilia was *not* Ribeiro's daughter, then why had he come? Was her tenuous connection to the Braganza his only motivation? It seemed a rather thin explanation.

And Bronwyn… she'd smiled up at Ribeiro as if she too might be taken in by the man's charm. The sight had sent a white-hot flash of anger through Gabriel, stealing his breath.

Outside, Gabriel was conscious of eyes watching them move up the street. He encountered Mrs. Pentreath outside the bakery, and though he tipped his hat pleasantly, she must have sensed a juicy bit of gossip, for he felt her gaze follow them with avid interest.

"Papá," Emilia said, "you're walking too fast."

He slowed but didn't stop. "My apologies."

His mind raced with plans. First and foremost, he must secure Emilia, and then he would settle matters with Ribeiro once and for all. He returned them to the alley behind the post office, where he'd left Hadley with the wagon.

His batman, on seeing the set of his face, stepped forward. "Sir?"

"Ribeiro is here," Gabriel said.

To his credit, Hadley didn't ask any questions but moved quickly to see to the horse.

Gabriel lifted Emilia onto the seat and tried to

ignore her accusing, tear-stained face.

"But Tio said—"

"Vasco Ribeiro is no relation of yours."

———

BRONWYN WATCHED GABRIEL stride from the inn, Emilia's small hand clasped in his. Something in his bearing—the rigid set of his shoulders, perhaps, or the way his hand gripped his daughter's—set off a warning in her mind. His expression on encountering Mr. Ribeiro had been one of anger, though she was at a loss to understand why. The man seemed respectable enough, and Emilia had certainly been pleased to see him.

But there had been something else in Gabriel's face. When his eyes had found his daughter, there'd been a flash of fear—raw and stark—before his features settled into stern lines.

Something was dreadfully wrong.

"I must apologize," Mr. Ribeiro said, recalling her attention. "I'm afraid the captain and I are not on the friendliest of terms."

Questions crowded Bronwyn's tongue, held back only by her awareness of the coffee room's other occupants. Mr. Pengilley and Mr. Evans had abandoned their game of draughts to watch the scene near the window with poorly concealed interest.

"If you'll excuse me, sir, I must be going."

Bronwyn didn't wait for Mr. Ribeiro's response but swept from the room, her skirts fluttering in her haste and Beth following close behind. She retrieved her cart from the inn's stable and with Beth pressing her cap and exclaiming at every bump and turn, they reached Penhale in short order.

"John," she said when he answered her knock. "I must speak with Captain Marsh."

John drew himself up. "I will inquire if the captain is at home."

While Bronwyn approved of his new discretion, she didn't have the time for it. Pushing past him, she entered Penhale's marbled foyer.

"Miss!" Beth squeaked as John blustered.

"For heaven's sake," Bronwyn said. "I know he's here, John. Will you announce me, or must I embarrass us all?"

The servant's throat worked as he swallowed. He gave her threat the consideration it deserved before finally nodding, an act that seemed to pain him greatly.

"Beth," she said, "why don't you go have a visit with your sister? I'm certain Mrs. Forsyth can spare her for a few moments."

"But miss, 'taint seemly—"

Before Beth could remind her of the folly of calling on a gentleman alone, Bronwyn said sternly, "I won't be long."

Beth tucked her chin and left them, and Bronwyn gave John an expectant look.

Reluctantly, he led her to the library like a man walking to the gallows. Before knocking, he cast her one final beseeching look, clearly doubting his chances for continued employment.

"Oh, do step aside." Bronwyn reached past him for the handle, but John, finding his courage, moved to stand between her and the door. With one hand on either side of the frame, he blocked her way, and no amount of her hands-on-hips displeasure would move him.

The door opened then, and Bronwyn peered around John to see Gabriel's thunderous expression. His cravat was loosened, and his dark hair fell across his brow in intriguing disarray. But the tight line of his mouth and the stark contrast of the scar against his cheek cast that observation to the back of her mind.

"I apologize, sir," John said over his shoulder. "She got past me."

"Yes, I imagine she did." Gabriel's jaw worked around a sigh. "I doubt there was much you could have done to prevent it, though I appreciate the effort."

"I will show her to the door—"

"Let her in."

John deflated with relief before moving aside for Bronwyn to enter his master's sanctum. There, she found Emilia collapsed in an attitude of despair on the settee near the hearth. Spying an ally, she straightened.

"Miss Kimbrell! Tell *o capitão* I wish to see Tio Vasco."

Though Bronwyn was no stranger to the occasional fit of temper, she felt suddenly out of her depth. Carefully, she said, "Oh, love, I think you must do as your Papa says."

Emilia frowned at this betrayal and crossed her thin arms.

"Go to the nursery," Gabriel said to her. "We'll discuss this later."

Emilia pulled herself from the settee, her small face set in mutinous lines. "You're being horrible and mean."

"Yes," her father agreed. "I am detestable. Now, go. Please."

When she'd gone, Gabriel summoned John back. "Your new duties are in the nursery. My daughter is not to leave the house," he said. "Her safety depends upon it. Remain by her side, and do not let her manage you as Miss Kimbrell has done. Do you understand?"

John's face paled at this direction, but he nodded. "I will not disappoint you, sir."

John left, and the room fell silent. Bronwyn searched for words. Surely, Gabriel's odd reaction to Mr. Ribeiro's arrival was more than one man deserved.

Before she could say anything, though, he turned to her, his eyes sharp. "Tell me, Miss Kimbrell, are you in the habit of making the acquaintance of every man who passes through Newford?"

She blinked at the accusation in his tone, then her ire rose. "Well, to be sure, I make a point to acquaint myself with all the dunder-headed ones."

He rubbed a hand over his face, and Bronwyn, sensing something deeper behind his mood but not knowing the cause, swallowed her irritation. "I apologize if I have given offense, though I confess I do not know how." She hesitated. "I was given to understand Mr. Ribeiro is acquainted with your family. Emilia called him her *tio*—that means uncle, does it not?"

Gabriel's voice was harsh and flat. "He is not her uncle. He was my wife's lover."

The admission startled her, as he certainly intended it would.

Gabriel went to the desk and sat—a rudeness she overlooked given his current state of upset. But when he removed a wooden pistol case from the desk, she gasped.

"Oh, but surely that is not the solution! What

d'you mean to do?"

His hands were sure as he checked the weapon. "Steady yourself. I do not mean to shoot the man outright, but I will protect my family. I'll not be at a disadvantage." Then, eyes narrowing, he said, "What gossip have you been hearing about my daughter?"

She hesitated at the abrupt change in topic, but it seemed a matter of some import to him. "There has been some talk amongst the matrons," she said slowly. And the man at the fair… Perhaps she ought to have told Gabriel about him then, though she couldn't see what purpose it would have served. Now, she admitted, "There was a man at the fair—"

"What man?"

She frowned at his brusqueness but described the man. "I didn't recognize him—there were so many people visiting from other parts that day—but he seemed rather interested in the ladies' gossip. I saw Mrs. P speaking with him as we left."

Gabriel nodded, though his hands remained focused on his task. Then, with a sigh, he set the pistol aside. "I wish you had told me."

She shook her head. "To what purpose? What could you have done?"

"I could have confronted him. At the least, I could have gone and taken my daughter elsewhere!"

Her stomach dropped uncomfortably. A heavy sadness filled her that, despite their friendship, despite what she'd thought to be a growing affection between them, he would consider leaving Newford. And all over… *gossip*?

"People will always talk," she said softly, "no matter where you go. But are you not, per'aps, making too much of't? Is it possible your… your…"

"My what? My anger? Pride? My sensibilities?"

"Well, aye. No one, I think, wishes to hear whispers about themselves. D'you think your pride has affected your reason? You've been wounded most grievously, after all, by your wife and Mr. Ribeiro."

Gabriel's expression darkened, his fingers tightening around the butt of the pistol. "It was not my wounded *pride* that brought Ribeiro to my doorstep," he continued. "His agents merely followed the sound of gossip. I did it often enough during the war, and it's very effective. Do you think a few whispers are harmless? I assure you, they are not." His cold, impersonal tone chilled her. "Ribeiro means to take Emilia," he said bluntly.

"But he cannot simply take your daughter. She is yours!"

Gabriel's jaw shifted, the scar on his cheek drawing tight. "That matters not. Ribeiro has the influence and resources of an entire government behind him. If he wishes to take my child, there is no one to stop him but me. Already, there have been two attempts, when she was en route to me in London, and Hadley was followed in Falmouth. I suspect his man and your eavesdropper were one and the same—an agent of some sort for Ribeiro."

"But… but why should Mr. Ribeiro wish to have your daughter? Regardless of what people say, anyone with eyes can see she is not his!"

Gabriel cut a sharp look at her. "I don't know his purpose, but I mean to find out."

She swallowed at the fierceness of his countenance, and her gaze went to the pistol cradled in his hand. What did he mean to do? Gossip may have brought Mr. Ribeiro to Cornwall, but how could the man think to simply steal Emilia away? More importantly, how could she prevent it?

"I will talk to my brother," she said. "Or my cousin! Gavin is the constable for our parish. He'll know what's to be done."

Gabriel's laugh was bitter. "Go home, Miss Kimbrell. I'm sorry to say it, but this is where our association comes to an end. You cannot manage everything, no matter how strongly you wish to do so, and I will not have you embroiled in this."

CHAPTER 25

OUR ASSOCIATION COMES *to an end.* Gabriel tried to banish the image of Bronwyn's stricken face from his mind. The words had to be said, though—one way or another, he meant to see the matter with Ribeiro put to rest, and he'd not have Bronwyn tangled in it.

And so, she'd left. She collected her maid and her cart and drove down Penhale's long drive without another word between them. Just as he'd intended.

Now, he set the pistol aside and drew out a sheet of paper. Dipping his pen, he scratched out a brief summons: *Penhale's stables, tomorrow morning, nine o'clock.*

Folding it, he applied a wafer and sent Hadley to deliver his message to the inn. He would meet Ribeiro on his own ground, at a time of his own choosing, and of course, he'd be waiting well ahead of the appointed hour.

Ribeiro's reply was both prompt and irritating: *I am yours to command. Shall I bring my sword or will you have pistols?*

Gabriel didn't dignify that with a response. He wore the all-too-visible reminder of Ribeiro's blade, though knowing his opponent's left arm must pain him in England's damp weather brought a grim satisfaction of its own. But this would not be a duel. He meant to have Ribeiro's purpose in Cornwall from him, and then he would send him packing. Without Emilia.

He spent the rest of the afternoon and evening checking and re-checking the doors and windows and not thinking of Bronwyn. He had far more success with the former than the latter.

When he ventured into the nursery, he found John had been conscripted into the lowest of duties. His butler-turned-nursery maid was serving imaginary tea and biscuits to a trio of dolls while an unhappily attired Sombra, dressed in one of Emilia's pinafores, chewed the edge of a pillow.

To John's credit, he'd taken to his new duties with his usual diligence. He made an exaggerated bow to Sombra, and Emilia giggled into her handkerchief until she caught sight of Gabriel in the doorway. Then, sobering, she gave him an imperial stare reminiscent of her earliest days with him.

He was not forgiven then.

He dismissed John with a nod and lowered himself into an armchair. Emilia watched him with wary eyes, the stubborn tilt of her chin much like Mariana's when she'd been set on something.

"You do not like Tio Vasco," she said.

"I do not." Resting his elbows on his knees, Gabriel added gently, "But I know that you care for him."

"He was my mother's friend. He is my friend." Her tone was defiant, though there was a thread of uncertainty beneath it.

"People—adults, mostly—are often not as they seem."

Emilia frowned. "What do you mean?"

Gabriel exhaled slowly, choosing his words. "They may act in a certain manner on the outside but feel very differently on the inside."

She gave a small nod and considered his words. "Like when I act brave even when I'm scared? Or when people smile although they're cross or sad?"

"Precisely."

His daughter's slim brow furrowed. "Like my mother?"

Gabriel swallowed. "Yes, I suppose. Like your mother."

"And you?"

"At times," he admitted.

"And my Tio Miguel?"

"Yes, even your Tio Miguel." He feared they'd lost the original thread of his argument. Before she could enumerate her entire list of relations, he added firmly, "But especially your Tio Vasco."

Her frown deepened, but he pressed on. "As your papa, it is my responsibility to keep you safe, *minha querida*. That means understanding a person's true sentiment before we count them a friend—seeing them as they *are* rather than as they wish to appear."

Emilia lifted her chin, her dark eyes flashing with quiet determination. "He is my friend. You will see."

Gabriel said nothing. He admired his daughter's conviction, but there would be no convincing her. She would see in time. He only prayed this lesson didn't cost them both more than they could give.

———

BRONWYN HELD THE reins loosely as Pippin trotted down the lane toward her home. Beth's chatter hummed in her ear, but she heard none of the words. She was too distracted by her fear for Gabriel and the sick, hot twist in her stomach his words had caused. *Our association comes to an end.*

Gabriel no longer desired her aid or her friendship. Much less anything of a more personal nature. She had been nothing but helpful to him, and now, when he and Emilia needed her most, it seemed her best efforts were inadequate.

Her eyes burned with hot tears, and she blinked. Sniffed and straightened on the bench. He had rebuffed her before. This was no different.

But why, then, did the tightness in her chest feel as though her heart were being squeezed?

After leaving Beth at the door, she brought the cart to the stables and climbed down. Jem emerged, wiping his hands on a cloth as she loosened Pippin's girth.

"'Ow'd he go then?"

"He was steady enough," she said, "though I wonder if he's caught a pebble in his near fore shoe."

"Aye, I'll check 'im."

Bronwyn left Pippin to Jem and strode into the house, wondering how she could speak of ordinary things like pebbles in the pony's shoe with such heaviness in her thoughts. But, as the afternoon stretched into evening, she found ordinary was just the thing to keep her mind from brooding overmuch.

After setting aside her bonnet and gloves, she tallied her mother's ledger. Satisfied there were no discrepancies, she drafted an order to the grocer for tea and sugar, and a request to the chandler for lamp oil.

Next, she inspected the linen cupboard, refolding an already-neat pile of napkins and squaring them up. All of these tasks she managed very capably, with the certainty that *someone* might appreciate them.

It wasn't until she'd confirmed their cook had all she needed to prepare their supper, that she stopped, only to find her thoughts drifting back to Gabriel. With a puff of her cheeks, she reached for the sewing basket—there was always mending to be done.

"Is there anything amiss, love?" her mother asked after they'd had their supper. Merryn was working late in his office, so there were only the two of them in the parlor, the lamps reflecting in the dark window as they stitched in silence.

"No, Mama. Why d'you ask?"

"Why, no reason. 'Tis only that you've been mending the same shirt this half an hour, and not a word from you. I thought you might be taking ill."

Bronwyn lowered her needle and looked at the garment in her lap—one of her brother's shirts. She'd been so distracted she didn't realize she'd stitched a tiny tear in the seam more than once. She tied off the thread and snipped it. "I only wish it to hold up properly. You know how rough my brother is with his shirts."

After a hesitation, her mother agreed. "Aye, he's some dreadful." When Bronwyn said nothing more, she added, "But you don't seem yourself. Something weighs on you, I think."

The blasted tears threatened again. Swallowing against them, Bronwyn said, "Mama, when Papa was courting you… did you ever doubt his feelings for you?" She bit her lip, unwilling to let her fear and confusion fully surface.

Her mother looked up, her face softening. "Oh, you can be sure, more than once! But doubts, love, are only natural. 'Tis better, I think, to have and sort them than to go into the thing stupidly. You have quarreled with Captain Marsh, I gather."

"'Twas not a quarrel," Bronwyn corrected with a frown, "so much as a parting. He faces a dilemma with his daughter and… and a past acquaintance of his wife's. He doesn't wish my help, though."

Her mother nodded knowingly, though she didn't look up from her sewing. "Edith Pentreath has been talking, you know. I've heard the speculation about the captain's wife and that dear child. 'Tis for certain, the stories are exaggerated—gossip always is. But your captain is a proud man. It cannot be easy for him to endure such things being said, much less discuss them with the lady he's courting.

No man wishes to be pitied."

"But I don't pity him! Only the opposite—I admire him. He has a strength of character that puts all other men in the shade."

Her mother looked up then and gave her a smile. "A person's self-perception seldom aligns with how others see him. A man who is vain will hold himself in a higher esteem than he ought to, while a noble man will be harsher on himself than any faultfinder. And offers of assistance, however well-meaning, may only add weight to his own critical thoughts."

Bronwyn considered this long after her mother left her alone by the flickering lamp. Setting aside her mending, she stood and paced from one end of the parlor rug to the other. If what her mother said was true—if her desire to aid Gabriel caused him more grief than ease—then what hope was there for them? She could not change her nature any more than he could change his. Nor would she wish either of them to do so.

But worse than any of these thoughts—worse than the loss of any future between them—was the thought of Emilia. If what Gabriel feared was true, then Vasco Ribeiro meant to take her away with him, and her heart ached for both father and daughter, who'd only just begun to find their way around one another.

She folded her arms over her middle as an unbearable longing swept her—a longing for the days of her girlhood, before her father had passed, before any thoughts of men or marriage had ever entered her mind. She longed for her father's arms and his gentle hand on her hair. She'd been fortunate to enjoy twelve years with him. Would Gabriel and Emilia never have more than these last weeks?

She was roused from these depressing thoughts by a noise outside—Merryn, returning from his office. The mantel clock showed it was nearing midnight.

He entered quietly with his key and came into the parlor.

"I saw the lamp," he said. "You're still awake."

"I am." She thought to ask him about his day, but the words wouldn't form around the lump in her throat.

He studied her for a moment and then, clearing his throat, he asked, "Is everything well?"

"Aye," she assured him. Then, to make the lie believable, she attempted a smile, but her chin wobbled.

Reaching out one long arm, he drew her to him. She resisted briefly before giving in, and he folded her in his warmth as she hiccupped against his chest.

"What has he done?" he asked, offering his handkerchief.

"N—nothing."

"Should I call him out, or dispense with politeness and simply toss him from the cliff?"

Bronwyn chuckled weakly and pulled back in his arms. The unsmiling earnestness on his face startled her into saying, "No! You will do neither of these things."

"D'you love him?"

Bronwyn blinked at the directness of his question. "Yes," she whispered.

After drawing a liberal breath, he set his jaw. "Then you must tell me what is wrong."

She blew her nose heartily. Pacing before the hearth, she told him in halting tones of the arrival of Emilia's "uncle" at the inn and Gabriel's subsequent rejection of her help. She shared what their mother had said of noble men and Gabriel's pride.

"He is far too proud for his own good," she said, "and arrogant, I think, but in the best way." Then, eyeing her brother critically, she said, "*You* are proud and arrogant. What d'you think I should do?"

He frowned at her assessment. "I suppose 'tis absurd to suggest you allow the man to see to his own affairs? Not every burden is yours to bear."

"But why shouldn't I do something to fix a problem if I am able to? How can I stand silent? 'Tis not my nature. Oh, I fear I am an unnatural female, but I don't know how to be any other way."

An expression of contrition crossed her brother's features. "Nor should you be anyone but who you are. Of course, I did not mean to say you are unnatural. You are strong, is all—too strong, per'aps, for many to accept. If his affection for you is true, he will see your worth. If he does not, then you are well rid of him now rather than later."

Bronwyn sniffed. "You are not helping," she muttered.

Merryn's eyes narrowed in the way they did when he studied the drawings for one of his building projects. The notion that she was but another bridge or stable set her back up, but she forced her tongue to silence while she waited.

Finally, he spoke. "He is not the gentleman I would have chosen for you." When she would have protested, he forestalled her with a hand. "He has too many complications for my liking, and now, there's this business with Ribeiro. But if your heart is set, then per'aps 'tis not for you to take his burden from him, but to help him bear it. Lend him your support rather than your aid."

"But he already has my support!"

"Then he has all that he requires."

She frowned, for that was little comfort. Sinking onto the settee, she admitted her fear. "I am just so worried for him and Emilia. I'm certain Gabriel means to confront Mr. Ribeiro. He was cleaning *pistols* when I left. D'you think I should—"

"No."

"But per'aps—"

"Let me be clear," Merryn said, his voice rising. "You are not to attempt to *fix* this particular problem. In fact, you are not to return to Penhale until this matter with Ribeiro is sorted. If Marsh means to confront the man, with pistols no less, then the situation is far too dangerous."

"Well, 'tis not as if I mean to ride in like some sort of Boudicca! I am not so lost to propriety or insensible to the danger." Despite the heat of her words, she couldn't ignore the dread in her belly. The fire left her and she sagged a little against the settee. "I merely thought I might consult with Gavin. He will surely know what can be done."

Frowning, Merryn shook his head. "He's away to the assizes." Then, with a relenting sigh, he said gruffly, "*I* will go to Penhale and offer my aid if Marsh should need it."

"You would do that? Oh, you are the very best of brothers!"

He shook his head. "Why is't the only time I'm so favored is when I'm doing something I'll surely regret?" He moved to leave the parlor, and she stopped him.

"Merryn." He turned. "Please—please!—be careful," she begged. "And, even if you did not do this thing, you are still the best of brothers."

"I know," he said with a teasing smile. "You are the most fortunate of sisters."

She refrained from throwing a cushion at his arrogant head.

CHAPTER 26

BRONWYN STARED AT the ceiling above her bed well into the small hours of the morning, pondering her brother's riddle: *He has all that he requires.* Now, dawn was beginning to peek around the lace curtain, but she was no closer to solving it.

All her pondering had yielded was the discovery of a tiny crack in the plaster, which Merryn would wish to know about. With a lusty punch to her pillow, she flopped onto her side. Heaven save her from men who thought they were clever.

There was one thing she did know, however. She would not allow Gabriel to dismiss their friendship so easily. She wasn't such a craven-hearted female as that. His stupid pride might not allow room for her in his heart—a thought which caused her chest to ache horribly—but she still counted him a friend.

So, she would let Merryn go to him, then she

would lend her ear if Gabriel needed it. She would not press him with offers to help or—heaven forfend!—suggestions for how he might go about things. And anyway, he had vastly more experience than she in matters of strategy and… and enemy engagement and such.

But… perhaps he might sort the matter with Mr. Ribeiro more easily if Emilia were tucked safely away at Oak Hill. The more Bronwyn thought of it, the better the idea sounded.

Tea and cake were what the situation called for. And perhaps some painting—the tin she'd purchased in Cadan's shop still sat, unused, atop her dressing table.

Throwing off the bedclothes with more enthusiasm than a sleepless night warranted, she rolled from the bed and called for Beth. Then, once she was washed and dressed, she went to find her brother.

———

"Do you see anything yet?" Gabriel called up to Hadley. His batman was in the loft atop the stables, leaning his elbows on the wooden ledge as he peered through a glass.

"No, sir. Not a soul on the lane." He lowered the glass and glanced down at his employer. "That's the third time you've asked."

Gabriel didn't acknowledge the remark. Instead, he continued to inspect the grounds, his gaze sweeping the long drive. He wanted no surprises. The house itself was secure, every door bolted, every window latched. The weight of the knife in Gabriel's boot and the pistols at his sides were a comfort.

The servants had been given the day off, save John, who'd been tasked once more with nursery duty. He kept a quiet watch over Emilia, who remained unaware of the preparations taking place outside, and of Ribeiro's imminent arrival.

Gabriel scrutinized the gentle rise and fall of the fields beyond the house and the copse bordering Oak Hill. There was no movement save the fluttering of the breeze in the trees.

"Keep watching," he ordered Hadley before turning his mount to circle the stables once more. He had a clear line of sight to the cliff path where he'd ridden with Bronwyn. It was empty, but his unease remained, his soldier's instinct on alert.

A moment later, Hadley's voice called sharply from the loft. "Sir! A horse approaches."

Gabriel checked his watch. Ribeiro was nearly an hour early, which was no surprise. Were their roles reversed, Gabriel would have arrived early as well, or late, but never at the appointed time. It was best to keep one's opponent guessing.

Fogo danced beneath him as they waited for the rider to emerge from the shadows on the drive.

"Sir, two more ride with him."

Gabriel's stomach sank. Though he'd not expected Ribeiro to come alone, he had hoped their numbers would be more even. It was no matter. He and Hadley had the advantage of the King's training. They would acquit themselves well if it came to a fight.

The approaching party cleared the thickest part of the trees. Gabriel lifted the glass to his eye and frowned.

"Sir?" Hadley said. "Do you see—"

"I see." It wasn't Ribeiro who came down his drive on a roan mare, but Merryn Kimbrell, flanked by Alfie Kimbrell and the innkeeper's husband, Roddie Teague. Gabriel urged Fogo ahead and met the new arrivals at the bottom of the drive.

"Kimbrell," he said tightly. "I gather you've been conscripted into this affair?"

"Conscripted? No. But my sister did apprise me of your dilemma. Against all reason, she's grown fond of your face. I thought to see how I might help you preserve what's left of it."

Gabriel muttered an oath.

"Just so." Then, drawing a breath, Kimbrell added, "We're yours to command, if you require us."

Gabriel almost told him to take his troops back to

Newford. There was no reason to risk all their necks, and Bronwyn wouldn't thank him if some harm came to her brother or her cousins.

But then he heard her words again. He couldn't forget them, for all the times they'd sounded in his thoughts these last hours. *D'you think your pride has affected your reason?*

He'd denied it, of course. No man wished to think his emotions had the run of his reason. Yet, in the quiet of his own mind, he was forced to acknowledge the truth—at the root of all his troubles lay his shame and mortification.

His wife had left him. With less than a year of marriage, she'd deemed him unworthy of the effort. And he'd let her go.

He'd left his post in London, fled the city, and shunned society in Newford—all to avoid the whispers of his disgrace.

Oh, there'd been truth in what he'd told Bronwyn—the matrons' gossip had no doubt hastened Ribeiro's arrival, though the man would have found them eventually. But Gabriel had managed Ribeiro before.

What he couldn't manage, it seemed, was his own conceit. And now, his daughter might suffer for it.

Kimbrell took his silence as a rejection of his offer. "We will withdraw, then," he said. He nodded to his cousins, and they turned their mounts.

"Wait."

Kimbrell paused, the mare shifting beneath him.

"I could use more men," Gabriel said, "if you're willing."

Kimbrell nodded, and Gabriel, conscious of the hour, hurriedly apprised them of the plan he'd devised with Hadley. As he explained John's role in safeguarding his daughter in the nursery, Kimbrell cleared his throat.

"My sister has suggested a meeting with Ribeiro might be easier done without the distraction of Miss Marsh's safety, and I have to agree."

Gabriel shook his head. "I'm not moving my daughter."

"Oak Hill is close, and Bronwyn is there now with my grandfather and his servants. They'll keep your daughter safe, if you allow her to go to them."

Gabriel eyed the distance across the field to his neighbor's home. It was too far, too open. He wouldn't expose his daughter when Ribeiro must be close. Then a thought occurred to him. Turning to Teague, he said, "When I first arrived in Newford, Mrs. Teague said something about smugglers and kings hiding at Penhale."

"Aye, in the tunnels."

"Bronwyn mentioned them, too, but she suggested they must be bricked up by now."

Alfie Kimbrell released an amused huff, and the others gave him wry looks.

"They're not bricked up, are they?"

"I imagine they haven't been used in some years," Teague said, "but I doubt anyone's gone to the trouble of setting bricks. Who knows when a tax might bring the trade round again?"

Gabriel's heart thumped. He thought they'd secured all the entrances, but if there were tunnels… "These tunnels lead to the sea?"

Teague scratched his jaw. "Aye, to the sea caves, mostly, though there's one that runs between Penhale and Oak Hill."

"Can Ribeiro use the tunnels to access Penhale?"

Kimbrell shook his head. "Not for some hours. The tide is up—the only access to Penhale is by way of Oak Hill, but he'd have to go through my grandfather first."

Gabriel nodded, his alarm somewhat abated as he considered this new information. Ribeiro couldn't reach them through the tunnels, but perhaps Gabriel could use them to his own ends.

"You're thinking to send your girl under the ground rather than over it," Teague said.

"Can it be done?"

"I don't see why not. 'Tis a sound plan, and your man John was here as a boy—he'll know where to find the entrance." Teague shifted before adding,

"And if he doesn't recall't, I daresay I can."

Gabriel ignored this confession to send Hadley for John, who said he did indeed know where to find the passageway. The entrance to it was hidden in the shadows of the cellar, behind a tidy stack of old barrels.

By the time Gabriel persuaded Emilia to follow John into the dank space to meet Miss Kimbrell—"Yes, you may take Sombra"—it was nearly time for Ribeiro's arrival.

———

RIBEIRO CAME ALONE. He was either that sure of himself, or he wished to keep Gabriel guessing at his intentions. Either way, Gabriel found the man's arrogance insufferable. As his opponent approached the stables, Gabriel motioned to Hadley to keep a watch on the trees for any followers.

"You've gathered an audience," Ribeiro said, his voice smooth and unconcerned as he gave a nod to the Kimbrell contingent. "I'm uncertain if I should be flattered or concerned, though I assure you there was no need for spectators. It is not as if we meet for a dawn appointment."

Gabriel's jaw tightened, but he kept his hand loose on Fogo's reins. "I would not be so smug about our last meeting," he said with a pointed glance for Ribeiro's left arm. "I may bear the mark of it upon my face, but you, I recall, were the one lying in the mud beneath my blade when it ended."

Ribeiro laughed then casually twitched his cuff. "So I was. We were such stupid youths, were we not?"

Gabriel held his growl in check. "Say what you mean to say. What is it you want?"

Ribeiro motioned for them to dismount. "Come, let us not talk over our horses' heads."

Gabriel ignored him. As a cavalry officer, he preferred the advantages of the saddle. "I'll tell you now, if you've come for Emilia—"

"Stubble it, Marsh, to use the vulgar language of your countrymen. I have not come for the girl." Ribeiro's voice lowered as he met Gabriel's gaze. "I am here to *warn* you, you foolish man."

Gabriel hid his surprise behind a derisive snort. "About what, precisely?"

"It is your odious brother-in-law with whom you should be concerned. He has had his ear to the ground, listening for you. My men have tracked him to Cornwall."

"Miguel? What has Mariana's brother to do with anything?"

"He is the one who means to take your daughter."

"Explain yourself."

Ribeiro scratched his chin with one long finger.

"Has he not already attempted to do so during your daughter's travels to England?"

He referred to the attacks on Brightwell. Still, Gabriel wasn't certain what his brother-in-law could want with Emilia, and he said as much to Ribeiro.

"Does your daughter keep a handkerchief, perhaps? One with the Silva crest?"

Gabriel's denial was swift. "Of course she doesn't carry the Silva crest," he spat.

The Silva family were notorious, both on the Peninsula and abroad, for their opposition to the Braganza court. Their dealings were secretive, their loyalties uncertain, and he wanted no connection with them.

But Emilia's handkerchief... the one she'd brought with her to England. He'd never looked closely at it. He'd always assumed it was a token of her mother's, but if Mariana had become tangled with the Silvas, then his daughter's reputation would suffer far more than the rumors of her birth. She could be branded the daughter of a traitor. His stomach churned with the implications.

With a tone of extreme patience, Ribeiro explained, "The Silvas signal their conspirators with some sort of social code—a snuff box left behind, or a dropped handkerchief. The one your daughter carries—Mariana recovered it from a woman her brother was meeting. I advised her to turn it over to the Regency as evidence of his treasonous activities, but Miguel had her killed before she could do so."

Gabriel didn't miss how the other man's voice roughened at the mention of Mariana. He hardened himself against the observation even as his heart pounded. Ribeiro spoke of treason and now *murder*.

"I was informed my wife died in a carriage accident."

Ribeiro's expression shifted. "An accident is one theory."

Gabriel considered all he'd heard. Ribeiro's men had tracked Miguel to Cornwall. He thought of Hadley's follower—the same man he was sure Bronwyn had spied listening to the matrons' gossip. Was he Miguel's agent or Ribeiro's?

"Do you have a man in Newford?" he asked.

Ribeiro laughed. "I have many men, but none I would waste in a place such as this."

Gabriel described the man Bronwyn had seen, and Ribeiro shook his head. "That sounds like Salvador Reis—he belongs to your brother-in-law."

"If Miguel has, in fact, come for Emilia, then what does he want with her? Even if she does carry her mother's handkerchief, what harm is a square of linen? My daughter has nothing to do with any of this."

But even as he said the words, the answer came to him. Miguel didn't know what knowledge Emilia might have, however unwittingly, of his meetings with the Silva family or their conspirators. Miguel's schemes were unraveling, and he was trimming the loose ends.

Ribeiro only confirmed his suspicions with his next words. "Your brother-in-law has just cause to panic. Our king returns soon from Brazil; when the full extent of Miguel's actions against the crown becomes known, he won't be exiled. He'll lose his head. Whether your daughter knows something or not, he means to see her silenced."

Dread filled Gabriel for the other man's words. Whether he could believe them or not, was another matter. He'd spent too many years hating this man to trust him now.

"You couldn't have sent someone else to warn me?" he asked, his tone suspicious.

Ribeiro held his gaze. "I wouldn't trust the safety of Mariana's child with anyone but you."

Before Gabriel could judge the sincerity of that, Hadley interrupted. "Sir, another rider approaches."

The horses shifted restlessly as the men waited. Miguel Alves appeared at the bottom of the drive with another man—Reis, Gabriel suspected. His brother-in-law reined in sharply and took in the scene before him without a word of greeting. It was clear he'd not expected a crowd.

Gabriel's grip tightened on Fogo's reins, the familiar tension of battle coiling in his gut. He didn't know whom to trust, but he'd not be a sitting target. With a motion too practiced to forget, he drew his pistol—just as Ribeiro reached for his.

In the same instant, Miguel pulled his own weapon, and Fogo sidled as the crack of a pistol shot echoed.

CHAPTER 27

BRONWYN POURED OUT the tea and passed a cup to her grandfather, willing her nerves to settle. She hated not knowing what was occurring at Penhale. Had Merryn issued her invitation? And once he did, would Gabriel even allow Emilia to join her at Oak Hill? What if he truly desired no assistance from her?

Even Brioc sensed the electricity in the air; the wolfhound paced before the cold fireplace before settling on the flagstones with a frustrated sigh.

"All will be well," her grandfather assured her.

"Aye," she murmured without thinking. Then, catching his eye, she allowed her unease to escape its tether. "D'you truly think so? What if someone is harmed or this Ribeiro person succeeds in taking Emilia with him?"

Parsons entered then and announced that Miss

Marsh had arrived without her hat again, this time in the wine cellar.

Bronwyn leapt from the settee. "Heavens! The wine cellar!"

"Clever," her grandfather said with an approving nod.

Bronwyn frowned down at him until his meaning dawned. "Oh! They've used the tunnels!"

She raced from the room, her slippers sliding on the marble in her haste to reach the servants' stairs. Skipping the last two steps, she hurried into the kitchen where the housekeeper had settled John and Emilia at the worktable, their clothing dusty and cobwebbed. Nearby, a pair of maids peeled potatoes into a bin, and Sombra inspected the floor at their feet.

Emilia's cheeks were bright from her adventure. "Miss Kimbrell," she said in a hushed whisper. "We came through the tunnel, and John has been telling stories. Did you know *smugglers* used to carry lace through the same tunnel?"

"Did they? You will have to come into the drawing room and share John's tales with my grandfather," Bronwyn said, though her grandfather probably had first-hand knowledge of John's tales and then some.

Sombra snatched a bit of peel from atop one of the maid's shoes, causing her to squeal in surprise.

As Emilia went to collect her pup, Bronwyn turned to John with a whisper. "Tell me John: what has occurred at Penhale?"

"Your brother and cousins are there, all right, and all was quiet when I left. The captain was worrit 'bout sendin' his daughter 'cross the open field. 'Twas a bit of brilliance 'e had to use the tunnels."

Bronwyn couldn't help her smile. "Wasn't it though?"

John held out a folded slip of paper. "He bid me to give you this."

Once more, I find myself in your debt. Thank you.

It was hardly a profession of love, much less a message of apology, but it was something. She folded it carefully and tucked it in her palm.

John stood. "I'm to return to Penhale," he said, "if you're agreeable to it."

"Go on," she urged. "We will be fine."

Before John could leave, a pop echoed from across the field, and Bronwyn's heart lurched. A gunshot—but not the thunderous report of a hunter's fowling piece. It had a sharper, fainter sound like the crack of a pistol.

She glanced at Emilia, who'd also heard it. The girl's eyes widened with uncertainty as she gripped Sombra's fur.

"John!" Bronwyn whispered. "You must hurry."

He nodded, his countenance hardening as he

left. Bronwyn's first impulse was to follow him into the cellar. Gabriel could be in peril, and her cousins and brother as well. But there was Emilia to consider. The girl came close, pressing against her side, the dog held tightly in her arms.

Bronwyn saw then, with a clarity she'd not possessed before, that aiding Gabriel—supporting him—was not about her own capabilities. It wasn't about the pleasurable satisfaction of being right, nor the admiration to be had for a challenge well conquered. It was about offering what *he* required of her in that moment, whether it was what she wished or not. And what he required of her now was to protect his daughter.

She swallowed her unease. John was strong. He was a capable ally, as were her brother and cousins. Gabriel would prevail. He'd entrusted her with his daughter's safety. In turn, she would trust that he knew what he was about.

This, she realized, was what Merryn had been trying to tell her, though why he couldn't have simply said as much was beyond her.

She summoned a reassuring smile and crouched to meet Emilia's gaze. "John and my brother are strong, and so is your father. They are doing everything they can to protect everyone."

"Even Tio Vasco?" Bronwyn hesitated a moment too long, and Emilia insisted stubbornly, "He is my friend. He is not mean like my Tio Miguel."

Bronwyn straightened. "Who is your Tio Miguel?"

Emilia told her then of the uncle who'd often been cross with her and her mother. "And he has bad men for friends who don't like the king. They tried to take my mother's handkerchief."

"Well, they should not have done that, but your uncle is in Portugal, is he not?"

Emilia shook her head. "I don't think so. I saw his friend Señor Reis at the fair."

Bronwyn considered this for half a beat before racing for the cellar. Pulling open the door to the tunnel, she called down to John. There was nothing but silence for a long moment before she heard his steps returning.

She quickly explained what she'd learned from Emilia. "You must go and tell Captain Marsh," she urged.

Returning to Emilia, Bronwyn said brightly, "Let us find my grandfather. Brioc is with him, and they will wish to hear all your tales of the smugglers. And I've brought paints!"

When they reached the drawing room, her grandfather greeted Emilia warmly, as if a young lady arriving at his cellar door was in the usual way of things.

Parsons reappeared as they listened to Emilia's tales of the free traders who'd once carried their tubs up from the sea to evade the revenue men. With a speaking glance, the butler set a wooden pistol case at her grandfather's elbow.

They'd heard the shot as well.

——

GABRIEL BARELY REGISTERED the crack of Miguel's pistol before Ribeiro jerked in the saddle. A dark stain spread across his fine blue coat as he fell, his boot catching in the stirrup and his weapon lying useless on the ground.

Swearing, Gabriel dismounted in a single motion and seized Ribeiro's reins before the frightened horse could drag the man. With nothing more than a nod from him, Kimbrell and his cousins thundered past in pursuit of Miguel and his man.

"Hold still," he ordered Ribeiro as he freed the boot, wrenching it from the stirrup. He dragged him free of the horse and into the stable. If there were a few bumps along the way, they couldn't be helped.

Ribeiro let out an amused breath, his face pale. "If you wish to be rid of me," he muttered, "there are more elegant ways."

Gabriel snorted and deposited his burden without ceremony against a hay bale. "All of which are tempting. Hadley!" he barked, but his batman's boots were already hitting the ladder as he climbed from the loft.

Gabriel bent his head to examine the wound. The ball had struck Ribeiro's shoulder, though how deeply, he couldn't tell. He removed his coat and pressed the cloth firmly against the flow of blood.

"I hate for you to ruin such a fine specimen," Ribeiro said mockingly.

Gabriel pressed harder, drawing a sharp hiss from his patient. "Not half as much as I loathe wasting it on you, but here we are."

"Go on, sir," Hadley said, taking over with the coat. "I'll manage 'is nibs."

"Keep him alive, if you can, but don't let him go. I'm still not convinced who our friends are in this."

Gabriel didn't wait for a response but raced for the house. On the steps, Teague held a weapon on Reis. He motioned with his head to where a morning room window had been broken. "Merryn and Alfie followed your brother-in-law."

Gabriel hauled himself inside and stepped over the shattered glass.

The house was quiet, save for the heavy footfalls on the floors above as the Kimbrells searched. Their instincts were good; if Miguel had come for Emilia, he would begin in the nursery.

Gabriel strode toward the stairs, but before he'd gone far, he heard the sound of running feet behind the wall. Someone was in the servants' corridor.

Hurrying into the dining room, he went through the narrow servants' door set in the paneling. He glanced to his left and right, but he couldn't determine the direction the steps had come from.

Then a muffled shout came up from the ground floor.

Moving swiftly, he hurried down the stairs. He passed the butler's quarters and the servants' dining room to find John on the floor outside the kitchen, propped against the wall.

Gabriel hurried to him. The servant's eyes were closed, and he bled from a wound in his side. Added to that injury, a knot was already forming at his temple—no doubt from the butt of Miguel's pistol.

Gabriel shook him. "John."

The servant's eyes fluttered open at Gabriel's address, and he opened his fist to reveal a bloodied knife and more wounds on his hand.

"I took his knife, sir, but 'e has a gun. Miss Kimbrell says 'tis not Ribeiro but another uncle—Miss Emilia's Tio Miguel."

"I know."

Even after Miguel had fired his shot, even as Gabriel had pursued his brother-in-law through the house, he'd still suspected Ribeiro's hand in all of this. But with the evidence of John's injuries before him and now Bronwyn's confirmation, Gabriel's uncertainty resolved itself.

He'd been blinded by his hatred for Ribeiro, but his daughter had been right. Ribeiro *was* her friend. Her revelation during the fair preparations—that she believed her grief was a weakness—now made more sense. She hadn't been speaking of her Tio Vasco then, but her Tio Miguel.

Behind him, the Kimbrells thundered down the stairs. Merryn reached them first with a dark expression that only grew when he took in John's pained wince.

"Where did he go?" Gabriel said to John.

"The kitchen, sir."

The corridor around them was quiet. Had Miguel escaped into the kitchen garden? Did he lie in wait in the scullery, ready to ambush the first man to enter? Or had he gone into the nearby cellar?

If Miguel found the entrance to the tunnel…

Merryn took two steps in that direction, but Gabriel called him back. "See to John and send for the surgeon," he said.

"My sister—"

"I will bring her to Penhale," Gabriel assured him. He would bring Emilia and Bronwyn home.

Merryn looked as if he might argue, but after a final, significant look, he relented with a sharp nod.

Gabriel found a lamp as the Kimbrells helped John to the stairs. Lighting it, he descended the narrow steps into the cellar, where the smells of damp earth and old wood were strong. At the back of the small, dank room, the barrels had been carelessly shoved aside.

Miguel had gone to Oak Hill.

Gabriel ducked to enter the dark passage where the air was thick and close. Water dripped steadily somewhere ahead, and his shoulders scraped the rough walls. He ignored the sticky cobwebs, and the sound of his breathing was unnaturally loud in the confined space.

He tried to keep his thoughts from dwelling on Emilia and Bronwyn. He couldn't allow the distraction, but the effort was useless. They were the two halves of his heart. He could hardly recall his life before the pair of them had upended it. To lose either of them now… it was a notion too dreadful to contemplate.

He hadn't gone far when he heard the faint scrape ahead of a shoe against stone. Gabriel quickened his pace.

CHAPTER 28

"JOHN SPEAKS TRULY of the smugglers in these parts," Parsons said as he placed a slice of seedcake before Emilia. "Why, I heard a tale of one night in particular, when the moon was full..."

Emilia picked at the crumbs of her cake as Parsons spun his tales. Her somber mood mirrored Bronwyn's own. What was happening at Penhale? Were Gabriel and the others injured, or worse? Bronwyn caught herself tapping her finger and forced her hand to still.

The minutes stretched on, and no further shots were heard from Penhale. Nothing disturbed the peace at Oak Hill. Bronwyn allowed herself to hope that all would be well.

When Parsons had exhausted his stories, she took out her paints, and he went to find paper and brushes.

With a smile for Emilia, Bronwyn said, "I thought a fine painter such as yourself might enjoy an afternoon with watercolors. This tin is fresh, never used, and I'm assured 'twill be a perfect diversion. D'you see? It even says so: 'Perfect for miniatures, landscapes and elegant diversions.'"

Emilia showed some interest in the endeavor, but before they could begin, a distant thud made them both jump. It was followed by muffled shouts and a disturbance on the servants' stairs. Brioc lifted his head, his ears pricked forward and hackles raised.

Bronwyn's grandfather reached for the case at his elbow and removed one of the weapons. Her stomach twisted as he checked the priming, but she went to him and held out her hand.

"No," he said softly.

"Granfer," she whispered, glancing back at Emilia. "She is my responsibility."

"And you are mine."

"You know my father taught me to shoot. If her uncle means us harm, I will not hide behind a locked door while you stand alone. If I must be afraid, then let me be afraid with a pistol in my hand, not wringing my hands in a corner."

When it seemed as if he would argue, she pressed her advantage. "Grandmother would have done the same."

"Demmed fiendish lass," he muttered before passing the weapon to her.

Despite the heat of her words, the metal felt cold and foreign in her palm. It had been years since her father's lessons. He'd taught her how to aim and shoot, believing any Kimbrell ought to be able to defend herself against highwaymen and revenue men, but those lessons had seemed more sport than necessity.

But she could do this.

Her grandfather took up the second weapon, his movements unhurried.

"Remember your lessons, lass. Steady hands. And aim away from me."

She nodded, but her heart pounded.

Emilia clutched Sombra close, her small face pale, paints forgotten. Setting aside the pistol, Bronwyn knelt beside her. "All will be well," she murmured. "You and Brioc must keep Sombra safe, there behind the settee."

Emilia nodded with wide eyes, and Brioc, seeming to understand his task, padded over to settle protectively beside his charges.

Heavy footsteps thudded on the servants' stairs, accompanied by muffled shouts. Her grandfather went out into the hall, limping against his cane, and Bronwyn followed, pausing only to brush a hand over Emilia's shoulder before pulling the doors behind them.

The commotion continued until a man burst into the hall, slamming the door on two pursuing footmen. His eyes were dark and slightly wild as he spied Bronwyn and her grandfather before the drawing room doors. He waved his pistol.

"Stand aside," he said in accented English. "I've come to take my niece home."

"She is already home," Bronwyn said, "with her father."

Behind him, the footmen pressed on the door. If she could delay the man long enough for them to come through—

But he raised his weapon, pointing it at her and putting paid to that notion. Bronwyn's grandfather lifted his own pistol and fired, but there was nothing but a dull click.

Without hesitation, Bronwyn squeezed her trigger. The report was deafening, the smell of gun smoke sharp. Miguel flinched, and a dark spot spread on his shoulder where she'd hit him. But then, moving his weapon to his other hand, he took aim once more.

Bronwyn's grandfather shoved her none too gently as another shot rang out. Miguel crumpled, and behind him, Gabriel lowered his pistol.

With disbelief, Bronwyn checked her person. She was unharmed; her grandfather was unharmed. Her hands began to shake. Her ears rang. Vaguely, she felt the cold weight of the pistol in her hand as Gabriel strode forward.

———

GABRIEL EASED THE gun from Bronwyn's shaking fingers and passed it to Parsons. The butler accepted it, as if this were the most normal thing in his day.

Gabriel spared a watchful glance for the scene behind him, where several of his neighbor's stoutest footmen secured Miguel. His brother-in-law groaned where he lay on the floor. His coat was wet with blood, but he lived.

"I shot him," Bronwyn said slowly. Her tone was one of amazement.

"Why do I take no comfort in the fact that you seem pleased by it?"

She smiled, though the action was a bit feeble when cast against her usual unshakable manner. Then, as he took in her small form and determined chin, her warm eyes and the slight tilt of her nose, the weight of the day made itself known. He'd endured much longer operations with much graver results during his time on the Peninsula. Each one had taken its toll on his thoughts and his heart, to say nothing of the lives of his men.

But this one... he thought it might end him. Bronwyn, along with her grandfather, had stood between Miguel and his daughter. They'd been prepared to give their own lives to protect hers. And if Miguel had found Emilia... He swallowed, unwilling to contemplate such an outcome.

"Emilia is fine," Bronwyn whispered, as if he'd spoken his thoughts aloud. "She's in the drawing room with the dogs. And cake."

He smiled at that, the knot loosening in his chest as he went to the drawing room doors. His hand reached for the knob, but then he stopped.

Turning back, he took three long strides and clasped Bronwyn to him. She stood stiffly for a moment before allowing herself to be held in his embrace. He bowed his head, resting his cheek against her temple, and closed his eyes. She smelled of lemon and gunpowder.

"Thank you," he whispered into her hair.

———

GABRIEL ESCORTED BRONWYN and Emilia to Penhale by way of his neighbor's carriage rather than the tunnel. The pair sat soberly across from him while Sombra napped at their feet. For once, Bronwyn seemed bereft of speech. Gabriel didn't miss the gentle way she held his daughter's hand, or the reassuring smiles she offered whenever Emilia pulled her gaze from the window.

In her other hand, Emilia carried her mother's handkerchief—the source of the day's troubles. An embroidered corner peeked out from between her small fingers. The stitching was ivory thread against an ivory ground, so the design was hard to discern from across the carriage. But now, with a critical eye, Gabriel could just make out the curved lines of the Silva crest.

He scrubbed a weary hand over his face. He'd have to part his daughter from the thing, but with Miguel incapacitated, that endeavor could wait a few moments more.

On reaching Penhale, they were swiftly met by Bronwyn's cousins, who collected her from the carriage and folded her in their noisy embraces.

Inside, Newford's surgeon attended his patients in the drawing room. A tray of instruments and bloodied linens took up the tea table, and John, looking less pale than he had been, balanced on the edge of a chair by the hearth. He drank brandy from a crystal glass and was clearly anxious over staining the chintz.

Across from him, Ribeiro sat—lounged, really— on the room's best settee. His coat and waistcoat were off, and the top of his shirt had been cut open to reveal his wound. Gabriel couldn't deny a perverse twinge of satisfaction that Ribeiro had been winged—again. As the surgeon wrapped a bandage about the injured shoulder, Ribeiro caught sight of them.

"I suppose you've come to revel in my misfortune," he said.

"I've come to see that you don't soil the settee."

"It is not enough to have one lame arm. With two, I'll hardly mount a horse again without someone heaving me up like your corpulent king."

"Does your arm hurt very much, Tio?" Emilia asked from Gabriel's side.

Ribeiro's gaze softened. "Do not worry about Vasco. It will require more than a poorly-aimed bullet to bring me low."

Emilia looked up at Gabriel with an unmistakable question in her eyes. Reluctantly, he nodded, and she hurried across the room to Ribeiro. A lump formed in Gabriel's throat as his daughter gazed up at the man with a broad smile.

"Now, *minha pequena*," Ribeiro said to Emilia. "I believe you found a handkerchief among your mother's things."

Emilia nodded, her gaze going to the linen in her hand.

"It was one she was holding for me, but I carry one of hers. It has a border of pretty jasmine flowers, and it smells of your mother's perfume. Perhaps we might make an exchange."

Gabriel closed his eyes in mortification. He was so tired of the feeling, but the fact that this man carried his wife's handkerchief could not have been overlooked by anyone witnessing the scene.

There was a moment of suspended silence—it couldn't have been more than a second or two, though it seemed much longer. Then the surgeon, having collected his instruments into his bag, cleared his throat and left them while Bronwyn gently ushered John and her relations from the room.

Emilia, on a moment's consideration of Ribeiro's offer, relinquished her talisman, and Ribeiro directed her to bring his coat. When she did, he removed a square from the pocket and passed it to her with a flourish.

"Now, this is a handkerchief meant for ladies. Go and put it somewhere safe until you are older and not likely to spoil it with jam or… other things."

With a ridiculous obedience, Emilia left to do as he bid her.

"Clear the scowl from your face, Marsh. It is unbecoming."

The effect of that directive was only to grow Gabriel's frown even more. He turned to go, but Ribeiro stopped him with his next words.

"She was rarely happy, you know."

Gabriel turned to find Ribeiro studying his nails. The other man's casual attitude fueled his anger anew, until Ribeiro looked up. A shadow of something—sorrow, perhaps—darkened his countenance before he spoke again.

"Mariana was rarely happy," he repeated, "even when she smiled. *Especially* when she smiled. But in the infrequent moments when her soul seemed to find peace, she spoke of you. You were her greatest regret"—his mouth twisted—"and my most despised enemy."

Gabriel knew not what to say to that. The admission was so unexpected, but hearing it had a freeing effect, as if the last knot around his heart had been loosened. "I no longer mourn my lost marriage," he said, surprised to realize it was true. "I'm sorry my wife was unhappy, but she brought our daughter into the world. She loved Emilia, in her way, and for that, I can never be sorry."

"Are we friends now?" Ribeiro said, standing and reaching for his ruined coat.

Gabriel huffed a surprised laugh. "You and I will never be friends."

Ribeiro smiled. "I suppose I ought to be glad you have not taken advantage of my infirmity and called me out." Then, his nose wrinkling with distaste, he added, "Now, I must collect Mariana's brother. My men will ride with him to Falmouth and see him secured aboard our ship."

Emilia returned, and she was smiling until she saw that her tio meant to leave. Gabriel knew a moment's anxiety. Would she demand to go with Ribeiro, to be permitted to return to Portugal? How could he let her go when he'd only just found her? But how could he keep her if it meant her happiness?

He held his breath while Ribeiro bowed over her hand and kissed the air above it in the old fashion. "Until we meet again, *minha pequena*, put your father through his paces for me. There is nothing wrong with a little mischief now and then."

She nodded, taking this nonsense for truth while Gabriel frowned. But then Emilia's fingers found his. He held her hand as they watched Ribeiro leave, hopefully for a long time.

Sombra chose that moment to toddle into the drawing room, sniffing the furniture legs in an alarming manner. Emilia jumped, pulling her hand from Gabriel's. "I will take him outside, Papá."

Gabriel followed her into the entry hall, where Merryn Kimbrell waited with his cousins. Gabriel shook the hand of each man in turn. "I thank you for your assistance. Were it not for your aid—"

"Nonsense," Merryn grumbled. "We did nothing but tend the wounded."

"An unfortunate but necessary task in every operation, I'm afraid. I couldn't help noticing, though, your absence in particular when we returned from Oak Hill—or the cobwebs in your hair."

Merryn snorted. "Did you truly think I wouldn't follow you into the tunnel with my sister at t'other end? Per'aps you're not as clever as I thought, though you do have a fine aim."

"You would have made an abysmal soldier."

"Aye, but a fine captain, I imagine."

Gabriel ignored that to search the entry for Bronwyn.

"She has gone," Merryn said.

Gabriel's stomach dropped as those three words recalled him to the day he'd learned Mariana had gone. But then, as quick as his panic had risen, it fell away. Bronwyn was not Mariana. In fact, the pair of them could not have been more different from one another.

If Mariana had been an exotic and complex port wine, then Bronwyn was a bright champagne—tart and effervescent, and utterly without artifice.

His wife had been fire and ice and beauty—a distant, untouchable star that burned hot and cold at the same time. Elegant and sophisticated, she'd mesmerized any company she graced with her smooth wit and cutting ripostes. She adored the attention of others. More than once, she'd made him feel ten feet tall, until a single, arch remark brought him back down to size—all in the space of a single evening.

But Bronwyn… Though pretty, she possessed more countenance than classical perfection. She hadn't engaged in flirtations to fix his notice or tempt his ardor. She was frank and managing, and she maintained just enough propriety to keep herself out of trouble. In short, she was not the sort of female he had ever desired. And yet, she was perfect for him.

But he'd been harsh with her the day before. He'd rejected her aid when she only wished to help. She'd accused him of allowing his pride to guide his reason, and she'd been right. He had an apology to make, and even then, he didn't know if she'd have him. There was still much to be said between them, if only he could figure out *how* to say it.

CHAPTER 29

THREE DAYS LATER, Bronwyn joined her family at Oak Hill. Kate and Ben would soon return to London, and this was to be a farewell party of sorts. Merryn was there, as were many of her cousins and Kate's family, but the day still felt flat.

Not only was her best friend leaving again, but Bronwyn had not spoken to Gabriel in three days, despite his shocking (but not unwanted) embrace after she'd shot Emilia's uncle.

He and Emilia had both suffered a horrid ordeal. She was allowing them time together, she told herself. Although, if she were truthful—and it was rarely sensible to deceive oneself—her pride had suffered a dusting.

Pride—yes, the very same pride she'd accused him of suffering. The awareness didn't make the sting any less.

But truly, what sort of man embraced a lady in such a manner and then said *nothing*?

Despite Wynne's dire prediction, though, she was not one for languishing sighs, no matter how strong the urge to cry might be. So, with a stern order for her pride to rise up and brush off its skirts, she invited Brioc to join her in a game of chase-the-stick. As the crack of her cousins' cricket bat sounded behind them, she tossed the stick farther and farther across the lawn until they found themselves, inevitably, at Penhale's wall.

She sighed to see the lock on the gate was still in place, and the garden was empty. And when she looked toward the crevice where he'd left her notes between the stones, it was to find it filled with fresh mortar. Mortar!

Her disappointment was acute. Then, she recalled Gabriel's words just days before when she'd told him about the matrons' gossip: *I could have gone and taken my daughter elsewhere.*

Would he truly leave Newford? He'd never put the knocker up. Was he even now ordering the holland covers put back on everything? With a lead weight in her stomach and an even heavier heart, she retraced her steps back to Oak Hill.

When she came round the hedge toward the terrace, it was to find a new figure sitting with Merryn and her grandfather. *Gabriel.*

Her heart skipped but pride raised its hand. So, rather than following her heart's example, she walked onto the terrace with a measure of decorum.

——

GABRIEL STOOD AS Bronwyn approached, more certain of his heart with every step she took, but less certain of hers. She came onto the terrace without her usual enthusiasm—though given his previous dismissal, he couldn't say he blamed her.

She dipped her head at him; he returned her greeting with a bow. "Miss Kimbrell."

"Captain Marsh."

He was conscious of her brother watching them, a frown creasing his brow, and of her grandfather's interested gaze. As he was about to invite Bronwyn to walk with him in the garden, the elder Kimbrell spoke.

"Bronwyn, lass, I believe I left my snuff box in the library. Would you be a dear and fetch it?"

Gabriel held a sigh of frustration as Bronwyn agreed to this request and left them.

"What d'you need with snuff, old man?" Merryn said. "I daresay you quit the habit years ago."

"I daresay."

And Gabriel, who was not slow-witted, said, "I shall go see if Miss Kimbrell requires assistance."

Bronwyn's grandfather gave him a conspiring wink even as her brother stood and crossed his arms. Then, seeing there were two against him, Merryn sighed. "Five minutes, Marsh, and not a moment more."

Five minutes was not enough to say what needed to be said. "Fifteen," he countered.

"Ten."

Jaw shifting, Gabriel accepted Merryn's terms and hurried after Bronwyn. Behind him, he heard Merryn speculating on the odds his grandfather's pistol would misfire twice in one week.

He found Bronwyn rifling the papers on her grandfather's desk in search of the missing snuff box. She looked up when he entered and smiled, though she didn't cease her search.

"Captain. I have been wondering how Emilia fares after the events of this last week."

"She does well enough. I believe she misses Ribeiro, but she'll recover. She's taken a liking to Newford, after all."

Bronwyn nodded, pulling open a drawer and rearranging its contents in her search. "And you?"

"I have taken a liking to Newford as well."

She paused and looked up. "Oh! I meant, how do you fare, but that—that is nice."

Nice. Not an auspicious beginning. Bolstering his nerves, he said, "How are *you*?"

"Me? Oh, well enough, though 'tis not every day I shoot a man, I can assure you."

"I am relieved to hear it."

She finally ceased her search and rested her fingertips atop the blotter, a smile drawing up one corner of her mouth. "Aren't you, though?"

Then, coming round the desk, she frowned at the library. "Where d'you suppose my grandfather has left his snuff box? I've searched the entire desk and the table by the fireplace."

"I doubt you'll find it here."

"But—" she began before realization struck. Then, eyeing the closed door behind him, a flush stained her cheeks. "'Tis my grandfather's scheme?"

He nodded.

"And my brother is agreeable?"

He tilted his head to one side. "'Agreeable' might be a bit generous."

"Then you'd best bar the door."

Gabriel's eyes widened. But, conscious of Merryn's clock, he did as she suggested and wedged a chair beneath the knob.

Then, drawing a breath, he took one of Bronwyn's hands in his. "The other day at Penhale, I was unkind. You accused me of allowing my pride to affect my reason." She opened her mouth to protest, or perhaps to restate her position, but he shook his head. To his surprise, she allowed him to continue.

"You were right, and I offer my humblest apologies for the harsh way I turned you away from me. It was poorly done, but I wonder if an explanation might help you to understand. It's no excuse, mind you, but… may I tell you a little more about my wife?"

"I—if you wish."

Studying their joined hands, he began. "You already know we were estranged, but I'll start at the beginning. I met Mariana at the royal court in Lisbon. She was a distant cousin to the king and sister to one of João VI's advisors—Miguel. Her beauty and sophistication were far above what a young lieutenant could have imagined for himself. She was… dark and bright, all at once, like a star fallen to earth. Her family—Miguel, in particular—had loftier aspirations for her than a British soldier, but she was of age and determined to forge her own path. She was very modern that way.

"We married within the month, and I took her with me when my company moved to Oporto. I thought—it hardly matters what I thought. She left before the year was out."

"With Mr. Ribeiro. I can hardly credit she would do such a thing."

He gave her a weak smile, her indignation doing more to bolster his determination than he'd have thought possible.

"Yes. Ribeiro and I—our association has always been one of contention. This"—he dropped her hand to indicate the scar on his cheek—"was the result of one of our earliest encounters, though it's less than the injury I left him with.

"But when Mariana left and I tried to follow, Ribeiro threatened to obstruct a crucial alliance between our forces and the Portuguese army. It would have made my men vulnerable to attack. I was unable to fight him, and Mariana made it clear she wouldn't return with me anyway. And so, I let her go."

"You were faced with an impossible dilemma."

Gabriel left her to pace, searching for the right words. He wanted to tell her everything, to make her understand. If they were to have any future together, he wanted nothing between them.

His voice was rougher than he intended when he said, "I failed in my marriage, Bronwyn. I have lived with the shame of her leaving these past years. I left London for Emilia, but also, if I'm truthful, I left for myself. I couldn't bear the whispers."

He stopped pacing and risked a glance, half expecting to find judgment for his cowardice. But, when he met Bronwyn's gaze, he found a flicker of understanding, a spark of warmth that reached into the shadowed places of his heart. He hadn't realized how heavy his burden had been until it began to lift.

He took a step closer, and Bronwyn tilted her head. "'Tis not your wife's failings that define you," she said, "but your own steadfastness and honor. Do not let her choices mar your view of yourself."

"It wasn't only her leaving that shames me, but my own inaction as well. I should have pursued her in earnest."

"But you were unable to do so."

"In my heart, I know I should have tried harder to persuade her to return, but the unvarnished truth is that I was *relieved*. I was ashamed by her leaving, but I was also relieved by it, if you can understand that." He'd been *glad* to have done with Mariana's tantrums and games. With her impulsive fits and starts one day followed by melancholic languor the next. He'd been relieved, and that had only fed more fuel to his shame.

"I think we can have more than one feeling for the people we love, and not all of them must make sense."

The people we love. She understood, then, that he'd loved his wife, even if that love had been broken and imperfect. But with Bronwyn… the feeling in his heart was strong and steady and *right*. Whole and unbroken. It was nothing like the harsh and jagged emotion he'd once felt for Mariana.

He'd not fought for love before, but fate was giving him another chance. He wouldn't make the same mistake again.

"I've been a fool," he continued, "but I adore you. You have charmed me from the moment you arrived on my doorstep with your broken wheel. I love you, and if you consent to be my wife, and Emilia's mother, I will do everything in my power to persuade you to stay."

Lifting her hand to his cheek, she looked in his eyes as she said, "I would not go." The certainty with which she uttered the words was a balm to his heart.

"No, I don't think you would."

"Nor," she added, "would I consent to *your* leaving."

"I would not go," he said, giving her words back to her.

"Then I accept, happily. But you should know I've an apology of my own to make."

He shook his head. "You've nothing to apologize for."

She moved her hand from his cheek and laid a finger across his lips. "But I do. When I first set my mind to helping you, I thought I was doing it for you, but I've come to realize I was doing it for myself." Her gaze searched his, and something in her expression held his silence. "Solving problems makes me feel… useful, but I never stopped to think about what you needed rather than what I wanted to give. If 'tis any comfort to you, I don't think I'm the same as I was when we met all those weeks before. I feel… older, per'aps—though not so old as you."

"Minx," he teased. "But we are well matched, you and I. I feel older, as well, but lighter."

She stepped closer then, and her gaze fell to his mouth.

Caring not for Merryn's clock, Gabriel leaned down and kissed her, gently at first, then more ardently. Her lips were soft and expressive, matching his fervor as her hands wound their way around his neck and into his hair. He explored her mouth, delighting in her scent and the curve of her smooth cheek beneath his fingers.

When he pulled away some moments later, it was to find a becoming flush on his intended's cheeks and a languid brightness to her eyes.

"Oh," she said, studying him in turn. "I do like this look on you, Captain."

"What look is that?" he said, bending to nuzzle the hair above her temple."

"Why, your hair is rumpled and your neckcloth nearly undone. You look… you look—"

"Thoroughly kissed and desiring another?"

That was the only invitation she needed to rise

up on her toes and press a kiss to the corner of his mouth. One kiss soon became another and another until he collected himself enough to rest his chin atop her head. He held her in his arms far longer than he ought to have done, but she fit him so perfectly.

Soon, though, the door rattled in its frame. Her brother called to them, but neither of them paid him any heed.

——

THAT EVENING, GABRIEL untied his cravat and draped it over the back of a chair. He smiled to recall Merryn Kimbrell's expression when Gabriel had emerged from Oak Hill's library with Bronwyn, the pair of them decidedly rumpled. He thought only the news that Bronwyn had consented to be his wife had prevented the man's fist from finding his face.

He'd yet to share his good fortune with Emilia. Though it was clear she adored Bronwyn, he wasn't certain how she would react to having a new mother. But before he could address that question, there was something else he needed to do.

Opening the top drawer of his dresser, he reached into the back, feeling among the cravats and small clothes until he found a small oval miniature. He removed it, allowing his thumb to trace the smooth glass covering the portrait.

The image of Mariana was set in a delicate gold frame, and a lock of her raven hair had been tucked into a pocket at the back. The portrait had been done mere weeks before she'd left him. In it, his wife's dark eyes sparkled with a mischievous light, as if she were about to share a secret. Had she known then that she carried their child?

He stared at the image, and a wave of sentiment washed over him. It wasn't the sharp, stinging pain of betrayal, but a softer, more melancholic ache. He allowed himself to recall the first time he'd seen Mariana, and the way she'd laughed at his then-clumsy Portuguese. She'd made him feel… alive amidst all the death of war.

He found Emilia in the nursery, having her hair brushed by Mrs. Forsyth while Sombra snored on the rug at their feet. Candles flickered on the nightstand and in the sconces.

He waited until the housekeeper left before taking a seat on the edge of Emilia's bed. He patted the counterpane next to him, and his daughter joined him there. As he turned the miniature in his hand, he considered his words.

Emilia leaned closer, her eyes going from his face to the portrait and back. "Papá?" she said softly. "Is that…?"

Gabriel nodded, his throat tight as he held out the portrait. "It is your mother."

Emilia took it from him carefully, her small fingers tracing the smooth frame. "It looks just like her," she whispered. "She was so beautiful."

"She was," Gabriel agreed, his voice rough.

Emilia looked up at him, her dark eyes rather grown up as they searched his. "Did you love her?"

Days before, his daughter's question would have caught him by surprise. Now, he met her gaze evenly. She waited, her shoulders high as if his answer mattered very much.

"I did," he said, and in her way, he thought maybe Mariana had loved him.

Emilia relaxed against him and studied her mother's half-smile. With her child's innocence, she said, "She looks happy."

Gabriel recalled Ribeiro's parting words to him. *Mariana was rarely happy.* He knew that now to be true. Despite her frequent laughter, Mariana hadn't been a happy individual—neither before their meeting nor after. But his daughter's smile was worth allowing her to believe it.

"She was," he said. "Perhaps she knew you were coming."

They sat for some time in silence, but when Emilia offered the miniature back to him, he said. "It's yours now, so you can always remember her."

Emilia's eyes widened, and she pressed the portrait to her chest. "Thank you, Papá."

"Now," he said, "I've a question to put to you: what do you make of Miss Kimbrell?"

Emilia's brows lifted and she pulled her legs beneath her nightgown. "I like her. She's funny and… and brave, I think, to defy Tio Miguel."

"She is both of those things, and many more besides." Gabriel swallowed. "I love her," he said, "and I have asked her to marry me."

Emilia gasped. "She will live here, at Penhale?"

"Yes. Bronwyn does not mean to replace your mother, but she will be your new step-mama."

"I will see her every day?"

"Yes, if that is agreeable." He didn't know what he would say if this *wasn't* agreeable, but to his relief, his daughter smiled as she began envisioning this new life.

"We can invite Brioc to play with Sombra," she said, "and we'll have breakfast together and… and luncheon and tea."

"You and Miss Kimbrell may share as many meals as you both desire. Does this mean you approve my marrying her?"

Emilia gave his question the consideration it deserved before nodding. More relieved than Gabriel cared to admit, he stood, and a new sense of peace fell over him. He would never forget the shadow of his first marriage, but he was coming to terms with it. And perhaps in doing so, he was finding a way forward with his daughter.

"Come," he said, extending his hand. "Let's sneak down to the kitchen and see if Mrs. Davies has put up any biscuits."

EPILOGUE

Spring transformed the gardens at Penhale. Where tangled brambles once choked the paths, roses now climbed the restored walls, their first buds promising a riot of color to come. The jasmine Gabriel had planted for Emilia flourished, its white stars sprinkling her bench and perfuming the air with their sweetness. Even Mr. Patterson, who generally regarded any garden not under his direct supervision with deep suspicion, grudgingly admitted the soil was much improved.

Today, after several days of rain, the sun was out, and the Marshes meant to enjoy their garden. John directed the footmen in arranging the tea things beneath the apple tree. His dark butler's coat suited him, though Bronwyn suspected he held a private envy for the footmen's fine blue coats.

He'd assisted her in ordering Penhale's new livery, and when the coats arrived, in a hue specifically chosen to match the coats of the 14th Light Dragoons, there'd been a suspicious brightness to his eyes that even his elevated position as butler-in-earnest could not prevent.

"Mind the spacing, Thomas," he said now. "Mrs. Marsh will not thank you for a crowded table, nor one so sparse it looks half-set."

Thomas, who'd fished the same streams as John growing up, struggled to keep his composure at his superior's directive. Bronwyn gave the pair of them a smile of broad approval before any domestic discord could upset her husband's tea.

"John, you've arranged everything so splendidly, I could scarce improve upon it myself. And Thomas, the table looks exactly as it should—gracious and inviting and not a thing out of place. I've yet to see a finer tea."

Both men preened until Sombra, who'd been investigating the fresh, rain-washed scents of the garden, emerged from beneath the tea table. He announced himself with a short bark before yielding to the distraction of the fluttering tablecloth.

John removed the linen from the dog's mouth and shooed the animal from the table with a scowl. Despite his irritation, Bronwyn suspected he would slip the animal an extra biscuit when he thought no one was looking.

Beside her, Gabriel ignored these distractions to frown over the letter in his hand.

Bronwyn lifted the pot to pour. "'Tis bad news?"

Gabriel set his letter aside. "No, it's merely another communication from Lord Rutland. He joins the squire's house party next month, and he wishes to see my mare before committing to her foal."

Lord Rutland, a baron out of Northumberland with more funds than sense, had a desire to expand his stables. Having written to Gabriel on the squire's recommendation some months before, he'd then gone on to challenge everything, from the price of Amante's foal—far too dear!—to the pure bloodlines of Gabriel's newest stud.

"But what more can he hope to learn that you've not already shared in your letters? I hope all the Quality are not so particular."

"He only wishes to put me through my paces," Gabriel said, unruffled by it all. "Once he sees Amante move, he'll understand why the fee must be high.

Bronwyn considered this. He was right, of course, and she told him so. "I've yet to meet anyone who is not staggered once they see your horses in motion." Then, lifting her cup to hide her smile, she added, "'Twas your horse that first caught my notice, after all."

"My horse! I don't think I've heard anything so lowering before."

"Well, to be sure, 'twasn't your amiable nature."

"Minx," he muttered, though he was smiling as he took a bite of cake.

"To be fair," she mused, "I should say that once I discovered your kissing abilities, you were redeemed."

"Only then? But you accepted my proposal *before* I kissed you. How do you explain that?"

"Mine is an optimistic nature," she said. "I was certain you had potential, and I was not disappointed."

"Count me relieved."

"As am I. As you've pointed out, I'd already accepted your proposal. What if you'd been dreadful at the kissing part?"

He laughed then and, lifting her hand, placed a kiss on the back of it. His gaze, when he lifted it, gave a clear indication of his thoughts. Just that morning, he'd caught her on his library ladder and had stolen a fair number of kisses.

She might have allowed him to indulge his thoughts now, were it not for the interruption that came through the open gate.

Brioc bounded into the garden from Oak Hill, followed at a more sedate pace by Bronwyn's grandfather. His knee still pained him occasionally, though he claimed regular walks to Penhale helped to ease the stiffness. Bronwyn didn't doubt it, but she suspected his pleasure in their visits was as much for the tales he shared with his new grand-daughter as for any alleviation of his ailment.

Bronwyn greeted him with a kiss for his cheek as Emilia came down from the house with Miss Enderby, her edition of Amadis de Gaula pressed close to her chest. She'd taken quickly to her new governess, a lady Bronwyn and Gabriel had chosen as much for her sterling references as for the smattering of Portuguese she was not averse to sprinkling in her lessons.

Their daughter had grown like one of the garden's weeds these last months, outpacing Bronwyn and Morwenna's efforts to let down her hems. She would need new dresses soon.

Emilia's face brightened on seeing their guest. "*Avô*! Miss Enderby and I have been reading about Lady Oriana. Would you like me to read it to you?"

"Why else have I come, if not to hear more of the lady's tale?" He allowed Emilia to see him settled comfortably on her bench while John brought him a cup of tea.

As Emilia read to her grandfather, Bronwyn leaned close to Gabriel. "I overheard the most intriguing story yesterday at the apothecary." She frowned as she tried to recall the tale's exact provenance. Ticking it off on her fingers, she said, "Mrs. Pentreath was telling Mrs. Tretheway that she had it from Mrs. Clifton that Mr. Carew has found himself a spot of trouble with the Stanton sisters."

Gabriel's lips twitched. "Is this your way of informing me the good ladies of Newford have discovered fresh blood?"

"Ha! I like what you did there, and I don't think anyone will argue our matrons' resemblance to vampires. But 'tis true, they've found another source for their gossip, though I don't think they needed poor Mr. Carew to fall on his sword for that. I overheard Mrs. Pentreath commenting to Mrs. Tretheway how closely Emilia's nose resembles yours. I suppose even a stopped clock has the right time twice a day."

He frowned. "Does it?"

"Well, aye, if the hands stand still—"

"I was referring to my daughter's nose, and well you know it."

Bronwyn held her smile. "The poor dear does indeed have your masterful nose. Thank the heavens she has her mother's eyes." Then, placing a hand over her growing belly, she said, "Shall we walk? The babe grows restless."

Her husband, who'd missed the birth of his first child, had been very attentive these last months. At her question, he stood with alacrity and helped her from her chair, drawing her arm through his.

A breeze ruffled the leaves overhead and

brought with it the scent of jasmine as he matched his steps to hers. She shivered a little as she wondered if Mariana watched her daughter from above.

"I do love you," she whispered to Gabriel. "I should not be selfish, but I am so grateful for everything, the good and the bad, that brought you and Emilia to Cornwall."

He looked down at her, his hazel eyes softening. A flurry of barking rang out as Sombra and Brioc chased a squirrel up a tree, drowning whatever reply he might have made.

He leaned down and kissed her instead, pulling her close with one hand on her hip as the other stroked her cheek. She didn't need to hear her husband's words to know his heart.

THE END

THANK YOU

Thank you for reading! If Bronwyn and Gabriel's tale brought a smile to your face, swept you away or simply provided a welcome escape, please consider leaving a star rating and/or review on your favorite book site.

Want more of the Kimbrell cousins? Subscribe at klynsmithauthor.com/dw and receive a free copy of the Hearts of Cornwall prequel, Discovering Wynne. It's a fun and flirty tale about innkeeping, smuggling and of course, swoon-worthy romance.

Don't miss the next installment of the Hearts of Cornwall series. Follow K. Lyn Smith on Amazon or BookBub or subscribe to her newsletter for new release updates.

BOOKS BY K. LYN SMITH

Something Wonderful
The Astronomer's Obsession
The Artist's Redemption
The Physician's Dilemma

Hearts of Cornwall
Discovering Wynne (Prequel Novella)
Jilting Jory
Matching Miss Moon
Driving Miss Darling
Kissing Kate
Saving Miss Swan
Charming the Captain
Engaging Miss Enderby*
Regarding Rebecca

Love's Journey
Star of Wonder
Light of a Nile Moon
Stars of Twilight Fair
Beneath a Brighton Sun

* Cadan's story appears in the
Hearts in Bloom Regency Anthology.
Visit klynsmithauthor.com
for the most up-to-date list of titles.

ABOUT THE AUTHOR

K. Lyn Smith writes sweet historical romance about ordinary people finding extraordinary love. Her debut novel, The Astronomer's Obsession, was a finalist for the National Excellence in Romantic Fiction Award, and many of her other titles have been shortlisted for honors such as the American Writing Award, the Carolyn Reader's Choice Award, the HOLT Medallion and the Maggie Award.

When she's not lost in the pages of a book, you can find her with family, traveling to far-off places and binging period dramas. And space documentaries. Weird, right?

Visit www.klynsmithauthor.com, where you can subscribe for new release updates and access to exclusive bonus content.

www.ingramcontent.com/pod-product-compliance
Lightning Source LLC
Chambersburg PA
CBHW020233010826
48973CB00006B/1496